ABIDING
CONVICTION

ABIDING
CONVICTION

A DUTCH FRANCIS NOVEL

STEPHEN M. MURPHY

OCEANVIEW PUBLISHING
SARASOTA, FLORIDA

ISBN 978-1-60809-565-0

Published in the United States of America by Oceanview Publishing

Sarasota, Florida

www.oceanviewpub.com

10 9 8 7 6 5 4 3 2

PRINTED IN THE UNITED STATES OF AMERICA

To Patty with love always

Proof beyond a reasonable doubt is proof that leaves you with an abiding conviction that the charge is true. The evidence need not eliminate all possible doubt since everything in life is open to some possible or imaginary doubt.

California Criminal Jury Instruction 220

ABIDING
CONVICTION

CHAPTER ONE

LIFE CAN THROW you curves, particularly when you least expect it.

Ginnie pulled the sheets over us as she nestled in beside me. We were in bed in her condo amid Manchester's red-brick mill housing near the Merrimack River. Outside the window above the headboard, I could see streaks of sunshine in the blue sky. We had been married only six months, but it felt like we were still on our honeymoon. I savored the touch of Ginnie's skin on mine, holding her tightly as if I never wanted to let go.

She was quiet for a few minutes.

"Where'd you go?"

"Just wondering if it will always be this good."

"What does that mean?"

We lay together quietly as I tried to figure out what was bothering my wife. The mood had suddenly changed.

I stroked her cheek. "Are you mad at me?"

She inhaled deeply and blurted out, "I'm pregnant."

I stopped breathing, not sure I heard her correctly. "You're joking."

She lifted her head off my arm, her eyes watery. "Would I joke about something like that?"

"That's . . . that's great news."

She stared at me, displeased. "I don't want a baby. I have a career to worry about."

"You can have both."

"Spoken like a lawyer. I have a choice, don't I? I can terminate the pregnancy."

I was so flustered I grasped at the first thing that entered my mind. "But you're Catholic."

"What difference does that make?"

"I know you stopped going to church but still . . . We did discuss having children. You said you wanted them."

"I don't want a child right now." She lifted her head to be even with mine. "Can't you at least support me? A little bit?"

"Ginnie." I gazed at her freckled cheeks. When she was on duty as a newscaster for Channel 9, those freckles usually were covered with makeup. I loved the look of them.

She threw the covers off and got out of bed. I also loved seeing her nude body and tried to imagine how carrying a child would affect this perfect figure. I imagined her keeping her figure perfect but with a slight bump for the baby.

"I feel sick," she said, bursting my daydream, as she hurried to the bathroom. I could hear her retching. My thoughts turned to what life would be like with a child: going to baseball games or dance recitals, school plays, band practice, soccer. I wanted all that; I would make time for it; I would be a good father.

Ginnie stayed in the bathroom and turned on the shower. I checked the clock and realized I had less than half an hour to get to court. I had a preliminary hearing in one of the most high-profile cases I'd ever had: a superior court judge accused of murdering his wife. Even Ginnie had reported on the case extensively.

I got out of bed and walked to the bathroom. The shower stopped. I knocked on the door and turned the handle. The door moved a few inches. "Hon, I've got to get a move on. Any chance you can hurry?"

She pushed the door shut and locked it. I was stuck. After the wedding I had moved out of my apartment and into Ginnie's condo. The condo was well located, near Channel 9, but was small with only one bathroom. Until now, that hadn't been a problem. I knocked on the door, gently at first, but when Ginnie didn't respond I pounded it. "Ginnie! I've got to get to court. Please open the door."

She unlocked the door and I turned the handle and went inside. She stood in front of the sink with a towel around her slim waist, exposing her small, firm breasts. Her hair color tended to change with the seasons but now it was rust, which blended perfectly with the freckles that covered her body. "Go ahead and shower while I finish putting on my makeup," she said, staring at a steamy mirror.

I turned on the shower and stepped inside. This was a terrible time to be in such a hurry since we had a lot to talk about. I showered quickly, dried off, and waited for Ginnie to finish with the mirror.

"We have to talk," I said.

"Not now," she said.

She moved aside to allow me to shave. Since I still had a full beard, I needed only a few minutes to shave around the edges. Then I dressed quickly and kissed her lightly on the lips. She didn't respond at all. "I love you."

"I love you too, but we need to work this out."

"We will. I promise." I put my arms around her and hugged her close.

She reciprocated, sinking into me. "We'll talk tonight, after the six o'clock broadcast."

❊ ❊ ❊

The Hillsborough County Courthouse was a short drive from the condo, and I made it there in five minutes. But I was already a few minutes late for the preliminary hearing. My client, the Honorable Carlos Garcia, was sitting alone at the defense table. He was rubbing his silver goatee as if worried I'd never show up. Prosecutor Wayne Tompkins, a heavyset white man in his mid-thirties with a shaved head, sat at the other table. A police officer was on the stand and Judge Denise Shane on the bench. Judge Shane usually sat in Lancaster, Coös County, two hours north past the White Mountains. She was the only judge in the state who didn't recuse herself from this case, most having some familiarity with my client. Recently appointed, Shane had quickly made it known that she disliked tardy lawyers. To embarrass them, she insisted everyone take their places on time, meaning the late lawyer would walk into a prepared quiet courtroom.

"Nice of you to join us, Mr. Francis," Judge Shane said, looking over her half-lens reading glasses. She had short grey hair and the build of an athlete even though she must've been in her late fifties.

"My apologies, Your Honor. It couldn't be helped."

"I'm quite sure," she said, staring at me. After I announced my appearance for the record, the judge asked, "Mr. Tompkins, are you ready to proceed?"

"We are, Your Honor. The People call Officer Richard Sambuchino." Normally you'd see the witness walking from the gallery to the stand to take the oath, but Sambuchino was already there, so he simply stood and raised his right hand. His soft belly jiggled over his belt.

I leaned over to my client and whispered, "Morning. Sorry I'm late."

"No problem." Garcia was in his early sixties with thick silver hair combed straight back and an equally thick silver mustache and goatee. He was tall and thin and commanded a distinguished appearance. He enjoyed telling people he was descended from Spanish royalty. I never knew if the story were true, but he acted like he was above the rest of us. I had had a few appearances in front of Garcia but didn't know him well.

After his arrest, he called me. "I need your help," he had said. I was flattered but tried to beg off, telling him I was a civil trial attorney, with a few decades' experience, who only dabbled in criminal law and he needed an experienced specialist. But he brushed that off. "I talked to Judge Taylor about your Walker murder trial. He said you were outstanding, that he hadn't seen a lawyer as good as you in front of a jury for a long while. So I want you, Francis. Name your retainer." I gave him a number I thought for sure he'd reject but to my surprise he said, "Fine. When can we meet?"

Now, sitting at the defense table, for the first time Garcia appeared uncomfortable. He shifted in his seat and stared at Sambuchino with disdain. He had been charged with poisoning his wife with an overdose of hydrocodone and emphatically asserted his innocence. Unfortunately, the state supreme court had suspended him from the bench after the charges were filed, which didn't matter much since he was in custody. Because of the seriousness of the charges, Judge Shane refused to grant bail, a controversial decision that garnered her a lot of publicity, both positive and negative. Some people thought Garcia should be locked up forever; others said he wasn't a threat to anyone so should be granted bail.

Tompkins took Sambuchino through his investigation, starting with the 911 call from my client, which he prepared to play for the judge. A crackling sound came through the speakers, which were set up facing the bench. Tompkins played the CD through his laptop, which sat on the prosecution table. I sat with Garcia at the defense table beside Tompkins. Both of us faced the judge who sat on the bench between the flags of the United States and the State of New Hampshire with its image of a ship on a blue background surrounded by yellow stars and leaves.

My client's deep, faltering voice filled the courtroom.

"Hello?"

"This is the 911 operator. How can I help you?"

"It's my wife."

"What's wrong with your wife?"

"She's not—not moving. I don't know what happened."

"Have you checked her pulse? Sir, I said, 'Have you checked her pulse?'"

"I'm sorry. I-I just did and oh my God there isn't any. You have to send help right away. Please."

By the time the operator had obtained his name and address, Garcia was yelling, *"Hurry, hurry."*

Tompkins shut off the audio and turned toward the witness. "Officer Sambuchino, did you respond to that 911 call?"

"Yes, the operator radioed me right after she dispatched an ambulance."

"And what did you find when you arrived at the residence?"

"The door was open and the EMTs were attending to Maureen Garcia who was lying on the bed in the master bedroom. She was on top of the covers, fully dressed in a white blouse and black-and-white checkered pants. Judge Garcia was in the room and

I asked him if we could speak privately. He agreed and we stepped into the kitchen."

Despite his slovenly appearance, Sambuchino was an articulate witness, confident and clear. Since this was a preliminary hearing, and not a trial, my job was to listen and learn. Chances were the prosecution had enough evidence to show probable cause that my client had committed the murder. This was my opportunity to get a preview of that evidence and see if there were any holes I could poke into it.

"What did the defendant say when you got to the kitchen?" Tompkins asked.

"He said he'd been working late and when he got home his wife ordered Thai food to be delivered. They ate dinner together, sharing a bottle of red wine. I got the sense they weren't on the best of terms. After dinner she complained of a headache and went to the bedroom to lie down. Judge Garcia watched TV for an hour or two before checking on his wife." Sambuchino spoke slowly without looking at his report, giving the impression that he had a clear memory of the conversation.

"And what did the defendant say next?"

"He said she was lying on the bed, her arms outstretched. He panicked and yelled, 'Mo! Mo!' but she didn't move. I asked if he touched her and he said he put his hand to her cheek. She was cold to the touch. That's when he called 911."

"Did you do any further investigation at that time?"

"There was something about his tone of voice that made me suspicious, so I called forensics and they came to the house and collected evidence."

Tompkins took a step toward the witness, holding a manila envelope in his hand. "Did you speak to the defendant at a later time?"

"A few days later, after the medical examiner's report came back showing she'd been poisoned, I returned to his house with the homicide detail and they made the arrest. I read him his Miranda rights and asked if he had anything to say."

Sambuchino paused and took a sip of water. "He said, 'I want to talk to my lawyer.' So that was it. He lawyered up after that."

"Your witness," Tompkins said, turning toward me.

I considered whether to ask Sambuchino anything, but this was a prelim so I could afford to fish a little bit. There was no jury here to pass judgment.

"Officer Sambuchino, did Judge Garcia ever say anything to indicate in any way that he was responsible for his wife's death?" I emphasized "Judge Garcia" to humanize my client as opposed to Tompkins referring to him as the "defendant."

Sambuchino glanced at Tompkins as if looking for help. "The prosecutor can't help you, Officer," I said. "What's your answer?"

"He did not," he finally answered.

"So you had no reason that night to suspect Judge Garcia of any wrongdoing?"

He shook his head. "Nothing other than you always look at the husband."

"Is that so?" I was surprised that Sambuchino had given me an opening. "So you suspected my client from the get-go?"

"I wouldn't say I suspected him. I kept an open mind, that's all."

"But your experience told you that the husband should always be considered a suspect when a woman dies suddenly?" I almost said "is murdered" but changed it at the last moment. I didn't want to give the judge the impression that we agreed Maureen Garcia had even been murdered.

"I'd say that's true."

"Because of your experience, you focused your investigation on Judge Garcia, isn't that right?"

"We focused on him because the evidence pointed to him. His fingerprints were on the bottle of Vicodin and the pills were crushed before they were put into the food."

"That evidence came from the forensics team, correct?"

"Correct, and the coroner."

"You're not qualified to testify on fingerprints or crushed pills in food, are you?"

"No, I'll leave that to the experts."

"I'm sure we'll be hearing from them. Getting back to my original line of questioning: Did you consider anyone besides Judge Garcia as a suspect?"

"We considered everyone."

"You did? Name one other suspect."

Sambuchino gritted his teeth and glared at me. He knew I had him.

"There were none."

"What's that?"

"There were no other suspects."

"So this was a biased investigation from the very beginning, wasn't it, Officer? You suspected my client of murder simply because he was the husband, isn't that right?"

"Objection," Tompkins said, jumping to his feet. "Compound and argumentative."

"Sustained as to compound," Judge Shane said. "Mr. Francis, move things along here."

"Officer Sambuchino, you suspected my client simply because he was the husband and then you focused your investigation on him. Am I right?"

Sambuchino took another sip of water. "I answered this already." He looked up at the judge.

"Answer again," Judge Shane said, "so we can get to the next witness."

"I focused on the defendant because the evidence pointed to him."

I stared at him and decided to let it go. I had made my point, I thought, at least as much as I could.

Next, Tompkins called several officers from the forensics team who had searched the home after the 911 call. The only fingerprints they could identify belonged to Judge Garcia and his wife. Both their fingerprints were on the Vicodin bottle. There were a few unidentified ones in the living room and on the front doorknob but none in the bedroom. I let their testimonies go unchallenged.

✦ ✦ ✦

During the lunch break I called Ginnie at the television station. "Are you feeling any better?"

"A little. How's the hearing going?"

"Okay. There were a few hiccups, but I think I smoothed them out." I paused. "How's your day going?"

"Oh, the usual. Digging up stories, salad for lunch, but I did get some interesting phone calls."

"How so?"

"A couple of unpleasant men wanted to express their displeasure with my reporting of recent stories. One said I'd better watch my back; the other told me to perform an impossible sexual act on myself."

"Ginnie, did you call the police?" I didn't like the idea of anyone threatening my wife.

"No. I think they were just blowing off steam. I get those kinds of calls sometimes. And the occasional nasty email."

"Well, you should at least tell management. Maybe they could trace the calls."

"I suppose." She became quiet.

"Are you all right?"

"Yeah, just thinking about this morning. I shouldn't have been so mean to you."

"Do you want to talk about it?"

"Not now. Let's wait until tonight."

"Okay. I love you."

"I love you too."

CHAPTER TWO

THE ENTIRE AFTERNOON session was taken up with one witness. Tompkins stood in front of the bench and announced, "The People call Arlene Downey."

Judge Garcia turned sharply toward the rear of the courtroom where Ms. Downey soon appeared. As Garcia watched her walk to the witness stand, he grimaced.

Then the heavy wooden door of the courtroom slammed open, causing everyone, including the handful of reporters in the audience, to turn and look. A fifty-something man with black hair spotted with bits of grey, perhaps five nine, stood at the back of the courtroom, glaring in our direction. I couldn't tell if his focus was on Garcia or me, but there was no questioning the hate in his eyes. As he moved to take a seat behind the reporters, Garcia leaned over toward me.

"That's my brother-in-law, Sam Collins. A real asshole."

"He doesn't look too happy."

"He hates my guts, always has. I'm sure now more than ever."

Meanwhile, Arlene Downey had arrived at the witness stand. She took the oath and settled herself in the chair. Thompson began his examination. "Ms. Downey, what is your occupation?"

"I am a psychologist. I treat patients with depression and anxiety."

"Then I will address you as Dr. Downey. You're in private practice?"

"Yes, I have an office on Elm Street here in town."

"And do you know the defendant, Judge Carlos Garcia?" Tompkins turned and held out his hand toward my client.

"I do."

"And how is it that you know him?"

Downey was in her mid-forties, dressed smartly in a black skirt and cream-colored blouse that was tight enough to display her impressive figure. She was fully made up but she was one of those women who don't need cosmetics. From my viewpoint at counsel table, she was quite attractive.

"I testified in his courtroom as a treating therapist."

"And did you happen to see him after that testimony?"

Downey hesitated and wiped her eye with a tissue. She seemed to be struggling to control her emotions.

"Dr. Downey?" Tompkins prodded.

"He called me and asked me to dinner."

"Did you have dinner with the defendant?"

She nodded. "I did."

"And how long ago was that?"

"It was before Christmas, late November, early December."

"Is it true, Dr. Downey," Tompkins asked, raising his voice, "that you and the defendant then conducted an extramarital affair?"

I glanced at my client, but he looked down at the table, not wanting to make eye contact with anyone. He was ashamed to have his affair discussed in open court. There were a few reporters sitting in back taking notes on laptops.

"I didn't know he was married . . . at first."

"But you did have an affair?"

She stared at Garcia, but he continued looking down. "We did."

"And how long did this affair go on?"

"From December until a few weeks ago when he was arrested."

"Dr. Downey, let me direct your attention to the evening of April 21 of this year. Were you with the defendant?"

She nodded, slowly then more quickly. "I was."

"At what time that evening did you first see him?"

"He came by my office after my last appointment, which ended at five."

"So he wasn't working late?" Tompkins turned to look at Garcia as if to say, "I caught you lying to the police." Just what I needed: a credibility issue.

"And how long were you with the defendant that evening?"

"We had a drink at Fat Tuesday's, then he dropped me off at my apartment."

Tompkins exhaled loudly, clearly exasperated. "The question was how long were you with the defendant?"

"Until six thirty or so."

"Did anything unusual happen while you were together?"

"Objection," I said, rising. "Irrelevant."

"Overruled." Judge Shane didn't even bother looking up from her legal pad.

"Dr. Downey, do you have the question in mind?" Tompkins asked.

"I do. Yes, something unusual happened. We got into a nasty argument. I didn't want to continue the way we'd been going, cheating on his wife, and I asked if he intended to get a divorce."

"And how did the defendant respond?"

"He said he loved me and would do anything for me."

"Did you believe him?"

"I did. He was crying when he said it. I wiped his tears with my napkin."

"How did the conversation end?"

She looked at Garcia again. "He promised I was the only one for him."

For the first time, Garcia looked up with a pained expression on his face. Downey had made a good impression; she was sincere, articulate, and credible. When I stood up to cross-examine her, I knew I had to treat her delicately to avoid offending the judge.

"Dr. Downey, is it fair to say you were in love with my client?"

She raised her fist to her nose and nodded, fighting back tears.

"You have to answer audibly, Dr. Downey," the judge said.

"The answer is 'yes.'"

"Thank you," I said. "And you wanted him to divorce his wife?"

"He had promised to divorce her."

"Please answer the question I put to you."

"Yeah, I wanted him to divorce her."

"Is it true, Dr. Downey, that Judge Garcia spoke about his wife with affection?"

Tompkins was on his feet. "Objection, Your Honor. That question is so hopelessly vague as to be unintelligible."

Judge Shane looked at me and I could tell she was going to sustain the objection. To save her the trouble, I said I would rephrase the question.

"Let me ask it this way: Did my client ever say anything about his relationship with his wife?"

"He did. He said it was a loveless relationship. They hadn't made love in a long time. He felt they had outgrown each other."

"Did he tell you he no longer loved her?"

She looked away, staring toward the back of the courtroom. "He never said that, which I couldn't understand."

"Dr. Downey, did Judge Garcia ever express any dislike for his wife?"

She shook her head. "None."

"Was it your impression that he still loved her?"

"I don't know."

I was doing pretty well so far but I was saving the key questions for the end. "Did Judge Garcia ever say anything at all to indicate he wanted his wife dead?" I was taking a chance with this one since I didn't know how she'd answer, but in a preliminary hearing, as opposed to a trial, it was better to learn the bad along with the good.

She bit her tongue and stared at me, as if deciding how to answer. "Not in so many words."

I froze. What was she saying? I couldn't leave the answer like that. I had brought up the subject so I needed to finish this line of questioning. I felt like I had stepped into quicksand but still hoped I could pull myself out.

"So he never said he wished his wife were dead?"

"As I said, not in so many words."

"Is the answer to my question 'no'?"

"Objection," Tompkins said. "Mr. Francis is arguing with the witness."

Judge Shane leaned forward. "I don't think he is. Are you, Mr. Francis?"

"No, Your Honor."

The judge turned to Downey. "Can you answer Mr. Francis' question with a 'yes' or 'no'?"

A petulant look came over Downey's face. "The answer is 'no.' He never said those words to me."

Judge Shane addressed me. "Please continue, Mr. Francis."

I hated to ask the next question, but I had to since it would be the first question Tompkins asked on redirect. "When you say 'not in so many words,' what do you mean?"

"He mentioned that they each had substantial life insurance policies." The courtroom went silent. I felt myself sinking further. Downey seemed to be getting pleasure out of making me and Garcia squirm.

"Did he say how substantial?"

"A million dollars."

I bit my lip. I didn't like where this was going. The prosecution hadn't even brought up life insurance as a motive for Garcia to murder his wife.

I had to keep swinging wildly. "What was the context in which this subject was raised?"

"The context?"

"Yes, what were you discussing when he mentioned life insurance?"

She seemed disappointed I had asked that question. "I had asked him for some advice."

"Advice about what?"

"About insurance generally. I was looking for new coverage for all my policies."

"Including life insurance?"

"Yes, including life insurance."

I was feeling better but still needed to eliminate life insurance proceeds as a motive for murder. "One of the things you wanted to know was how much coverage you should have for your own life insurance policy?"

"That's true."

"And it was in that context that my client mentioned his own coverage, right?"

"Yes."

"And his wife's coverage?"

"It was the same conversation."

I had to finish on a high note. "Did you ever know my client to be in any kind of financial distress?"

"No, he was always quite generous."

"Finally, Dr. Downey, did you ever hear my client say he wanted to harm his wife in any way?"

"Harm her? No, not to me."

I breathed a sigh of relief and sat down. There was a shuffling noise from the back of the courtroom as the reporters stood up to leave. But Garcia's brother-in-law stayed in his seat, continuing to glare in our direction. He didn't move until the bailiff rushed him along so he could lock up the courtroom.

CHAPTER THREE

As soon as the hearing recessed for the day, I stopped by the office to work on other cases. Although Judge Carlos Garcia was a well-paying client, I couldn't survive on a murder case alone. I needed civil cases, in which I charged a contingency fee, cases that paid handsomely. Of course, the trick was to select cases I could win. I liked the concept of being partners with my client, having the same goal in mind: to squeeze as much money out of the defendant as possible. My favorite cases were ones against cocky corporate lawyers, so sure of their righteousness that they underestimated a simple sole practitioner like me. I knew how they thought because I used to be one myself.

Since leaving my corporate practice in Boston and moving to Manchester, I had developed a David-and-Goliath complex. I loved representing the little guy and slaying the more powerful opponent, usually a big corporation that had wrongfully terminated my poor client.

That afternoon I had one meeting scheduled and I wasn't looking forward to it. The case involved an employee of a financial services firm who got fired after he ignored my advice not to send a bombastic letter to his boss, complaining about not getting a higher bonus. Although we filed a wrongful termination lawsuit, it was promptly dismissed on summary judgment since the client was an at-will employee who could be fired for any reason as long as it was not an illegal reason. The case had a tragic ending when my client later hanged himself. Now his distraught wife wanted to meet with me and collect his entire case file. I suspected she might be contemplating a legal malpractice suit but felt secure that I hadn't done anything wrong.

She arrived fifteen minutes late. I had not met Grace Handford until now and was struck by how awful she looked. Her long stringy hair hung over her face as if it hadn't been brushed in weeks. Her clothes were wrinkled. She was thin though appeared muscular, almost mannish, her biceps bulging from the collared short-sleeved shirt. Her husband had told me she was an avid weightlifter, a New England champion, and hinted that she had taken steroids. From the looks of her, I didn't doubt it.

When I opened the door, she didn't bother saying hello. "You must be Francis." She had a deep, almost masculine voice.

"Yes. Mrs. Handford?"

"That's me. The widow. Do you have the file?"

"Would you like a cup of coffee, glass of water perhaps?"

She walked past me and ignored my question. "The file?"

I picked up the brown accordion file that sat on the edge of the assistant's desk. "Here it is." I handed it to her. "I'm sorry for what happened."

"You ought to be. You advised him to write that letter. You should've known it would get him fired."

I was taken aback. "But I didn't advise him to send the letter."

"That's bullshit and you know it." She held the accordion file to her chest and her eyes watered. "Robert told me you helped him."

I didn't know what to say. She was obviously angry at me, and there was nothing I could say to change that. I did help him write the letter, but that was only after advising him not to send it. The file contained my edits to his draft, which I was afraid would reinforce her opinion that his firing was my fault.

She turned to leave but stopped suddenly. "I hear you're defending the judge who dismissed Robert's case."

"Yes, Judge Garcia's preliminary hearing started today."

"I hope he loses."

I could think of no response that wouldn't set her off so I remained quiet.

She continued in a low, flat tone. "I'll just have to go on without my husband. And my children will have to live without their father."

She opened the door. "And we all have you to thank for that."

Sometimes this David-and-Goliath thing can get ugly; David doesn't always win.

❋ ❋ ❋

By the time I got home, I was exhausted and in need of some downtime so I popped open a bottle of Molson and turned on the TV. There was a rerun of last night's Red Sox game, a blowout loss that I didn't feel like watching. I turned to Channel 9 and waited for the live news show to come on. I loved watching Ginnie at work. She was so self-assured; no matter what she said, you couldn't help believing her.

I sipped the Molson, smiling. I didn't care what she was reporting; it was enough to know that this beautiful, articulate woman was my wife. I was so proud of her. She could've taken a higher paying, higher profile job in Chicago but turned it down because of me. That had made me love her even more.

While I waited for Ginnie to come home, I pulled some papers from my briefcase and prepared for tomorrow's hearing. The prosecutor said he would be calling the medical examiner to prove time of death. I glanced over the medical examiner's report and reached to my bookcase to pull down *Forensic Pathology* to brush up on autopsy protocols. The Channel 9 news program ended so I shut off the TV, leaned back into the soft leather couch, and turned the pages. I read for a while before falling asleep with the textbook open on my chest. By the time I woke up, it was eight o'clock and Ginnie was not yet home. She must've stopped at the store, I thought, or had some work to catch up on. I grabbed another bottle of Molson from the fridge and turned the TV back on. I didn't know what I was watching since I kept glancing at the clock. Finally, after an hour, I got up, grabbed my cell phone from the kitchen table, and speed-dialed Ginnie. The phone rang several times before her voicemail came on. "Hon," I said, "let me know when you'll be home. I'm missing you. Love ya."

It was not like Ginnie to be late without calling. I wondered if she was still upset about the pregnancy; maybe she didn't want to have that talk we'd planned. I was troubled all day about her reaction; it had never occurred to me that Ginnie would have an abortion. She was raised in a strict Catholic family in what was now called St. Anne-St. Augustin's Parish. Her mother still attended weekly Mass. Before her father died, he had stopped going altogether. He still held strong Catholic beliefs but pulled back from the established Church, so disgusted was he by the molestation scandals.

I couldn't stand waiting so I called the station and asked for Ginnie's co-anchor, Dennis Cassidy. He took several minutes to get to the phone. Knowing Dennis, who openly competed with me for Ginnie's attention, he probably did so purposely. When he finally picked up, I said, "Dennis, this is Dutch. Ginnie hasn't come home yet and I'm wondering if she told you of any plans for after work."

"No, nothing. She's probably at the mall. You know these women: can't have enough clothes or shoes."

"I don't think so, Dennis. That's not like Ginnie at all. Do me a favor: go to the parking lot and check if her car is still there."

"Hold on, I'll be right back."

I waited with the phone to my ear, pacing the condo from one end to the other. I could feel my face flush and my temperature rise. My t-shirt had turned damp under the armpits. I couldn't stop thinking about the threats Ginnie had reported to me. I was probably being ridiculous; there could be a million explanations for why Ginnie hadn't called.

"Dutch," Cassidy said, panting. "I don't know what this means."

"What're you talking about?"

"Her car's there."

"It is? So she must still be in the building."

"I don't think so. But let me check. I'll call right back."

The few minutes it took for Cassidy to call me back dragged on while I again paced the condo. As I passed through the kitchen, I stared at the photos of Ginnie on the refrigerator door. There was one of her at work, sitting at her desk, obviously surprised that her photo was being taken. Her desk was strewn with papers and her laptop was open in front of her.

Finally, Cassidy called. "Dutch, I don't know how to say this but Ginnie's nowhere to be found. I even had one of the girls check the bathroom. Maybe she took a walk. It's a warm evening."

I inhaled deeply and tried not to panic. "I don't think so, Dennis. She doesn't answer her cell phone. But just in case, I think I'll drive down there and look around."

I was torn between calling the police and looking for Ginnie myself. But if Ginnie had just gone for a walk, I would feel ridiculous. Canal Street was well lit, but the side streets were not. I took my time, driving with the high beams on down one side street after another until I covered a half-mile radius. The only pedestrians were couples leaving the Mill Club. There was no sign of Ginnie.

At the station, I parked next to Ginnie's car and searched the ground in case something had fallen. Amidst the dirty newspapers and gravel near the driver's door was Ginnie's cell phone. It was powered on and showed the missed call from me. By now nearly an hour had passed since I first talked to Cassidy. My anxiety level had shot up considerably so I dialed 911.

"Hello," I said. "My wife's missing and I need the police at Channel 9 right away."

"Yes, suh," the female operator said. "First, can I have your name?"

She had a strong Southern accent. "My name is Dutch Francis and my wife is Ginnie Turner." I then explained what had happened.

"Couldn't your wife be with friends or relatives?" She talked in a slow drawl, which I normally found charming. Now it was infuriating.

"If she wanted to go visiting, she would've taken her car, but it's sitting here in the Channel 9 lot. And her cell phone wouldn't be lying here on the ground."

"Have you checked to see if the car's operable?"

Are you kidding me? This was driving me crazy. "Ma'am, I don't have the keys," I said slowly. "Can't you send a squad car out here now?"

"Just a moment." Thirty seconds passed. "A cruiser will be there within the minute. Stay on the line." I waited in silence until I saw the flashing lights of a police cruiser.

"They're here." I hung up.

Two officers exited the police cruiser. The driver I recognized as Bill Delahunty, a poker buddy of mine. "Bill," I yelled. "It's Ginnie. She's disappeared."

He hurried over to me. He was broad-shouldered with a thick neck and red cheeks. "When did you last talk to her?"

"At lunchtime. She said she'd received some threatening phone calls today."

"What kind of calls?"

"Both from men." I tried to remember Ginnie's exact words. "One said she'd better watch her back; the other told her to fuck herself, though that's not exactly how she put it."

"Did she give you any other information?"

"She said they weren't happy with some recent stories." Delahunty wrote in his notepad.

"But she reported the six o'clock news. She was supposed to come home before eight. Her car's here and she's nowhere to be found."

"Marie," he said to his partner, "gather everyone in the station and let's get statements. I'll be right in." Short, with dark hair and a solid build, Marie stared at me as she walked through the parking lot to the front entrance.

Delahunty walked around Ginnie's car, looking in the windows.

"Here's her phone." I tried to hand it to him but he held up his hands.

"Let me put on gloves." He then took the phone and placed it in a plastic bag. "We'll run it for prints, which means we'll need your prints since you touched it."

"Got it. Where could she be?" I asked no one in particular. "I can't believe this. Ginnie is loved by everyone."

"Don't panic. We'll find her."

"I can't help panicking. This is my wife."

"I know, but let us do our jobs. Does she have any family nearby?"

"Her mother lives in Manchester." I hadn't even thought to call her mother. "Let me call her."

With Delahunty standing there, probably thinking Ginnie was sitting comfortably at her mother's house, I called Barbara Turner. "Hey, Barb, it's Dutch."

"How're you, Dutch?" She had a raspy voice from smoking unfiltered Chesterfield Kings for nearly forty years.

"I'm afraid I'm not well at all. I'm looking for Ginnie. Does she happen to be with you?"

"No. I talked to her yesterday and she seemed preoccupied, but I haven't seen her today. What's happened?"

I explained that Ginnie was missing but her car was still at the station.

"This is crazy. Who would take her?"

"We don't know yet, but she told me she received some threats today."

Her mother gasped. "Oh, my God."

"Sorry to hit you with this, Barb, but I've got to go. I'll keep you posted."

"That's not good news," Delahunty said as I followed him inside the station where the staff was gathered in the conference room, which had a twelve-foot-long oak table with black leather high-backed chairs lining both sides.

There were seven or eight people standing around and Bill's partner was addressing them. "I'm Officer Marie Leary and this is my partner, Bill Delahunty. We need to know if any of you has any idea where Ginnie Turner might be." There were gasps among the group; this was apparently the first time some had heard of Ginnie missing.

"She was on her way home," a young woman said.

"What's your name?" Leary asked.

"Katrina Levine." She pushed back her dark glasses. She had short brown hair and was dressed in hole-filled dungarees.

"How do you know?"

"I asked her to go for a drink and she said she had to go home."

"Anything else she say?"

"Only..."

"What?"

"She wasn't going to drink for a while. Which was strange because we've had drinks many times and she's never been drunk."

Maybe Ginnie had decided to have the baby, I thought. That would be great news. I had to find out.

"Did anyone hear of any threats against her?" Leary asked.

Dennis Cassidy spoke up. "She came into my office this afternoon and said she'd received another nasty phone call. But she was laughing; she didn't seem to think it was anything to worry about."

"Did she give you any details?"

Cassidy knew no more than I did. "But this happens to all of us some time or other."

"Are you aware of other threats?" Like Delahunty, Leary was busy writing in a notepad.

"In the past she's mentioned receiving angry phone calls or emails, but nothing stands out. I never mentioned it to anyone." Cassidy looked at me as if wanting me to say he had done fine.

"Can you take me to her desk?"

Cassidy gestured for her to follow him. After dismissing the other employees, Delahunty sat with me at the conference table. "Marie is checking your wife's desk phone for today's incoming and outgoing calls. I'll do the same for her cell phone after we check it for prints. Do you have her password?"

I gave it to him.

He scribbled in his notebook just as Leary returned. She sat down beside Delahunty right across from me. "Cassidy gave me your wife's laptop," she said. "Do you have the password?"

I shook my head. "You can try the cell phone password, which I gave to your partner."

"No problem. If we have to, we'll run a password scanner."

Then they looked at each other before Delahunty said, "There's no easy way to say this. We've got to search your home."

"What?"

"Standard practice," Leary said. "After a kidnapping."

"You mean I'm a suspect? Just because I'm the husband?"

Delahunty shrugged. "You know how it is."

"You got a warrant?"

"You're not goin' to play it that way, are you?" Leary asked.

"Why shouldn't I?"

"It'd go easier for you if you cooperated," she said, squinting her eyes as if she had a hard time focusing on me.

"Bullshit! That might work with your usual suspects but I know better."

"Look, Dutch," Delahunty said, "let us look around just so we can put it in the report. That way no one's gonna be asking questions later on."

I considered what he said. Delahunty was a decent sort but I didn't like Leary. She had an attitude that was hard to figure out. In the end, I decided to cooperate. Anything to help the cops find the kidnapper.

"All right. I'll let you search the condo. Do you geniuses have any other ideas on who might've taken Ginnie?"

They looked at each other, probably thinking I had just complimented them. "We're going to check out these phone calls," Delahunty said, "then surveil the neighborhood for any video."

"What about the station? Didn't they have a camera on the parking lot?"

"Hard to believe," Leary said, "but the answer is no. They've got all these cameras inside but none outside."

CHAPTER FOUR

I DROVE HOME in a blur and waited for the police to arrive to search my home. It was devastating to think I was a suspect.

Fifteen minutes later, Delahunty and Leary pulled up to the side of the condo. Delahunty sat down at the round Formica kitchen table and ran his hand over his face and hair, at least what was left of his hair. He seemed nervous. "Sorry to do this to you."

"Yeah, I know. You've got a job to do."

Leary stood nearby. Staring at me, without so much as a nod, she said to Delahunty, "Shall we?" Leary went right to work, pulling up the cushions on the sofa, emptying the hall closet before going into the bedroom. She was making a mess and I didn't like it. Delahunty checked the medicine cabinet, linen closet, kitchen cabinets, even the refrigerator. He was giving things a cursory look as if going through the motions. Before long they were finished.

"You find anything?" I asked.

Delahunty shook his head as Leary crossed her arms and said, "I got something to ask you."

"Yeah."

"Anything unusual happen today?"

"I told you about the phone calls. As far as I'm concerned, that was unusual."

"Anything else?"

"As a matter of fact, Ginnie revealed she was pregnant. She wasn't sure she wanted the baby; I did."

"First pregnancy?" Leary asked.

"Yeah, far as I know."

"Could be she decided to terminate the pregnancy."

"Without telling me?"

"She knew you'd get mad, didn't want to argue anymore," Delahunty said. "Might be worth talking to her gynecologist?"

I gave him her name and contact information, actually feeling hopeful for the first time. Maybe Ginnie just freaked out and decided to get an abortion, take a few days off. I actually tried to convince myself that was the truth, that she was fine and would be home soon. Then I thought about her car. If she wanted to get away by herself, why wouldn't she take her car? And her phone. No, Ginnie had been kidnapped; there was no doubt about it.

Ignoring my distressed look, Leary got right back to business. "We'll need your fingerprints."

"No problem." I waited while she gathered an ink pad and fingerprint sheets. She pressed my fingers onto the sheet, pressing a bit too hard for my taste. I let it go.

After finishing, Leary said, "One other thing: we need to take your laptop."

"Go to hell."

"Won't look good for you if you don't cooperate."

I looked at Delahunty. "I need that laptop for work. There's also a lot of privileged attorney-client communications so I can't let you have it."

"Understood," Delahunty said. "Do you mind at least if we look at it?"

I swallowed a few times. I had a few clients whose laptops were seized by the police and never worked the same. I wasn't going to make the same mistake. "I do mind, but I'm not going to get in your way as long as you stay out of my case files."

"Okay, turn it on," Leary said.

I turned on the laptop, entered my password, and opened to the desktop. I pointed to a folder. "This has my case files so stay away from it."

Delahunty pulled the laptop in front of him. The first thing he did was search my internet browsing history and, finding nothing of note, looked through my files. "There's nothing here."

"Not surprising. Now I recommend you two focus on finding Ginnie and not hassling me. You know this will get a lot of media attention. I'd hate for the public to think you botched this investigation right from the beginning."

❋   ❋   ❋

After Delahunty and Leary left, I placed a call to Glen Hedges, my ponytailed private investigator, and explained the situation. Even though it was after eleven p.m., Hedges agreed to come over as a personal favor. I didn't really know what Hedges could do but I had to talk to someone. Over the past few cases, we had become good friends. Occasionally we would drive to Boston for a sporting event or hang out in Manchester at one of the local pubs. Not a typical investigator, he had started as a fireman until a back injury forced a career change. Although he had a license to carry a gun, I generally asked him to leave it at home. I had no use for guns and believed I could talk my way out of most situations.

The doorbell rang and Hedges came in without waiting for me to answer. He was wearing a long-sleeve grey New England Patriots t-shirt, dungarees, and red suspenders. When I first met Hedges some time ago, his ponytail was dark brown. Now it was sprinkled with bits of grey, giving him a more distinguished appearance.

"You think you're back on the fire department?" I asked, pulling on the suspenders.

"Babes love them. Christy got them for me."

I smiled, thinking of his early-twenty's girlfriend, who was smart and funny and a perfect match for Hedges. For the first time since I'd known him, he'd stopped womanizing and focused only on Christy. For the last six months anyway, which was a lifetime for Hedges.

Hedges looked around the condo. "I like what you've done to the place. Monet prints."

"Ginnie wanted some grown-up decorations."

At my mention of Ginnie, Hedges turned toward me. "I'm sorry about this whole thing. It'll work out; you'll see."

"I know it will." I directed him to the couch, grabbed a couple of bottles of Molson from the fridge, and sat down beside him.

"Anything I can do, just ask. Let me tell you up front: this is pro bono. I'm not going to charge you for helping find Ginnie. That just wouldn't feel right."

"I appreciate that, Glen." Ginnie and I had gone out with Hedges and Christy a half dozen times, usually to a local restaurant or a Red Sox game at Fenway. They had hit it off, perhaps because they were so different, Hedges informal and irreverent and Ginnie straitlaced, always "on."

I told him everything I knew so far, including about today's phone calls to Ginnie. "The cops said they'd look into her recent stories."

"Why don't I do the same. I might see something the cops miss." He took a sip of his beer.

Hedges had provided great help on some of my biggest cases, including the Walker murder case and the Howard sexual harassment case, both of which had garnered extensive local publicity. I trusted him; he had good instincts and could handle the unexpected.

We made small talk for a few minutes then he chugged his beer. "I'm going online to watch as many of Ginnie's recent reports as I can. I'll let you know if I find anything."

After he left, I turned on the TV to see a full-screen photo of Ginnie sitting at her newscaster's desk, wearing a maroon dress and a necklace with four connected strands of pearls. A most professional appearance. It was taken when her hair was a bit longer and redder. She was smiling with a twinkle in her eyes. I stared at her photo, missing her all the more, thinking of our life together, our life to be, the good times we had, the good times we planned to have, the family we might have together, and the tears started dripping down my cheeks. Thinking of a family with Ginnie reminded me she was pregnant, our unborn child in her womb. Had I lost both my wife and my child?

The camera zoomed to Dennis Cassidy, his wavy silver hair still perfectly in place, who said the police had no leads on his dear colleague's disappearance. He pleaded with the public to call the station with any information about Ginnie as a phone number flashed on the screen. For once I actually agreed with Cassidy. On this issue, there was no doubt, we were on the same side.

CHAPTER FIVE

I COULDN'T SLEEP at all, constantly thinking of terrible things happening to my wife. My mind couldn't stop going to the dark side. There didn't seem to be any bright side to this situation so I guess I shouldn't have been surprised. I was still having a hard time believing someone would kidnap Ginnie.

Despite my weariness, I made it to court on time for day two of the preliminary hearing. Tompkins was sitting at counsel table. As if on cue, Judge Shane entered the courtroom and strode to the bench.

After we stated our appearances, the judge asked if we were ready to proceed.

"Your Honor," I said, "I'm afraid I have to ask for a continuance."

"Is this because of your wife?" the judge asked, looking concerned. As expected, everyone had heard about Ginnie's disappearance.

"Yes, it is."

Judge Shane turned to Tompkins. "Any reason why we can't continue this hearing for a few days?"

"Well, Your Honor," Tompkins stammered. "The People are most sympathetic with Mr. Francis' situation, but the problem is, our next witness, Dr. Marie McAulley, leaves tomorrow for a conference in New York City. She'll be gone the rest of the week. We need her testimony."

"Why can't we continue this hearing until next week then?" Judge Shane asked.

"We could except the defendant has invoked his right to a speedy trial so the trial must start next week. Assuming the court issues a holding order."

Judge Shane grimaced. "How'd my calendar get so crowded?"

"Well, Your Honor," said Tompkins, "we tried to schedule the prelim three weeks ago, but Your Honor had a three-week vacation planned."

"I see," Judge Shane said. "So it's my fault you gentlemen can't coordinate your calendars."

Judge Shane was clearly not happy to have her calendar jammed. She turned to me. "It seems, Mr. Francis, that the matter of a continuance is in your client's hands. I suggest we take a brief recess while you consult with the defendant in the holding cell."

The bailiff accompanied Garcia and me to the holding cell and stationed himself outside the door. I knew from experience that the cell was not entirely soundproof so I told Garcia to keep his voice low.

Before we sat down, Garcia held out both hands and grabbed my shoulders. "Dutch, I am so sorry. I can't imagine what you're going through."

I was feeling numb. "Thanks for your concern. What about waiving the speedy trial?"

He hesitated, looking away. "We both know Shane's going to find probable cause. Why not just get it over with?"

I couldn't believe he was saying this. He was a lawyer before he was a judge and he knew the importance of a preliminary hearing. "I can't do that."

"Dutch, I think you can. It will be a diversion from what happened to your wife. What will you do otherwise: sit home and stew?"

I slammed my fist on the table, which brought the bailiff into the cell.

"Everything okay?" he asked.

"Yes, sir," I said. "Sorry for the disturbance."

He nodded and then shut the door.

I tried to keep my anger inside. It was my business if I wanted to sit home and stew. At least then I'd be spending my time thinking of Ginnie and not Carlos Garcia. "For your information, Carlos, what I'll do is look for my wife." I didn't really have a plan for doing that, but I wanted my focus to be on Ginnie.

Garcia looked down. "I'm afraid I don't agree. I want this trial over as soon as possible."

"Why?" His desire for a speedy trial seemed irrational.

"I don't want to stay in jail a moment longer than necessary."

"What? You can't give it another week or two? What game are you playing?"

"It's not a game."

I had heard enough. I stood up and said, "I'm withdrawing. Get yourself another lawyer."

"I never took you for a quitter."

"You know what I'm going through. I have to find my wife." I started choking up saying these words and Garcia looked away. This was no way for a lawyer to behave in front of his client, but I couldn't control myself. Finally, Garcia turned back to me, his bushy grey eyebrows pointing inward.

"I'm sorry about your wife. I really am. But I hired you for a reason. You know how to win the impossible case. You've proven yourself. Do you think I'm going to risk spending the rest of my life in state prison? That's what I risk by changing lawyers now. I won't do that."

"I'm withdrawing."

He seemed shattered. "You can't do that; I won't agree."

I opened the door. "Let's see what Judge Shane says."

The bailiff said the judge was on the phone and would take the bench shortly. I pulled my seat a few feet away from Garcia, not wanting to be within punching distance, which is what I felt like doing to him. In a few minutes Judge Shane took the bench and I explained my client's position. She was sympathetic. "It's understandable that you want to focus on your wife. I think we'd all feel the same way if we were in your shoes. Mr. Garcia, let me ask you directly: Will you agree to change lawyers so you can get a speedy trial?"

"Judge, you know that's not going to happen. Any lawyer worth his salt will ask for a continuance so he can get up to speed on the case. I want Mr. Francis."

"You realize, Mr. Garcia, that Mr. Francis will be distracted until his wife is found. That could harm your defense."

"I'm willing to take that risk. From what I hear, a distracted Dutch Francis is better than most fully focused lawyers."

"I'm sure Mr. Francis appreciates the compliment." She turned toward me. "Mr. Francis, is there anything else you'd like to add?"

"Only that Your Honor is right: I won't be able to concentrate on this case. My only priority is to find my wife."

She nodded. "I understand the Manchester Police Department is investigating your wife's disappearance. Realistically, I'm not sure what else you could do."

"I could make sure they're doing their job."

"Understood, but I find myself between a rock and a hard place. If I let you out, the defendant will still insist on a speedy trial. It would be very difficult, if not impossible, to find someone to jump in at the last minute."

"I'm sure I could find someone, Your Honor."

"Be that as it may, I believe it would be prejudicial to the defense to grant the motion to withdraw. Therefore, I will have to deny your motion."

I asked for a fifteen-minute break, which Judge Shane quickly granted. I made my way to the rest room, wondering how I was going to get through this hearing. My reflection in the mirror revealed dark circles under my eyes. I splashed water on my face and wiped the back of my neck then dried off using the paper towels.

Outside in the corridor, I placed a call to Hedges.

"Garcia won't let me out. I've got to do this hearing, then the trial."

"Damn! The guy's got no heart. I'll do what I can from this end. There're a couple of recent stories I'm looking into."

"Great. Leave me a voicemail if you find any solid leads." I returned to the courtroom, my thoughts a jumble as Dr. McAulley took the stand. I tried to put Ginnie out of my mind and reflected on Dr. McAulley's testimony in the Walker trial. She had been forthright, not really helpful, but willing to concede points that hurt the prosecution. She still favored tartan skirts and wearing her grey hair in a short ponytail.

After Tompkins established her background, Dr. McAulley went through her examination of the corpse. "I used the standard formula to determine time of death: Hours since death equals 98.6 less corpse core temperature divided by 1.5. I used a rectal thermometer and also checked her liver by making a small incision in her abdomen and inserting a thermometer. At midnight her body temperature was 95.7 degrees."

"And, Dr. McAulley, what conclusions did you draw from the body temperature?"

"Mrs. Garcia had been dead at most two hours," she said with an assurance that startled me.

"On what do you base that conclusion?"

"Her body temperature had dropped less than three degrees. One and a half degrees drop per hour is the standard forensic pathologists use. Plus, there was no evidence of rigor mortis."

"What's the significance of the absence of rigor mortis?"

McAulley brushed a strand of hair from her eyes and leaned forward. "Rigor mortis typically sets in within two hours of death. Usually, it's seen in the small muscles of the face and neck. I examined that area carefully and found no evidence of rigor mortis."

"If you took her temperature at midnight, would it be safe to say she died around ten o'clock?"

"That would be my opinion."

Tompkins turned his notes and cleared his throat. "Did you determine the cause of death?"

"I did."

"How did you go about determining the cause of death?"

McAulley pursed her lips. "I tested her blood and found toxic levels of hydrocodone, nearly 0.50 milligrams per liter. From an examination of her stomach contents, I concluded she had eaten two to three hours before death. The drug appeared to have been crushed before being ingested."

"On what do you base that conclusion?"

"There were traces of hydrocodone throughout her stomach contents rather than concentrated in one area. She had eaten Asian noodles, the kind called drunken noodles."

"Hydrocodone has a trade name of Vicodin, is that right?"

"That's correct."

"And what significance is there in the drug being crushed?"

McAulley straightened up. "You want my opinion?"

"I certainly do."

"Crushing the hydrocodone causes a faster effect. If the tablet is crushed, that would make it act much more quickly. It's hard to tell how many tablets she ingested but whatever the quantity, it was enough to kill her."

"Do you have an opinion on the cause of death?"

"In my opinion—this is opinion only—someone poisoned her. There's no reason for her to crush a hydrocodone tablet before taking it. I believe someone crushed the drug and mixed it with her food."

I jumped up. "Objection. Speculation. Move to strike."

Judge Shane looked at me over her glasses. "The objection is sustained but the motion is denied."

"Your Honor," I said, almost pleading. "May I be heard?"

"Yes, Mr. Francis. What is it?"

"I agree Dr. McAulley can testify that the crushed hydrocodone caused Mrs. Garcia's death; however, there is no basis for her testimony that someone poisoned her. As you know, the defense is that Mrs. Garcia poisoned herself."

She looked toward the ceiling as if searching for her response. "Well, Mrs. Garcia certainly is 'someone,' is she not?"

"True. However, I don't believe that was the import of the witness' testimony."

"Mr. Francis, we're wasting time here. I've sustained your objection and I will give the testimony as much weight as it deserves."

Beside me, Garcia stiffened and stopped breathing. He stared at Dr. McAulley, his eyes squinting. "Easy," I said. "Don't show any emotion." Truth was, at that moment, I was feeling a lot of emotion, most of it anger at my client for putting me in this situation.

He seemed not to pick up on my anger and turned toward me and nodded, his lips pursed.

Tompkins straightened his papers, signaling he was nearing the end of his questioning. "Did you find anything else of significance?"

"Yes. Mrs. Garcia had a blood alcohol level of 0.09 percent, higher than the legal limit if she were driving a vehicle. There were significant traces of red wine in her system."

"Do you believe the alcohol contributed to her death?"

"It may have enhanced the effect of the hydrocodone and . . ."

"What is it, Doctor?"

". . . and drinking that much wine would have disguised the taste of the hydrocodone so she wouldn't detect it in her food."

"Thank you, Doctor, nothing further."

I put my hands on the table, trying to decide whether to stand up and question the doctor or wait until trial. Thinking it over, I pushed myself up and took my place behind the podium. "Doctor, I have only two subjects to ask you about."

"Please, Mr. Francis, don't limit yourself. Ask me anything." She was feisty, wanting to pick up where we'd left off in the Walker trial.

"One is how in the world you know, as a respected forensic pathologist, that the deceased did not crush the pills herself?"

"I don't know. It just seems unlikely."

"Is that your professional opinion as a forensic pathologist?"

"I examine a lot of corpses, Mr. Francis."

"No doubt. But isn't it true that all you can say from your examination of the body is that the drug was crushed?"

"The drug was crushed, that's right."

"You can't say the drug was crushed by Mrs. Garcia or someone else. That goes beyond your area of expertise, does it not?"

"If you say so."

"Not what I say; wouldn't you agree?"

She looked at Judge Shane as if wanting to be rescued. But the judge was writing on her legal pad and paid her no attention. "You are correct, Mr. Francis."

"So you agree that it's beyond your expertise as a medical examiner to opine that someone else crushed the hydrocodone tablets?" I wanted to pin her down so she couldn't give the same testimony at trial. I had to make sure she stuck to her area of expertise and not plant prejudicial ideas in the minds of jurors.

"I said you are correct."

"Thank you, Doctor. My second question has to do with your opinion that the red wine masked the taste of the Vicodin. What training do you have as a forensic pathologist that allows you to offer that opinion?"

"Don't forget I am a trained medical doctor, Mr. Francis. I am well acquainted with the tongue and its 5,000 or so taste buds."

"I haven't forgotten. Perhaps you could tell me how many times you have testified as an expert witness on the ability of wine to mask the taste of a drug."

She leaned back, thinking. "This is the first time."

"I see. And I understand you've done a fellowship on forensic pathology. Have you done any kind of fellowship on the study of taste buds?"

"I can't say I have."

"You've written extensively for professional journals on forensic pathology. How many articles have you written on taste buds?"

She exhaled loudly. "None."

"And you've lectured extensively on forensic pathology. How many lectures have you given on the subject of taste buds?"

She mumbled something. The court reporter hesitated. "I'm sorry. I didn't catch that."

"Neither did I," I said.

"I said, 'none.'" Dr. McAulley's tone had turned decidedly hostile.

I had one more question to put the nail in the coffin. "So you're really not an expert in the masking qualities of red wine, correct?"

"That's . . . that's correct. But it makes sense."

"I trust, Doctor, that you won't be testifying to such a thing at trial." I took my seat. "No further questions."

CHAPTER SIX

STRAIGHTENING HIS PONYTAIL, Hedges hovered over my desk. I had just come from court and was feeling exhausted. Hedges had been busy checking out Ginnie's recent stories, trying to figure out who had threatened her.

"There're a couple of possibilities," he said. "The night before her kidnapping, Ginnie had covered the arrest of the girls' soccer coach. My research revealed he has some shady friends."

"How shady?"

"Mobster types. Loan sharks, bookies, the usual."

"Why would they care about a child molester? Doesn't seem like their type."

"I agree." He sat up in his chair. "But this guy—his name's Billy Conti—is the grandson of a New England crime boss. The family thinks Billy got framed, that Ginnie blew things out of proportion. They say all he did was give an innocent hug to a twelve-year-old girl, that Ginnie got the girl to say it was much more."

"Have you talked to him?"

He shook his head. "Not yet. I've watched all the video of the TV coverage and talked to a few Conti family members. It's clear they're pissed at Ginnie, but I don't know that they'd go so far as to kidnap her."

"We definitely need to talk to Conti. Any idea who's defending him?"

"Marco Liberatore, a Nashua lawyer. Handles all Mob business."

"I've heard of him. Most of it not good." I thought about whether to approach Liberatore. Would he really allow his client to talk to Hedges? I doubted it. "Let's talk to Conti first, then try Liberatore." I swallowed, not liking this development. "You said there were a couple of possibilities. What's the other one?"

"Ginnie broke the story about St. Andrew's not long ago. Lots of alumni are pissed off, claiming it was a handful of upperclassmen who had concocted an elaborate challenge with financial rewards for sexual conquests of underclasswomen. They say these kids are not representative of the school."

"So where does that leave us? Check out everyone in the St. Andrew's alumni directory?"

Hedges scratched his head. "I hear what you're saying. Let me try to narrow the search."

"And let's not overlook the obvious," I said. "Ginnie covered Judge Garcia's arrest extensively so that's another lead worth checking out."

"Got it." He got up to leave but turned back to face me. "Oh, almost forgot. I spoke to Katarina Levine. Seems she was one of Ginnie's best friends at the station. She confirmed what she told the police but also said Ginnie had seemed unhappy lately, not her usual chipper self. You notice that?"

I thought about the last few weeks. "Nothing out of the ordinary." Had I been so insensitive to my wife's situation that I didn't notice signs of depression? Could it have been the pregnancy that was affecting her mood? Or even worse, could it have been something else? Could it have been me?

❄ ❄ ❄

I didn't feel any better after Hedges left. If the Mob were involved, then I feared for Ginnie's life. If it were a St. Andrew's alum, then perhaps he'd let her go, just scare her a bit. That's what I hoped anyway. I wanted to talk to Delahunty so I called him and said I'd be right over.

The police station is on Valley Street in a boxy red-brick building with windows of differing sizes, almost like a Mondrian painting. The receptionist directed me to an elevator, which took me to the second floor where Delahunty greeted me. We walked to a small conference room. The table was dark brown, six feet long, made of laminate with chips on the edges. I sat on one side on an orange plastic chair; Delahunty sat across from me.

"I wanted to be up front with you," I said. "I've got my friend Glen Hedges, a private eye, helping out with the case."

"Why're you doing that? We're checking out everything."

"I can't sit around doing nothing. Besides, your department seems to think I had something to do with Ginnie's disappearance."

"I admit Leary was leaning that way, but she's a suspicious sort. Between you and me, she's had some bad experiences with abusive boyfriends. I've no doubt you're clean. So what do you have Hedges doing?"

"He's looking into Ginnie's recent stories." I told him about Conti, the St. Andrew's sex scandal, and Judge Garcia's case.

"We've checked those out already. Conti's lawyer instructed him not to talk to us and so far the St. Andrew's story hasn't produced any suspects. And Garcia . . . I don't know. It's been weeks since he was arrested."

"Yeah, but his prelim just started the day of Ginnie's kidnapping." I thought of Garcia's brother-in-law Sam Collins and told Delahunty to check him out. I thought Hedges might have better luck with Conti. "Any other leads?"

"We're following up on her calls from yesterday, on both her work and cell phones. Too soon yet to know where that'll lead. We also canvassed the neighborhood around the station, talked to the neighbors. Found some video that has potential. We posted flyers on the telephone poles in the neighborhood with a photo of Ginnie. And I have the results of the fingerprint analysis on Ginnie's phone."

"Anything?"

"Your prints, of course. A few matched prints on Ginnie's laptop so my guess is they're hers. Some unidentifiable ones. We ran them through the database and came up dry."

"So now what?"

"We'll keep looking for witnesses. Leary is with our IT people now going over the video."

"So what am I supposed to do, sit home and wait?"

"There's nothing you can do. Why don't you take your mind off this and go to Sam's. Tonight's the poker game."

"That's crazy. I need to find Ginnie."

"Dutch, let us work the case. I'll call you if anything comes up."

❂ ❂ ❂

Before my anxiety could get the better of me, I took Delahunty's advice and drove over to Sam Dolorio's place for our monthly poker game. Sam greeted me at the door.

"Didn't think you'd come," he said. "With all that's going on."

"I wasn't but I need a distraction or I'll go crazy."

Sam was from the Dominican Republic, an early immigrant who had scraped his way through Massachusetts Law School, then moved north. He was also a baseball nut. "My grandfather played ball with Satchel Paige," he'd told me. "When he pitched for the Kansas City Athletics back in '65. Gramps was on the bench when ol' Satch shut out the Red Sox for three innings. Satch must've been sixty years old. They even had a nurse at the ballpark to help him get around."

Sam handed me a sixteen-ounce can of Pabst Blue Ribbon, the only beer he ever drank. "Delahunty won't be here tonight. Something about a conflict of interest."

I took a seat in the parlor. "Sonuvabitch's partner thinks I kidnapped my own wife. Or worse."

"Nah. They're just being careful. Delahunty knows you better'n that."

An ex-public defender, Sam practiced criminal defense full-time, unlike me. When Judge Garcia first approached me, I recommended Sam but he rebuffed me, spitting out a racial epithet. I should've turned him down right then but he quickly apologized.

"And I'm still defending Garcia. He wouldn't let me withdraw."

"The sonuvabitch. How're you going to do that?"

I shrugged. "Somehow I have to prove his wife committed suicide. You have any experience with that kind of defense?"

"Nearly had one go to trial but my guy pleaded out. What you need to do is get a shrink to do a psychological autopsy."

"What the hell's that?"

He smiled. "It amazes me that you get a high-profile murder case when you don't know jack shit from shinola."

"Me too. I told Garcia he should hire you."

That took him by surprise. "No kidding. I appreciate that."

"Should've guessed he'd be a difficult client; he didn't take my advice then so why would he listen to me when I asked to withdraw." I took a sip of beer. "So tell me about this psychological autopsy."

"You get a shrink to examine the victim's relationships, medical history, and background and come up with the conclusion she committed suicide."

"Sounds like bullshit."

"Yeah, but what else you got?"

"Do you have a referral?"

"Do you mind going to Boston?"

"You know I love Boston. It's my hometown. '*I love that dirty water*,' as the song goes."

"Not dirty anymore. Anyway, there's one expert everyone says is the best."

"That's great. You ever use him?"

"Her. You sexist pig. Doctor Marilyn Gumina. She's a Harvard-trained psychiatrist with a private practice in Cambridge."

"You're a peach. I'll check her out."

The doorbell rang. "Who else you expecting?"

"Gerry and Ray. Tim's got another date, the lovesick fool, so it'll be a cozy foursome."

Gerry Reilly and Ray Monroe arrived together. They made an odd pair. Reilly was about five foot six, clean-cut and nattily dressed with wavy black hair while Monroe towered over him at six foot one and wore undersized clothes.

The game started promptly at eight. The pot got to ninety dollars. I wasn't winning, but that didn't stop me from raising the bets. As my losses mounted, tension seemed to fill the room. No one wanted to talk about Ginnie though it was obvious she was on everyone's mind. I couldn't concentrate on the game and kept throwing my money away.

Monroe tried to loosen me up. "Business has been slow, Dutch. So I appreciate your supporting me. Perhaps you might invest in a duplex I'm remodeling. I figure when it's finished, I can sell it for half a mil, easy."

Monroe owned a small construction company with four employees. He did mainly residential projects, remodels mostly with some new construction.

"Hey, you promised that one to me," Reilly said.

"You can't afford it on a FedEx salary," Monroe said. "Don't be kidding me."

Reilly was a route transport driver for FedEx, driving a fifty-five-foot trailer between stations and the airport. He was constantly on workers' comp leave with neck, back, and shoulder pain. He consulted me about his employment and I referred him to a workers' comp attorney. But fortunately for him, I had read the FedEx policies closely and noticed that the company could fire him after ninety consecutive days of medical leave. I thought the policy was grossly unfair, and probably illegal, but convinced Monroe to go back to work before the ninety days ran out. He got his doctor to write a return-to-work slip that got him back to work for a week before going out again. At least he started the ninety days running again.

I raised the ante, oblivious to my losing streak. "I need to make some money for the ransom, if there is one." That brought things to a standstill, everyone quiet and staring at their cards. "Sorry to be such a downer."

"No problemo," Dolorio said. "We all feel for ya."

"We miss seeing Ginnie on TV, too," Monroe said. "She brightened my nights."

"Nice of you to say that, Ray," I said.

The game continued until I ran out of money. I looked at Sam and said, "Sam, I forgot to ask if you know someone named Marco Liberatore, a Nashua lawyer."

"Yeah, I know him. He's bad news. Why do you ask?"

"Might have some connection to Ginnie. I don't know yet."

"I hope not. I'd want nothing to do with that guy."

"What's the problem?"

Sam gathered up the cards and boxed them. "Bad reputation in the ethics department."

Sam's assessment of Liberatore didn't make me feel any better. I stood up. "Thanks, Sam; I've got to go."

Monroe also stood up and handed me a fistful of bills. "You take these. For Ginnie."

I held up my hands. "No, I was kidding. I don't need the money. You won it; you keep it."

Before I left, each guy gave me a hug and a pat on the back, the first time they'd ever done that.

CHAPTER SEVEN

THE PRELIMINARY HEARING was scheduled to resume at 1:30 so the next morning I worked from home.

I was amped up, unable to sit still. I dropped down and pumped out fifty push-ups. Then I rolled over and did a hundred sit-ups. Feeling somewhat better, I tried drafting a settlement demand letter for a personal injury client, but I had a hard time empathizing with my client's back injury. So I picked up a mystery novel by a popular Norwegian author. After reading the first chapter, a bleak depiction of a cold, desolate landscape, I threw the book across the room, realizing it was only making me feel worse.

My misery was interrupted by the sound of mail dropping through the slot in the front door. Most were bills except for a small manila envelope without a return address. I stared at the stamps, all U.S. flags, overnight mail, and my address typed right on the envelope. I should've known better but I couldn't help myself and ripped it open, nearly tearing the envelope in half. At first, I thought the envelope was empty then I blew it open and looked inside. At the bottom of the envelope were several strands of hair. I gasped as I pulled out the hair. It was rust-colored, about ten inches long, and bound together by an elastic band.

I held the hair up to the light. Some of the original brunette could still be seen, but I had no doubt it was Ginnie's hair. I stared at the envelope, realizing I had contaminated it with my fingerprints and dropped the hair on top of it. Then I grabbed my cell phone and called Delahunty.

"Get over here right away."

"What is it?"

"I got a delivery. Bring your crime scene kit."

Delahunty arrived ten minutes later with Leary in tow. I let them in and led them to the kitchen. Before examining the envelope, Delahunty handed me Ginnie's laptop. "We've cloned it so you can have it back."

"Find anything on it?"

"Too early to tell."

I pointed to the table. "This arrived today in that envelope. That's Ginnie's hair; there's no doubt about it."

Delahunty and Leary looked at each other. Delahunty seemed to have a smug look, as if saying, "I told you so." Delahunty put on a pair of latex gloves and placed the envelope in a plastic bag.

"What's the postal stamp on the envelope?" Leary asked.

"Manchester," Delahunty said. "It was mailed yesterday. That's something, anyway."

"You get anywhere with the gynecologist?" I asked, remembering what Delahunty had said before.

He shook his head. "The doctor confirmed the pregnancy but hasn't heard from Ginnie in the past few days."

"So you believe me now?"

"We always believed you."

"Sure," I said, turning to look at Leary.

❈ ❈ ❈

It was after ten when Delahunty and Leary left. I placed a quick call to Hedges. "Have you located Conti?"

"Yeah, in Nashua."

"No kidding. Pick me up as soon as you can."

Hedges drove a beat-up Dodge sedan, dark green, with dents in both bumpers. On the drive I told him about the envelope with strands of Ginnie's hair.

"He's sending you a message."

"What's the message?"

"The obvious one: that he's got Ginnie. This is a good sign. I would expect him to follow up with a ransom demand."

"I just want to know she's safe."

Hedges had set up the GPS with Conti's address in Nashua and we arrived in about twenty minutes. Conti's house was on a tree-lined street with well-trimmed front lawns. Across the street, several boys and girls, nine or ten years old, were shooting at a hoop set up in the driveway. I wondered what their parents thought of living so close to a suspected child molester.

As we walked toward his front door, my phone rang. It was Delahunty.

"Dutch, we tracked one of the calls Ginnie received the day of her kidnapping."

"What'd you find?"

"Now I don't want you to do anything, and I probably shouldn't tell you this, but she got a call from Billy Conti."

"That sonuvabitch!"

"That doesn't mean he took her."

"I'll find out for myself."

"Dutch—"

I hung up and knocked on the door.

A dark-haired woman with purple lips answered the door. "Is Mr. Conti home?"

"Who wants to know?"

"My name is Dutch Francis; I'm a lawyer. And this is Glen Hedges, my investigator."

She licked her purple lips. "You're the one whose wife is missing?"

"I am; that's what I want to talk to your husband about."

She pursed her lips. "He don't know nothing about that."

"If it's okay with you, I'd like to ask him myself."

Suddenly there came a booming voice from the top of the inside stairs. "It's all right, Anita, I'll talk to them."

Conti came to the front door. "Come in. I don't need the neighbors watching this."

We sat in his living room, Hedges and I on the brown leather couch, Conti and his wife on the dark pink chairs across from us. They made a sharp contrast: he was heavyset and short with a pockmarked face; she was stick thin with a smooth angular face. He was edgy, unable to keep his hands still; she sat calmly with her hands in her lap.

I glanced around the house, noticing the stairs leading to the second floor where Conti had been. A plan formed in my mind.

"I'm sorry for what's happened to your wife," Conti said.

"Are you? You said some unkind things about her."

"She said some unkind things about me." He folded his arms and looked down at the worn Oriental rug.

Hedges shifted beside me. I could sense that he wanted to take a shot at this guy. "You watch what you say about Ms. Turner," Hedges said, leaning forward.

"You don't get to tell me what I can say in my own house." Conti raised his voice. "Who the hell are you anyway?"

"I'm your worst nightmare. That's who."

I held up my hand to head off an argument. "Let's not get testy. Mr. Conti, did you have anything to do with my wife's disappearance?"

I stared into his eyes and he kept his gaze on me, letting his arms fall to his lap. "I did not." Did he hesitate before answering? This is what I had wanted: to sit down man to man with Conti and assess on my own whether he was guilty. Now I couldn't be sure. He hadn't said anything to indicate his guilt.

"Your wife caused me a lot of trouble. But I wouldn't do anything that crazy."

"What about your family?"

"My family?"

Hedges couldn't control himself. "Don't be bullshitting us, Mr. Conti. We know all about your family connections."

Conti glared at Hedges and then turned toward me. "Far as I know my family had nothing to do with your wife's disappearance."

"You won't mind, then," I said, standing up, "if Mr. Hedges has a look around just to be sure." I nodded to Hedges to go upstairs.

"Who the hell do you think you are?"

"Mr. Conti, I know you threatened my wife the day of her kidnapping and I just received strands of her hair in the mail. So excuse me for considering you a suspect."

Hedges scampered up the stairs as Conti and his wife stared at him, then back at me. "You'll be hearing from my lawyer."

Hedges returned in less than a minute, shaking his head. "No luck."

As Hedges and I walked toward the door, Conti said, "When you find your wife, tell her something for me."

"What's that?"

"Tell her I never touched that girl."

❖ ❖ ❖

When I got home the phone was ringing. I picked it up on about
the fifth ring.

"Hello."

There was a heavy exhale. "Who is this?"

"Francis, I got to say I'm disappointed in you. I expected more."

"What the hell are you talking about?"

"Why'd you bother my client today?"

"Is this Liberatore?"

Another heavy exhale.

"Don't bother him again is all I'm saying."

"My wife is missing."

"He doesn't know anything about that."

I still wasn't sure whether to believe that, but there was nothing I
could do. I had no evidence against Conti, only a theory.

"Look, I'm sorry about your wife, but kidnapping's not Conti's gig."

"He'd rather molest little girls, is that it?"

"I got no comment on that. Consider yourself warned."

He hung up and I pondered what he had said. To my knowledge
I had never met Liberatore, but he acted as if he knew me. Perhaps
he'd read about the Walker case and didn't expect another criminal defense attorney to contact his client, particularly when the
case was active. Thinking it over, I realized that he had a point. I
wouldn't be happy if someone had done the same thing with one
of my clients.

❋   ❋   ❋

I was not in the right state of mind to be working but I had no choice
because of the Garcia case. Around one o'clock I went to the basement jail of the Hillsborough County Courthouse. I thought of how
far the mighty had fallen, in Garcia's case literally. Previously he had

presided over a courtroom on the top floor; now he was as far down as one could go.

Deputy Sheriff Hank Lerner sat at his desk, playing with a paper clip.

"Hank, good to see you again. The judge is expecting me."

"I bet he is." He put his feet on the desk, signaling to me that he was in charge and I would see my client when he was good and ready. "First you get the Walker murder trial then this Garcia case. How do you get these clients, Francis?"

"It's my wit and charm that attracts them."

Lerner now used the paper clip to clean under his fingernails. "That's horseshit and you know it. I got as much wit in my little finger as—"

"I wouldn't call that chubby thing 'little.'"

"What would you call this thing?" Lerner extended his middle finger in my direction.

"Hank, you're getting a bit touchy in your old age."

"Day I take shit from a Hah-vad lawyer is the day I hang up my badge."

"I apologize to your little finger for calling it 'chubby.'" I was losing patience. "I didn't mean to exclude your other chubby fingers, or your chubby hand, or chubby fuckin' face. Normally I'd love this little repartée but I got a lot on my mind these days."

Lerner threw the paper clip onto the floor and moved his feet off the desk. "Fuckin'-A. It slipped my mind. Do accept my apologies for being so insensitive."

"Accepted." I waited for him to lead me to Garcia's cell.

"Any word on the wife?" He opened the door.

I shook my head.

"Damnedest thing," he said as he walked back toward his desk.

Garcia cleared his blanket from the bench to make room for me to sit. He leaned his head back against the wall and sighed. "What're your thoughts about where we stand?"

I turned to look at him. "Tompkins thinks he's got you dead to rights. No question Maureen died from an overdose of hydrocodone. You're the only one with access to her so he suspects you laced her dinner."

Garcia leaned forward quickly. "I didn't even know the damn stuff could be lethal. God knows I've taken it myself when I had a torn meniscus. It made me a bit loopy but that was all."

"Ever hear that it worked more quickly in powdered form?"

He shook his head, seeming to be lost in thought. "But I wonder how Mo figured that out."

"Maybe she did an internet search."

"I wouldn't put it past her. She was always thorough that way. I still can't believe she did this."

"You'd better believe it because that's the only defense you've got. We should have someone look at Mo's laptop, see if we can find her internet browsing history."

He shook his head. "Her laptop has been on the fritz for a few weeks. She was going to take it to the shop but never got around to it. She'd been using my laptop since then."

"Where's your laptop?"

"The cops seized it when they arrested me. They had me pinned as the murderer right from the beginning, so they probably don't realize that she and I both used it."

"So let's go over that night."

"Again?"

"It never hurts to review the facts. Something we didn't think was important can take on significance as we collect evidence."

He stared at the ceiling. "When I got home, she confronted me about Arlene, claiming a friend reported seeing us together." He stood up and faced the bars with his back to me. "So I told her; I came clean and said I loved Arlene. She demanded I stop seeing her."

"Did you tell her you wanted a divorce?"

He nodded. "She got real quiet, went to the bathroom for a long time, then came out seeming to be calm. I thought she had accepted the divorce. By then dinner had been delivered so she opened the take-out boxes and served the drunken noodles. She even poured us some wine. I told her how impressed I was with how well she had taken it and she said, 'We're not the same people who got married thirty-four years ago. So I guess we'll just go our separate ways.'"

Moisture formed in his eyes as he relived his wife's last night. He seemed genuinely sad at her passing.

The events he related could explain why his wife would kill herself, but then again, they could also point to Judge Garcia. Maybe, Tompkins would argue, the judge couldn't handle the shame and bad publicity of a divorce, particularly when he was involved with a younger woman, so he took the easy way out. Ground up some hydrocodone and mixed it with her Asian noodles, thinking no one'd be the wiser. He should've known better, Tompkins would say, but he was emotional and wanted to take action. So he acted in the heat of the moment, rather than thinking things through logically. If that were the direction Tompkins was going, then he'd box himself in a corner. If Garcia acted in the heat of the moment, that would be manslaughter at best, not first-degree murder. My guess was Tompkins wouldn't go in that direction, but perhaps I could work out a plea bargain with that argument.

"It's not too late to try a plea," I said.

"Plea to what?"

"I think I could convince Tompkins that his best case is manslaughter, maybe plead to ten years in prison."

"No way." He turned toward me. "Don't even think about it. I didn't hire you to plead me out. Either I beat this thing all the way or I do the time."

"I'm willing to try the case but I got to tell you it's not looking good right now. If we're to have any chance, we've got to hire a psychiatrist to do a psychological autopsy."

He raised his thick grey eyebrows. "I don't believe in that."

"Why not? It's pretty standard in a case like this, so I'm told."

He raised his hands, emphasizing his words. "Every time I've seen a shrink testify on that, I haven't been impressed. Juries don't buy it either."

"It's our best chance, goddamn it!" I was frustrated at him for giving me a hard time. He was lucky I was even helping him. I was not going to let him get in my way.

He could sense my mood and decided against arguing. "Then get on it." He put his hand on my shoulder. "Show me what you got."

Still annoyed, I turned to look at him, deep wrinkles on both sides of his mouth. I'll show you what I've got, I thought. I'll pop you right in the mouth. At least that's what I felt like doing.

CHAPTER EIGHT

ON THE ELEVATOR to the courtroom, I placed a call to Dr. Gumina, the psychiatrist in Cambridge Sam had recommended, and left a voicemail message. When I entered the courtroom, I had a sinking feeling in my stomach. I wanted to be anywhere but with Carlos Garcia. I should have been looking for my wife. While the bailiff led Garcia to the defense table, I tried to picture the front page of the *Union Leader* announcing his conviction for murder. There would follow, no doubt, Garcia's claims that he had ineffective assistance of counsel, justifying a new trial. I wouldn't let that happen. It was bad enough that I might have to fight a legal malpractice case by Mrs. Handford; I wasn't going to let my reputation be further ruined by Garcia.

Tompkins had rounded up the rest of his witnesses. Officer Douglas Anderson testified that he had reported to the Garcia house shortly after the 911 call. His job was to fingerprint the deceased, the defendant, and parts of the house. The most damaging part of his testimony was that Garcia's prints were found on the bottle of hydrocodone. After Tompkins finished his questioning and sat down, I had a feeling Anderson was hiding something.

"Officer Anderson, you say you found my client's prints on the bottle. Where exactly on the bottle?"

"The right index finger and right thumb were near the top of the bottle." He stared at me as if daring me to ask the next question.

"I see. And did you conclude from this that my client had picked up the bottle?"

"I did. Seems pretty obvious."

I was about to sit down when something occurred to me. "Officer Anderson, did you search for prints on the lid of the bottle?"

He smiled. "I did."

"And did you find any?"

"Yes," he said, making me work harder.

"Whose prints did you find on the lid of the bottle?"

"The deceased Maureen Garcia's."

"And which of her fingers?"

"Her left index finger and left thumb."

"So you didn't find my client's prints on the lid?"

"There were some partial prints I couldn't distinguish so I can't say."

"You can't say they were my client's, can you?"

He shook his head. "You're correct, I can't say that."

I was feeling my way, sensing Anderson was still holding something back. "Would you agree, Officer Anderson, that the location of my client's prints is consistent with his picking up the bottle and moving it but not removing the lid?"

"He could've removed the lid, I don't know."

I let out a sigh. "Could you answer the question I put to you?"

"Is it consistent, that's what you want to know? Sure, it's consistent with that and probably a dozen other possibilities."

"Thank you." I turned to sit but stopped suddenly, realizing another question I forgot to ask. I must've really been distracted by Ginnie.

"Just a moment, Officer. You said you found my client's prints on the bottle, but I forgot to ask whether you found any other prints there."

Again, he smiled. "In fact, I did."

"Whose prints did you find?"

"The deceased's."

"And which fingers?"

"Her right index and thumb."

I thought about what he was saying. "So you found the deceased's right index and thumb prints on the bottle and left index and thumb prints on the lid. Have I got that right?"

"That's correct."

"Did you conclude that those findings are consistent with the deceased holding the bottle then turning the lid?"

He hesitated. "I could see that."

"It's entirely consistent with the deceased opening the bottle, isn't it?"

"I would agree."

Next was Beverly Branson, a waitress at Fat Tuesday's. She had witnessed the interchange between Garcia and his mistress Arlene Downey the night of Maureen's death. There was not much I could do with her, but I saw a way to buttress an argument for manslaughter over first degree murder.

"Ms. Branson, you say you heard my client say Dr. Downey was the only one for him. What exactly did you hear?"

A twenty-something young woman with pink-dyed hair, Branson put her hand over her chest as if to stop what was about to come out of her mouth. She looked over to the judge and asked, "Can I say the b-word in court?"

The judge nodded. "Tell us exactly what you heard. Don't be afraid to use the actual words."

"Okay. Judge Garcia said, 'Then I'll divorce the bitch if that's what you want.'"

I swallowed then steadied myself and asked, "When Judge Garcia made that statement, was he crying?"

"Yeah, he was."

"You could see the tears?"

"I could. I also heard him sobbing."

"So you would agree that he was in a distressed state at that time?"

She gave me what I wanted. "No doubt about it."

Tompkins' final witness was the police IT specialist Victor Gaspari, a medium-sized middle-aged man with brown hair who was wearing a most uninspiring brown suit and brown tie.

After the preliminaries were over, Tompkins asked, "Did you examine the defendant's laptop?"

I jumped up. "Objection. No foundation. There's no evidence my client owned that laptop."

"Your Honor . . . ," said Tompkins.

"Mr. Francis is right," Judge Shane said. "Objection sustained."

"Let's start again," Tompkins said, sweat forming on his bald head. "Did you go to the defendant's home?"

"I did."

"Did you find a laptop there?"

"Yes, in the kitchen."

"Did you seize that computer?"

"I did. I took it back to my lab at the station." Gaspari spoke in a flat tone.

Tompkins glanced at me. "Did you examine the computer you seized from the defendant's home?"

I couldn't help myself. "And the decedent's home as well."

"I object, Your Honor."

"Mr. Francis," Judge Shane said. "Save the argument for closing. The court very well knows who lived there."

"Mr. Gaspari," Tompkins continued, "do you have the question in mind?"

"Yes. I did examine the computer."

"Did you find any identification of the owner?"

"Indeed. In 'Settings,' Carlos Garcia was noted as the owner."

So much for that issue. I suspected Tompkins would eventually get this information out of the witness, but I still wanted to make him work for it.

Gaspari testified at length about his forensic analysis of the computer. He checked the internet browsing history and found sites describing the toxic effects of an overdose of hydrocodone, the increased risk of ingesting the drug in powder form, and the enhanced effect of taking the drug with alcohol.

There was nothing shocking in what he said. McAulley had already covered this ground. There were only a few points I wanted to make.

"Officer Gaspari, did the computer have a password?"

"No, it did not."

"So anyone could have accessed it?"

"That's true."

"Did you find any evidence that my client accessed the computer?"

"Yes." Although I was hoping for another answer, I wasn't surprised.

"What evidence was that?"

"His email was accessed regularly, which required a password."

"Were you able to examine my client's emails?"

"Yes, I ran a password detector and accessed them pretty easily." Gaspari was proud of himself.

"How many emails would you say he had sent? Thousands?"

"Easily."

"In any of those emails that my client sent, did you see a hint that he had plans to murder his wife?"

"I wouldn't expect him to put that in writing."

"Please answer the question, Officer Gaspari."

"No, nothing in his emails."

"Let me broaden the question: Excluding the internet browsing history, which we'll get to, did you find any evidence indicating my client intended to kill his wife?"

He shook his head, seeming to will his lips to remain closed. It was clear he didn't want to answer this question. Finally, he said, "Not really."

"Not really? What does that mean?"

"Okay, no."

"Let's be clear, Officer. Excluding the browsing history, you found no evidence my client intended to kill his wife. Correct?"

"Correct."

"Let's turn to the internet browsing history. Could you determine from anything on the computer who accessed those sites about hydrocodone?"

Gaspari puffed up his lips, indicating this was another question he didn't want to answer.

"No."

"So you can't say it was my client?"

"He had access to it."

"Again, I would ask you, Officer, to please answer the question."

"All right, can you repeat the question?"

"I'd be glad to. From your examination of the computer, can you say that my client accessed the websites about hydrocodone?"

"No, I can't."

"It could've been the decedent, correct?"

"That's correct."

I was exhausted by the time the preliminary hearing ended. Judge Shane concluded by saying she would have a decision for us in a few days.

* * *

After a quick dinner in front of the TV, I sat down at the kitchen table with Ginnie's laptop open in front of me. There was no password required. I didn't know if she just never set one or if the police simply deactivated it. I clicked on Facebook and her page came up. What struck me at first was that she had over 3,000 friends. The posts were mostly typical comments about what she was doing: hiking with friends in the White Mountains, shopping at the Mall of New Hampshire, dining with her "loving hubby" at Sam's Seafood Café in Portsmouth.

I checked posts from the past few days and there was one about Conti with a link to a video of Ginnie breaking the story on Channel 9. The video showed Conti being led from the police car to the station, holding his jacket over his head. There were dozens of "likes" and several comments. One comment was disturbing. "This is the height of irresponsible journalism," it began. "You have no evidence linking Conti to any inappropriate conduct except the word of a twelve-year-old girl. Don't you think you should have more solid evidence before destroying a man's reputation? You will be sorry."

The comment was signed by "Concerned Citizen." I went to Concerned Citizen's homepage. There were posts about natural gas fracking, Israel's occupation of Palestine, and the CIA's responsibility for the 9/11 attacks. I perused the posts, which revealed a person with an active social conscience and a bit of paranoia about government and big business. I clicked on the "About" tab. The "Overview" was blank; on "Work and Education" it said, "School of Life" and "School of Hard Knocks." For "Places Lived" it said, "USA." The "Basic Information" tab had nothing for "gender" and under "Political Views" said, "anarchist." The remainder of the "About" tab was blank.

I was a novice on Facebook. Some time ago I set up a page at Ginnie's urging but rarely looked at it. Occasionally I would get friend requests and ignore them. I tried finding Concerned Citizen's identity but was getting nowhere so I placed a call to Hedges. "Why don't you come over tonight. I just got Ginnie's laptop back and may need your expertise." Even though Hedges was nearly my age, he was young at heart—perhaps immature—and kept up on the latest technology. He was the first person I knew to buy an iPhone, iPad, and even an iWatch.

Hedges arrived within fifteen minutes, helped himself to a bottle of beer from the fridge, then sat down beside me. I explained what I had found out and he took over the laptop. With me looking on, he quickly perused Concerned Citizen's Facebook page then did a Google search. He was moving so fast I couldn't keep up with him. I sat at the end of the table staring out the window.

Time passed as I thought of Ginnie, replaying in my mind the last time I saw her. I regretted that our last contact had ended in an argument. She wasn't sure she wanted a baby; I could understand that. She had a high-profile career, at least in New Hampshire. But I had a twinge of guilt since I had held back her career rise. When she turned down the Chicago job, I was grateful at the time but concerned she would harbor some resentment, though she never expressed any. I wondered if she still had bigger ambitions than Channel 9, if perhaps she wanted to move to a bigger, higher-paying market. Was that one reason she didn't want children?

I prayed that I would learn the answer to that question. That would mean Ginnie was alive, that she and my unborn child had been returned to me.

"I found something," Hedges said, interrupting my thoughts.

"What is it?"

"Here, take a look at this." He turned the laptop toward me. It was opened to a blog. The subject of the blog was "Media Dangers."

The post was by Concerned Citizen and began, "I am sick and tired of this so-called newscaster Virginia Turner with her sensationalist stories that bear very little resemblance to the truth. She appears to want to broadcast any story with a sexual component solely to garner attention, without regard for the evidence. I'm talking about the Conti molestation story. Even writing that, I realize I'm falling into the trap of convicting Conti. I should have written 'alleged' molestation story. That's all it is: an allegation from a crazy twelve-year-old girl. Then Turner ran with that story about St. Andrew's male students having a competition to see who could have sex with the most women. So what! That's not a story; that's life. Men want to have sex with women. What's wrong with that? I recommend that everyone in New Hampshire boycott Channel 9. Watch the Boston news if you want to know what's happening in the world. But stay away from WMUR if you want the truth. As for Turner, someone has to teach her a lesson. Are there any volunteers?"

"Jesus Christ!" I said. "He's practically begging someone to hurt Ginnie. Who is this guy?"

"I've looked at other posts and he seems to write about things happening in Southern New Hampshire, mostly Manchester or Nashua. He's got a social conscience and seems well educated. Not much to go on."

"We've got to find him."

"He must've provided some contact info for one of these sites. There are a lot of 'Concerned Citizen' sites and blogs. I need some time to filter through them."

He stood up to leave and walked toward the front door, taking Ginnie's laptop with him. I walked with him until he turned around and said, "Dutch, we will find her. I guarantee it." He leaned toward me and gave me an awkward guy hug, which only made me feel worse.

CHAPTER NINE

THURSDAY WAS MY third morning waking up alone, my wife's side of the bed empty, my heart aching. I called Hedges to get an update on Concerned Citizen and left a voicemail. Then I had to turn my attention to Judge Garcia's case and finally got through to Dr. Gumina. She was most gracious but couldn't meet with me until Monday morning. "If I get a cancellation before then," she said, "I'll let you know."

"I appreciate that."

She paused before saying, "Dutch Francis. Are you the husband of the missing newscaster?"

"Yes. It's a terrible situation."

"I'm sorry you're going through that. Are there any leads?"

Dr. Gumina's voice was soft, soothing, empathetic. I was immediately struck by the urge to share information with her. "She received some threatening phone calls the day of the kidnapping. The police are looking into that angle. So far nothing."

"I have some experience with kidnappings. I've worked on a few cases with the Boston police. Have the Manchester police put out a profile of the kidnapper yet?"

"No, they haven't said anything about that."

"I don't want to step on their toes, but in a case like this the police should go on the air and ask people to look at their neighbors, friends, relatives for signs."

"What sort of signs?"

"There are certain behaviors we see with kidnappers immediately after the kidnapping. For example, he may miss work. The absence will be sudden and unplanned. He may either be a 'no show' or he may offer a plausible excuse such as illness, death in the family, car trouble, etcetera. He may miss scheduled appointments or commitments and be unaccounted for during this period. These may include such things as medical appointments, meetings with a parole officer, that kind of thing. He may suddenly leave town, either with no explanation or with some plausible reason."

"That could cover a lot of individuals."

"It could. It's a lot of legwork but it's got to be done. Once the police make a public appeal, they'll get hundreds of leads. It's important to follow up on all of them."

"I'll have to talk to them. Anything else they should be looking for?"

"The kidnapper may express an intense interest in the status of the investigation and pay close attention to the media. However, some offenders may quickly turn off media accounts or try to redirect conversations concerning the victim or her family. There may be changes in the usual consumption of alcohol or drugs. All of these things are telltale signs."

"I appreciate your insight, Doctor."

"Oh, one other thing. The kidnapper may change his appearance or alter something to prevent identification, such as changing the look of his vehicle, cleaning or discarding his vehicle."

"So they've got to look for someone who fits all these categories?"

"The more he fits, the better chance of finding him."

I thanked Dr. Gumina for her advice and, as soon as I hung up, put a call into Delahunty. The phone rang several times but went to voicemail. I told him to call me right back.

A short time later the mail arrived. To my surprise, there was another manila envelope. My heart sank. It was the same size as the first one but had a Nashua postmark with no return address. As soon as I realized what it was, I dropped the envelope on the floor. I couldn't imagine what was inside and didn't even want to think about it. As I stared at the envelope, my phone rang. It was Delahunty.

❀ ❀ ❀

Wearing latex gloves, Delahunty picked up the envelope by the corner, careful not to smudge any prints. "We'll have to bring this to the lab so they can steam it open."

I didn't want to wait; I wanted to know now what was in it. "How long will that take?"

"Depends on their workload," Leary said.

I ignored her and turned toward Delahunty, who was making his way to the door as he held up the envelope. "I've talked to a Harvard psychiatrist with experience in kidnappings. She says you should go on the air with a profile of the kidnapper, try to smoke him out." I filled him in on the information provided by Dr. Gumina.

"I think it might be premature to do that. We've got some leads on the videos we're following."

"What sort of leads?"

"A few homeowners near the station had cameras that recorded traffic around the time of the kidnapping. We're tracking everyone."

"When do you think you'll have something?"

"In a day or two. I'll let you know if we find anything."

By the time they left, I was going stir crazy. The walls of the condo seemed to be closing in on me. I couldn't sit still. I'd sit on the couch, turn on the TV, then walk to the kitchen and look in the refrigerator. Then I'd repeat the same scenario. Finally, I gave up trying to keep calm and put on my jogging outfit: old-school blue sweatpants and a blue Red Sox t-shirt. I set off at a leisurely pace, tracking the river, trying to move my mind from the dark places it had been going. I couldn't think of Ginnie without wondering about the awful things happening to her. Just being apart was bad enough but knowing some maniac was controlling her, cutting her hair, and God knows what else overwhelmed me. I picked up the pace as my flat feet plop-plopped on the pavement. There were crowds of people on Elm Street, the men in short-sleeve dress shirts on this warm spring day. I watched the women in bright summer dresses and skirts, hoping to find Ginnie among them. No matter where I looked, Ginnie was on my mind.

After running the length of Elm Street, I turned left and made my way to St. Augustin-St. Ann's Church. I stopped in front and, even though I hadn't been to Mass in years, blessed myself, then prayed to God to return Ginnie to me safely. I walked a few blocks to Ginnie's childhood home where her mother still lived. I hadn't talked to Barbara Turner since the night of the kidnapping. I rang the bell and she answered right away.

"Dutch, I wasn't expecting you."

"I know. I was jogging in the neighborhood and thought I'd stop by and see how you're doing." In truth, I could see how she was doing. Her usually meticulously groomed red hair was a mess, unbrushed, and her eyes were dark and teary.

She put her arms around me, pulling me into a desperate hug, then let me in. "Any word yet?"

I hadn't told her about the envelopes and didn't want to alarm her so I kept that information to myself. "The police say they're following all leads but so far they got nothing."

She shook her head and pointed to a seat at the kitchen table. "Coffee?"

"Sure." She poured the coffee then, remembering how I liked it, grabbed milk from the refrigerator and sugar from the cupboard. I was pleased she remembered. It had taken a while for Barbara to warm up to me. Ginnie said her mother thought I was too old for her and, because I was divorced, she considered me "damaged goods." I worked hard to show her how much I loved Ginnie. At the wedding reception she gave a speech saying how much Ginnie had matured since she'd met me and that I was the best thing ever to happen to her daughter.

"Why hasn't he asked for a ransom yet?"

"Doesn't make sense. I wish I knew what's going on."

She sipped her coffee. A red lip mark was visible on the edge of the cup. I couldn't tell if it was old or new, though Barbara didn't appear to be wearing any makeup. She stared at the ceiling and the drop-down light fixtures, not saying anything. I took a sip of coffee and closed my eyes, wondering what to say to this mother whose daughter had been taken.

Suddenly Barbara turned her gaze on me. "The police were here," she said in an accusatory tone.

"Really?"

"Yeah."

"They say anything?"

"Plenty." She stood up and opened a drawer near the stove. There was a pack of cigarettes there and she smacked the pack against her palm, causing a cigarette to pop out. "I almost never touch these things anymore," she said as she lit it.

Once she settled back into her seat, her coffee in one hand, cigarette in the other, she again looked at me intently. I didn't like the silent game but cut her some slack, knowing what she was going through.

"You going to share with me what the police had to say?"

"They've got a suspect."

"They do? They never told me that." I couldn't believe Delahunty would've held back on me.

"Yeah, at least the female one said so. She said nine times out of ten in these cases it's the husband. She thinks you did something to her."

I was floored. I knew that Leary had acted like I was guilty, but I had no idea she would go so far as to tell someone I was a suspect. I stood up and approached Barbara. She froze for a moment then softened when she saw I wanted only to give her a hug. We hugged silently, the smoke from her cigarette filling my nostrils, and I returned to my seat.

"I know you don't believe that."

"I don't want to believe it."

"Barbara..."

"I'm sorry." She put out her cigarette in the brown onyx ashtray on the counter. "You do love her, Dutch? Still?"

"More than ever." I wiped my eyes. "There's something you should know."

"What?"

"I didn't want to tell you after what's happened. It's just that Ginnie is pregnant."

"Oh, my God! You mean I'm going to be a grandmother?"

"Well..."

I couldn't look at her and knew I shouldn't tell her. This was Ginnie's news to share, not mine, but under the circumstances I thought she had a right to know. "Ginnie's not sure she wants to keep the baby."

"Not keep the baby. I don't understand."

"She's awfully busy at work and doesn't think she'd have the time."

"But, Dutch, we're Catholic. She's got to have the baby."

I swallowed. Barbara looked at the ceiling, blessed herself, and grabbed the cigarette pack. Again, she slapped it against her palm and lit a cigarette.

"What else did she say?"

"That was it. We had a brief discussion then I had to leave."

"It sickens me that she would even think of an abortion. That goes against how she was raised." She took a long drag on the cigarette, releasing her anger. "Her father would turn over in his grave."

"I know." Frank Turner was a long-haul truck driver who died shortly after I started dating Ginnie. Gruff on the exterior, Frank was kind, honest, and very funny. He would call Ginnie from the road and always tell her a joke. On her birthdays, he would take her to dinner at the restaurant of her choice and he always made a point of listening to whatever she wanted to tell him. As a result, Ginnie and her father developed a very warm relationship. She still teared up when talking to me about him.

"Now I've got to worry about both my daughter and my grandchild." Barbara wiped the tears from her eyes. "This is unimaginable. What can we do?"

I got up and walked to her side of the table, putting my arm around her shoulder. "I'm doing everything I can. The police are working full-time on the case. There's not much else we can do."

"Dutch," she said, her voice pleading, "tell me again you didn't hurt Ginnie. I need to know you had nothing to do with this."

I didn't like hearing this again and became testy. "Goddamn it, Barbara!"

I walked to the other side of the kitchen. "I would give my own life to get Ginnie back. You have no idea how much I love your daughter."

"I want to believe that. I do. It's just that . . ."

"What?"

"I'm so scared, Dutch."

"So am I."

❀ ❀ ❀

Just as I stepped out of the shower, my phone rang. It was Hedges. "I've finished looking through Ginnie's laptop."

"Anything useful?"

"I scanned the chat rooms that Ginnie frequently visited. There was a lot of moaning and whining, people complaining about what lousy lives they had."

I never understood the attraction of baring your soul online. I guess I was too private a person, not willing to expose myself to strangers. I wondered why Ginnie spent so much time monitoring chat rooms and whether she was as willing to share her personal feelings online. Perhaps she was simply looking for stories.

Hedges continued. "Her username was the same for each site I visited: GinDut, an obvious abbreviation for Ginnie and Dutch. It took a while to figure out how to search through so many different chat rooms, but somehow I managed to find chats Ginnie had sent. Most of them were silly responses to other chats, some chastising others for bad language. Then there was one that caught my eye. I copied it and will email it to you. Hold on a sec."

I put the phone on speaker, toweled down, and dressed.

"Here it is," he said. "I just sent it."

I checked my emails.

"You got it?" he asked.

"Yeah. Who the hell is 'Bad Husband'? I hope she wasn't referring to me."

"Nah, keep reading."

Ginnie's chat message said, "U shld pay more tention to ur wife. I've got best hubby ever. He takes good care of me."

I wondered about my wife's writing style. I had never seen that side of her, so informal, but I felt relieved that she considered me a good husband.

"Thanks for sending that. I need the affirmation right about now."

"No prob. So then I checked out the blogs she had bookmarked. There were a lot that were obviously work-related: journalists, newscasters, politicians. She read a lot of these blogs. There're thousands on the internet: sex blogs, gossip blogs, confessional blogs, political blogs, mommy blogs, fiction blogs, video blogs, cartoon blogs, soldier blogs, and many more."

"I'm guessing you spent some time on the sex blogs."

"*Moi*? Who do you think I am?"

"Please."

He laughed. "Seriously, I may have something to show you. I'm on my way over."

CHAPTER TEN

HEDGES WAS WEARING blue overalls and a white t-shirt, professional attire for him. He placed Ginnie's laptop on the table and began fiddling with the keyboard. Somehow he accessed a page of code and was scanning it carefully.

"I took a class at the junior college on how to code. It's come in useful, especially for internet geolocation technology."

"What the hell is that?"

"I'll show you. Look, here's Concerned Citizen's IP address. Now I've got to search for the physical address. It'll take some time."

"How much time?"

"Hard to say." He stared at the screen, his fingers typing furiously. I had no idea what he was doing but I let him run with it. Within a few minutes, he had the latitude and longitude of the IP address, which was on a computer in Amherst, New Hampshire, less than twenty miles from here. Then he input the latitude and longitude into another website and the street address suddenly appeared. I was impressed with Hedges' skill, a different side from the rough-and-tumble guy I knew.

"Let's go," he said as he wrote down the address.

"Shouldn't we let Delahunty know?"

"Call him from the road."

With Hedges driving, we quickly made our way to Route 101 west. I called Delahunty.

"Bill, I wanted to fill you in on something. Hedges and I are heading to Amherst to track down a guy who posted some threatening things about Ginnie."

"Do you have a name?"

"Not yet. Just an address."

"Why don't you let us handle it?"

I paused. I didn't want the Manchester PD to think I had no confidence in them, at least not yet, but I was not happy about what Leary had told Barbara. If the police still considered me a suspect, they might not be working as hard as they should to find the real kidnapper.

"Why did Leary tell Ginnie's mother I'm a suspect?"

"Dutch . . ."

"What the hell!"

"She's a hothead, what can I say. She needs some seasoning."

"She needs more than seasoning."

"Go easy, Dutch. This is difficult for all of us."

I held the phone away from my ear and inhaled deeply before bringing it back. "Oh, really. Is your pregnant wife missing? Are you the one who's accused of kidnapping her or worse? Don't you realize how hard this is on me?"

"I do. I feel for ya, Dutch." He paused, shuffling papers. "Listen, we just got the report back from forensics. They're working overtime on this case. Again, there were no useful prints on the envelope and no note inside."

"What was it then?"

"I don't know what this means but it appears to be fingernails."

"Oh my God."

"Sorry. Clipped fingernails, not the whole thing."

My stomach wretched and I groaned.

"You okay?" Delahunty asked.

"What color?"

"Light red."

"That's Ginnie's color."

"I don't know what to tell you."

"Where do we go from here?"

"We're following up on the videos, I've got someone watching Conti, and I'm looking into the Saint Andrew's story. I spoke to the president, got the names of the students involved in the sex scandal. All were expelled and transferred to schools out of the area. I doubt they were involved in this, but we'll track them down."

"I'm going to find out what I can about this guy in Amherst. I'll keep you posted."

❀   ❀   ❀

In no time we arrived in Amherst and quickly made our way to Concerned Citizen's address. The door was answered by a woman in her late forties with thick blond hair cut short. She was dressed in a pink sweatsuit and sneakers.

"What can I do ya?"

"We're looking for someone whose online handle is Concerned Citizen," I said.

"Is that a fact?" She pulled on the end of her hair. "Might I ask just what business y'all have with Concerned Citizen?"

"Routine investigation, ma'am," Hedges said. "Just following up some leads."

"Uh-huh," she said, still pulling on her hair. "Well, I'm afraid I can't help ya."

"Is that because you don't know Concerned Citizen?" I asked.

"Well..."

"Or because you have something to hide," Hedges said, raising his voice.

"It's neither, gentlemen. Perhaps y'all could tell me who ya are."

"I'm a lawyer and this is my investigator. We're looking into a missing person case."

She twisted her mouth, sucking in her cheeks. "This isn't about that missing newscaster, is it?"

"Why do you ask, ma'am?" Hedges said.

"It's just... I don't know. My husband has been paying close attention to that situation." She looked past us as if searching for help. "I've said enough already."

I tried to keep my excitement contained. It was obvious this woman knew something and didn't want to share it. I glanced at Hedges who looked as if he were going to grab her by the throat and shake it out of her, though I knew Hedges would never lay hands on a woman. Then I turned back to her.

"Can I have your name, please?"

"Name's Tina. Why?"

"Tina..."

"Bernard. B-e-r-n-a-r-d. Like the dog."

"Where might your husband be, Ms. Bernard?"

"He's working. His schedule has been somewhat sporadic lately, but he probably won't be home until late."

I pulled out a business card and handed it to her. "Have him call me as soon as he gets home. Doesn't matter the time."

"S-sure," she said, acting nervous as she stared at the card. "I don't think he could help ya. I'm sure he can't."

"Thank you, Ms. Bernard," Hedges said. "You've been a big help."

We returned to Hedges' car and circled the block a few times, before deciding to conduct a stakeout, parking a few houses down from Bernard's.

"Dr. Gumina said the kidnapper may have altered his schedule, missed appointments, that kind of thing. Also might show an inordinate interest in the case. We may have our man."

"You think he would keep Ginnie here, with his wife around? I didn't get the sense she was covering up a kidnapping."

"Maybe not, but there was something off about her."

We waited for forty-five minutes. In that time, we both conducted online searches for Bernard. His wife's Facebook page disclosed that his name was Curt, but we couldn't find much else. The sun was starting to set when a blue Honda SUV drove past us and parked in the Bernard driveway. A large man, perhaps six three, 220 pounds, a bit bigger than me, balding, exited the car and unlocked the front door.

"Let's go get him," Hedges said.

"Wait, let me check something." I called Delahunty. "Bill, Hedges and I are outside the home of the guy I told you about. His name's Curt Bernard. You said you were looking at cars on the videos. Was one of them a Honda SUV?"

"Yeah but, Dutch, you shouldn't be there."

"What color?"

"We can't tell the color. The video's in black and white. What's Bernard's address?"

I gave it to him.

"Don't do anything. I'll get the local cops on it."

"We'll wait here, but they'd better come soon. I won't leave Ginnie with that guy much longer."

Five minutes went by as I stared at Bernard's house, waiting for any sign of movement. Hedges did another internet search of Bernard and came across a recent post from Concerned Citizen on a blog called "The Devil's Dilemma."

"Seems to be a place for people to spout whatever hatred they hold in their hearts," he said.

"What's the title mean? What exactly is the devil's dilemma?"

"You got me. You're not going to like this post: 'I hear that bitch got what's coming to her. She thought she could report on any damn thing she wanted but she got whatfor. Damn right! I couldn't be happier. Things are only going to get worse for her. I guarantee it!'"

Hearing this I got more and more incensed, to the point I wanted to punch someone, in particular Curt Bernard. I opened the car door and started getting out. Hedges reached over and tried to grab my arm. "Dutch!"

I moved to shut the door when I noticed Bernard's front door open. He hurried down the stairs and got into his SUV. "Get in," shouted Hedges. When I hesitated, he said, "You know Ginnie's probably not in the house. He'll take us to her."

Realizing he was right, I sat back down. Keeping a safe distance behind Bernard, we followed him down Route 101 to Route 122. He drove slowly toward Main Street and parked near the town library. We pulled in several spaces behind him where we had a good view. He sat in his car playing with his phone for a few minutes then quickly walked down an alley, which curved out of our line of sight. Just like that, we lost him.

Hedges and I jumped out of the car and ran toward the alley. "Where the hell could he have gone?" Hedges said. The alley contained the back doors to a laundromat, a Chinese/Polynesian restaurant, and a bar that emitted the stench of sour beer. Above the businesses was a row of apartments, each window covered by maroon shades. I nodded to Hedges to check out the restaurant while I searched the bar.

There were about a dozen people in the bar, mostly men with a handful of couples. I walked the length of the bar, checking the faces of everyone I walked by. I could sense hostility at my presence. Perhaps it was because I wasn't known there or because I acted a bit rudely by staring at everyone. Bernard wasn't there. Before leaving, I checked the men's room with no luck.

Hedges was already in the alley. "Anything?" he asked. I shook my head. He had come up dry as well.

"What about the apartments?" I asked. "Could he have ducked in there?"

"There's an entrance beside the laundromat."

The entrance was locked. I read the names on the mailboxes and didn't see Bernard's. I was about to walk away when Hedges ran his hand along the line of doorbells, ringing each one. A few seconds later, the door buzzed and we were in.

As soon as we entered, a woman's voice sounded from the stairwell on the second floor. "Who is it? Who's there?"

We climbed the oak stairs and told her we were looking for a man who had just come in. She was about seventy, bone thin with greyish brown hair, leaning on a metal cane. "It's usually pretty quiet in here, but I just heard a door down the hall open and close."

Hedges smiled. "Thank you, ma'am. Nothing to worry about. We're just checking on something."

"It's the third door on the left."

She stood watching as Hedges knocked on the door. The door opened a crack and Bernard peeked out.

"Who are you?"

Before Hedges could answer, I kicked the door open, pushing Bernard onto his ass. From a back room, a woman yelled, "Who is it, Curtis?"

"I have no fucking idea." He sat up.

"Yes, you do, Mr. Bernard," I said. "I'm sure your wife told you we stopped by the house."

"This is about Ginnie Turner? I've got nothing to do with that."

"From your online posts," Hedges said, "it sure seems like you wanted to do her harm."

"I don't much care for her newscasting, but that don't mean I'd kidnap her for Christ's sake."

A woman walked from the back room. She was about thirty-five, heavyset, with thick makeup, wearing a purple sweatsuit. "What's the meaning of this?"

Hedges walked toward her with his hands out. "We're looking for Ginnie Turner? Is she here?"

"Are you fucking kidding me?"

"You won't mind, then, if I have a look around?" Without waiting for an answer, Hedges walked around the corner.

"This is outrageous!" the woman shouted. "I'm going to call the police."

"No need," I said. "We already did. In fact, they're probably searching Mr. Bernard's house right now."

"You sonsuvbitches!" He stood up and moved closer to me, his face a few inches from mine. "You have no right to involve my wife."

Hedges reappeared. "There's no one else here."

"Obviously," the woman said.

I backed away from Bernard. "We're not through with you by any means."

"You won't get away with this."

As he walked toward the door, Hedges put his hand on Bernard's shoulder. "Curt, if I were you, I'd keep this little incident between us. I suspect you'd have a hard time explaining your girlfriend here to Tina."

We could hear Bernard and his girlfriend both cursing us as we descended the stairs.

"That was fucked," Hedges said.

"Yeah, you got that right." While walking to the car, I called Delahunty. "We found Bernard; Ginnie's not with him."

"She's not at his house either. His wife reluctantly gave us permission to search. For what it's worth, my buddies in the Amherst PD say they know him. He's got a screw loose though nothing really criminal."

"Great," I said, punching the air. "Back to square one."

CHAPTER ELEVEN

I WENT HOME to an empty condo once again. The silence was more than I could bear so I turned on the radio to a station that played hits from the '80s and '90s. I was surprised to hear the DJ call them "oldies." When I was growing up, songs from the '50s were considered "oldies." I picked up a framed photo of Ginnie and me from the Empire State Building. We had traveled to New York for a long weekend and enjoyed playing tourists. I shot the photo myself holding the camera at belt-level aimed at the mirrored wall. The photo showed Ginnie and me smiling broadly, my free arm around her, the New York skyline in the background.

I put the photo down as my eyes watered and thought of the envelopes with Ginnie's hair and fingernails. What kind of a man would do such a thing? I tried to imagine what he would have against Ginnie that drove him to such measures. God knows what else he was doing to her. I tried very hard to block my mind from speculating.

❈ ❈ ❈

As soon as I awoke the next day, I checked my emails and noticed one had a red flag. It was from Judge Shane's clerk, informing me she would announce her decision on the preliminary hearing Tuesday morning. I called the jail to let Garcia know. Hank Lerner answered.

"Hank, Dutch here. Would you mind putting my client on?"

"For you, the world," he said, pausing. He was never going to play it straight with me. After a few seconds passed, he asked, "Haven't heard anything about your wife. Any progress?"

"None I can talk about." I didn't want to disclose the two envelopes I had received.

"I'm keeping my chubby fingers crossed. Hold on while I get the good judge."

I could hear Hank's keys jiggling as he walked back to Garcia's cell. It took a minute for Garcia to come on the line. "Have you heard anything?"

I told him about the clerk's email. "My guess is we should plan for trial."

"You still think a suicide defense is the best way to go?"

"What else do we have? You know anyone who wanted to kill her?"

"Everyone loved Mo," he said, missing the irony. "There might be another way."

"What's that?"

He hesitated. "I'll have to testify."

"Too risky. Tompkins'll tear you apart."

"I don't think so," he said quietly. "Come visit so we can kick this around."

"As soon as I can."

Right after hanging up, I looked through the front window and noticed the mail carrier walking toward the condo. I opened the door and he handed me a pile of envelopes, magazines, and brochures. I found the manila envelope in the middle of the pile. This was the third one in a row and I was numb. I called Delahunty.

"Bill, there's another one. I don't know how much more of this I can take."

"Sit tight. We'll be right over."

"No, I'll come to you. I want to know now what this is. Get your forensics team ready."

At the station, I headed directly to the elevators. In the second-floor conference room, I found Delahunty and his techie, a young woman with short hair on top and long in the back, stringing down her neck like a rat's tail. I handed her the envelope and sat down at the table.

"This'll take a few minutes." She took the envelope and left the room.

"Coffee?" Delahunty asked, sitting across from me.

I shook my head.

"You know, you shouldn't have chased down Bernard. That whole situation could've gotten real ugly."

"What else am I supposed to do? I can't sit around and hope you come up with something."

"I know it's tough. We've been following up every lead. The department has made Ginnie our top priority."

"I appreciate that but I need to be involved. I've been thinking about Dr. Gumina's profile. Maybe I should go on the air."

He frowned just as the techie returned. "We're ready," she said as she laid a paper towel on the table. "There're a few prints on the envelope. I'm sure some are Mr. Francis's but the others I'll have to run through the database. I've steamed it open. Let's see what we got."

She emptied the envelope's contents onto the towel. Out came ten clipped toenails the same color as the fingernail clippings. I recognized them as Ginnie's. I folded my arms on the table and leaned my head on them. There was a steady pounding coming from inside my head, as if someone were jumping up and down on it.

"Where was it mailed from?" I asked.

"This one's from Nashua again," said Delahunty. "Looks like our guy's moving back and forth."

I lifted my head from the table. "What's next?"

Delahunty glanced at the techie and said, "We'll check with the postmaster again. Normally the clerk wouldn't process an overnight mail envelope without a return address so they figured the kidnapper put the envelopes in the overnight boxes in front of the post office."

My frustration was building and the pounding in my head was killing me. "Goddamnit!" I yelled. Before I realized what I was doing, I began slamming my fists on the table as if beating the table would somehow find Ginnie.

"Dutch," Delahunty said, "we'll find her."

"I'm sure you will," I said, sounding more hopeful than I actually felt. "But when?"

❖   ❖   ❖

Later that day, at 6:05 p.m., I was sitting at the anchor desk beside Dennis Cassidy. After leaving the police station, I had called Cassidy and begged him to let me go on air. His producer agreed to give me two minutes. I had put on a clean dark suit and red tie, blue shirt. On the drive over I composed in my mind what I would say. Two minutes was not much time, but I could get my message across. After all, many commercials run only a minute so I should be able to say a lot in two minutes.

As I stared at the camera, I swallowed several times. The light blinked red during a commercial. My cue was when the producer raised his hand just before the light turned green. When he raised his hand, a chill swept through me as I thought of the importance of what I was about to say. I had to sound convincing, not threatening, and appeal to his basest instincts. The light turned green.

"My name is Dutch Francis. My wife, Ginnie Turner, is a newscaster for this station. Last Monday night she was kidnapped. I'm asking for the public's help in finding the kidnapper. You may recognize the kidnapper among you. He's someone whose schedule suddenly changed. He may have missed work or doctor's appointments or meeting with a parole officer or someone else important. He may go out for long stretches and not want to talk about where he went. I realize this may describe a lot of people, most innocent. But this is one sign you should look out for. Another sign is that the kidnapper may have taken a sudden interest in the investigation of this kidnapping. Or he may react in the opposite way, insisting you shut off the TV when there's a story of the kidnapping. Yet another sign is that he may have changed his usual consumption of alcohol. Finally, the kidnapper may change his appearance or the look of his vehicle by suddenly cleaning or even discarding it.

"If you know of anyone fitting this description, please call the number flashing on the screen. Someone from the Manchester Police Department will take your call.

"I would now like to address my wife's kidnapper directly. You know that if Ginnie is harmed in any way, the police won't stop until you're behind bars. So don't hurt Ginnie, please. I know you're not a monster. From the items you sent me, it's clear you don't want to hurt Ginnie. I can't go on without my wife. Please release her."

The red light came on, indicating we were off air. Cassidy approached me and to my surprise put his arm around my shoulder. "You did well. That was very effective. But what's this about items he sent you?"

I shook my head. "I can't talk about the details, Dennis. The police want to keep them quiet. I probably said more than I should have."

"You did what you had to."

"Right."

CHAPTER TWELVE

WHEN I GOT home, I put on a vinyl record of Carole King's *Tapestry*. Recently I had found a great deal on a record player on eBay, bought a new high-quality cartridge, and retrieved my old albums from storage. Ginnie thought I was crazy. "How can you listen to all that scratching and crinkling?" she had said. "Who doesn't like the clean, fresh sound of a CD or digital music?"

I told her the records brought back good memories from my teen years, especially hanging out with friends in my basement. We played pool with Creedence Clearwater Revival's *Cosmo's Factory* blaring in the background, hit the heavy bag to the Rolling Stone's *Hot Rocks*, and played cards to the Allman Brothers' *Eat a Peach*. Our tastes tended to be the same though I leaned toward Dylan more than my friends who thought his voice terrible.

The record player took more effort than a CD player: you had to put the record on the player, swing over the cartridge arm, and place the needle just so to avoid it slipping off the edge. Then when one side finished you had to get up and turn the record over and repeat the process. There was some physical effort involved; you had to really want to listen to the record to go through all that. It wasn't like playing CDs in a five-CD player, which could go on for hours without any effort on your part, or a digital music player, which could play forever.

I lay back on my couch and thought of Ginnie as *Tapestry* scratched through "So Far Away." "*Holding you again could only do me good. How I wish I could but you're so far away.*" Perhaps, I thought, this wasn't the best choice.

❁ ❁ ❁

Saturday morning started earlier than I had planned when my doorbell rang at seven thirty. Hedges was standing at the door holding a Starbucks coffee in each hand. "Got you a grande latte," he said, handing it to me.

"Thanks for the head's-up. I had planned on sleeping in today." I took the coffee and let him inside.

"I saw you on TV last night. You looked good."

"I had to do something."

We sat down at the kitchen table and sipped the coffees. "The profile you provided was pretty broad; it'll cover a lot of people. Are the cops ready for all the calls they'll get?"

"They'd better be. Something's got to give. We're running in circles."

"Conti and Bernard seemed like such good leads." He shook his head. "Thought for sure one of them had Ginnie."

"Yeah, both had recently threatened her, and Conti had even called her the day of the kidnapping. For Christ's sake!"

"I've been thinking."

"I'm listening."

He leaned forward over the table. "What if we're approaching this from the wrong direction?"

"What do you mean?"

"We assumed Ginnie was kidnapped by someone with a grudge, mostly because of the phone calls that day. What if the phone calls were only coincidental?"

"I don't follow."

"We know from the blogs and Facebook posts that Ginnie received lots of threats. But none resulted in her being kidnapped."

"Until now."

"Well . . . That's what I'm saying. Maybe the threats had nothing to do with Ginnie's kidnapping."

"Then why would someone take her?"

He threw up his hands. "I don't fucking know! That's what's killing me."

"I forgot to tell you: yesterday I got another envelope. With Ginnie's clipped toenails. So that's locks of her hair, clipped fingernails, and clipped toenails. What do you make of that?"

"Must be torture for you."

"Yeah, you got that right. I don't know what I'd do if the guy hurts Ginnie or the baby."

"Let's keep the faith." He finished his coffee and stood up. "I'll continue searching for clues online. Keep me posted on any developments."

After Hedges left, I paced the condo, antsy, wanting to do something but not knowing what. Then I remembered there was something I meant to do in Garcia's case. I had planned on waiting until after the judge's ruling but now seemed as good a time as any. So I got in my car and drove over to Garcia's home.

On the way, my cell phone rang. I put the call on speaker.

"Hello."

"Dutch, it's Rodger."

What the hell? Rodger Dodds, my ex-partner, ex-father-in-law, and—at least I thought—ex-friend. We had disagreed over my handling of his niece's sexual harassment case and I hadn't seen him since my wedding last year. He was now a federal court of appeals judge in Boston.

"The Boston stations carried your appeal from last night. Sorry to hear about Ginnie. How're you doing?"

"Not good, if you want to know the truth."

"Understandable. It's a terrible thing. Any leads?"

"Nothing concrete. So far every lead has fallen through."

"If there's anything I can do, don't hesitate to ask."

"I appreciate that, Rodger." I inhaled deeply. "I'll be near Boston on Monday. Can I take you to lunch?"

"Happy to have lunch, but it'll have to be dutch, Dutch."

"You love saying that."

"I do, but seriously, judicial ethics are involved."

We set a time and place to meet and before he hung up, he showed his often-hidden tender side. "Dutch, I really hope you find Ginnie safe and sound. I can only imagine how difficult this is for you."

In a few minutes I arrived at Garcia's home on River Road in one of the most exclusive neighborhoods in Manchester. I parked across the street and knocked on doors of neighbors on each side of his home. No one answered, though in one house I swore someone was watching me. I decided to wait for someone to come home. I wanted to interview Garcia's neighbors to see if they knew anything about the Garcias' relationship or even Mrs. Garcia's mental state. If we were going to go with a suicide defense, I needed some solid evidence.

Ten minutes passed and no neighbors appeared, but a postal truck parked a hundred yards from me. The mail carrier bounded out of the truck, opened the back, and filled her bag. Then she began walking door-to-door. She was short and stocky with long stringy bleached blond hair. As she neared the Garcia home, I got out of the car and approached her. She seemed startled at first, but I held out my hands.

"Don't worry. I just have a few questions."

"I've got a route to cover."

"A moment of your time. That's all I'm asking. My name is Dutch Francis. I'm the lawyer for the judge who lives here. You may have heard he's accused of killing his wife."

"I heard something about it. What of it?"

"I'm trying to figure out who really killed her. You must've gotten to know Mrs. Garcia. She was home a lot."

"Sure, I talked to her from time to time. Nice lady. Sad what happened to her. I hope they crucify whoever did it."

She was loosening up, relaxing, so I asked her, "Do you remember the day she died?"

She nodded. "Typical day. Sunny and clear."

"Did you happen to see her that day?"

"Not that I remember."

"Did you notice whether she had any visitors?"

She looked at the ground and adjusted the bag of mail on her shoulder. "None of my business."

"I understand that, but it's important you tell me whatever you know. A man's life might depend on it."

"Like I say, I mind my own business. What people do on their own time is up to them."

"What did the visitor look like?" I was sensing that she was holding back.

"I didn't say there was anyone there, did I?"

"It really is important, Ms.—?"

"DaRosa. Abby DaRosa. I like my job and don't want to do anything to jeopardize that."

"Sure, makes sense, but you won't be risking your job. You'll be aiding the search for justice."

"Justice, huh? I doubt that. But you seem like a nice gentleman so I'll tell you what I seen. Just as I was delivering the mail, a guy pulled up in front of the house. He sat in the car, a spanking new silver Tesla. I haven't seen many of those. Then I went on my route to the next house. Only I looked back and saw him get out of his car and walk to the Garcia house. He rang the bell and then stepped inside."

This was a bonus. Who was this mystery man? "What did he look like?"

"Not much to tell. He was medium height, wearing a dark suit. Bald with a circle of dark, thick hair. Broad shoulders."

"Caucasian?"

She nodded. "Yeah, could be anyone."

"Did you hear any of the conversation at the door?"

"Nothing. I was too far away." She shifted her bag to the other shoulder. "I better get moving; the mail needs delivering."

I thanked her, got back in my car, and drove home.

❀ ❀ ❀

As I opened my front door, I kicked a pile of mail on the floor, exposing another manila envelope. "Jesus Christ!"

I picked it up. The postmark was from Manchester. I couldn't bear to open it and threw it across the room like a Frisbee.

I sat down on the couch and put my head into my hands, dejected and dismayed. What could this sicko be sending me now? Could it be because I went on the air? Before I knew what was happening, I broke down, inhaling deeply. I started to hyperventilate, my breathing becoming so quick I could hardly control it. It took a few minutes to compose myself, and when I did, I called Bill Delahunty, who agreed to come right over. He said he'd bring a techie and equipment to steam open the envelope.

By the time they arrived, I had washed up and made myself somewhat presentable. "Thanks, Bill. I appreciate it."

"Let me see it." I retrieved the envelope from behind the drape in the parlor and dropped it on the kitchen table. Bill stared at it without moving then looked to the tech, who immediately pulled some items from his briefcase. He put on rubber gloves, spread some powder on the envelope, and lifted prints, photographing each step. Then he turned the envelope over and repeated the procedure.

"Are you ready?" His name was Warren and he was thin and bony. Bill responded, "Go ahead."

Warren then took from his briefcase a small machine the size of an electric razor, went to the kitchen, and filled a glass from the cabinet with water. After plugging the machine into an outlet, he poured in the water. A cloud of steam rose from a hole at the top. He placed the envelope into the steam and soon the flap opened. After laying a paper towel on the table, he turned the envelope upside down. Small dark hairs fell onto the towel. While Warren photographed the hairs, I stared at them, fearing the worst.

"Do you know what these are?" Delahunty asked.

I swallowed. "They can't be."

"I'm afraid so. They're short, dark, and thick. I don't think there's much doubt."

The realization shook me deeply. "That means he has violated her. For God's sake, he cut her pubic hair. What kind of animal are we dealing with?" I tried not to think of how Ginnie must've felt while he forced her clothes off and held her down.

"I've never seen anything like this," Delahunty said.

"I know it's bad," Warren said while packing up his equipment, "but it could've been worse."

I said nothing, though inside I was seething.

CHAPTER THIRTEEN

MANILA ENVELOPES IN the mail for four straight days. At least there was no mail delivery on Sundays. What else could the kidnapper be planning to send me? What other parts of my wife's body could he cut? I struggled not to lose hope. I had to persevere, to continue the search for Ginnie, to bring her home safely.

I called Hedges around noon to see if he was able to find anything helpful online.

"I looked into any negative comments about Ginnie's reporting on your Garcia case. Nothing really came up. Some comments, but mostly lambasting your client. But there're a lot of miscellaneous threats going back months. Same kind of shit as Conti and Bernard. Nothing recent though."

"Makes me wonder if anyone liked Ginnie."

"Oh, yeah. People liked her. Some were over the top, swooning about her. Seems she was a hit with a lot of guys."

I had never thought of Ginnie as a sex symbol though of course I found her incredibly sexy. "Wait a minute. I've been thinking about what you said yesterday, about looking at this from a different angle."

"Yeah?"

"What if the kidnapper is not someone with a grudge against Ginnie, but someone in love with her?" I told him about receiving pubic hairs in yesterday's mail.

"You think maybe a guy with a sexual hang-up? Damn, I don't even want to imagine that."

"Me either, but we can't ignore the possibility. Think you can track down any guys who declared their love for her in the week before the kidnapping?"

"I'll look into it."

"Let me know."

❋   ❋   ❋

Part of me was hoping this new theory wouldn't pan out. I wanted to find Ginnie, of course, but I didn't want her kidnapper to be a pervert, though anyone who would send her husband her body parts definitely had a screw loose. To get my mind off this possibility, I drove over to the jail to see Carlos Garcia.

The deputy was a young woman I hadn't met before. She tried to give me a hard time about visiting on a Sunday, claiming visitors weren't allowed. I suggested she call Hank Lerner. She made me wait outside while she called Hank's cell phone.

Ten minutes later, she returned and let me in. "Hank said to tell you he's thinking about you and your wife."

"I appreciate that."

She shut the door behind me and led me down the hall. Garcia was sitting on the bench staring at the floor. He looked miserable.

After the deputy let me in, I sat down beside him. "Tough day?"

"Every day's a tough day."

I nodded.

"I'm meeting with Dr. Gumina tomorrow. She'll want to interview people close to Mo. Who do you suggest?"

"Is this for the psychological profile?"

"Yeah, we've got to get a head start on that."

He looked toward the ceiling. "I appreciate what you're trying to do, but let's say—hypothetically—that I have reason to believe Mo didn't kill herself. Where would that leave our defense?"

"What're you saying?" One of the problems of having a judge for a client was he tried to keep several steps ahead of me. He knew if he disclosed facts disputing a suicide defense, I might have an ethical duty not to assert that defense.

"If I were to testify to a different reason for Mo's death, one that exonerates me, how do you think that would go over?"

I nearly fell off the bench. "What the fuck? Where's this coming from?"

"I'm just wondering about your honest assessment of me as a witness. Do you think the jury would believe my testimony?"

There was something about this guy I didn't like. Over the years I had learned to trust my instincts about a client. If I doubted his or her credibility—whether in a criminal or civil case—it was likely the jury would have similar doubts. I couldn't see a jury accepting anything Garcia said.

"Are you saying you're the only witness to this 'different reason' for Mo's death?"

He faced me directly. "Hypothetically speaking, yes."

"Carlos, I don't know what you've got in mind but from my review of the evidence there are only two possibilities here: Mo committed suicide or you killed her. If you testify—no matter the substance of that testimony, but especially if it relates to some other reason for her death—you're inviting the jury to question your credibility. If that happens, you will turn a case with a lot of holes into a sure conviction. My advice is: don't testify."

He stared into my eyes for several seconds. From down the hall came the clicking of a keyboard, probably the deputy updating her report. In the silence of the cell, the clicking sounded more like pounding.

"You hired me for a reason," I continued. "And you're paying me for my advice. I'm advising you not to testify. Obviously, you don't believe your wife killed herself so you will blow away our only defense. Besides, if you testify, the focus of the case will have shifted from Mo to you. Instead of deliberating on whether Mo killed herself, the jury will be questioning your credibility. If they don't find you credible, they'll convict you. We can't take that chance."

"I appreciate your candor. Let me mull it a bit longer. In the meantime, shall I tell you about Mo's family?"

"Please."

"Her parents are long deceased. Her older brother, the plumber, is fifty-eight; his name is Sam Collins. You saw him in court the first day of the prelim. The younger brother, Joe Collins, is a meth addict, spent six years in state prison. Works construction, handyman kind of thing when he can find the work. Far as I can tell, he's a useless human being. Both have short fuses. It seems every family dinner we had at the parents' house ended up in a fight. Screaming, finger pointing, the whole thing. Bunch of nutjobs. Mo was the only sane one."

"When's the last time you had contact with them?"

"A few weeks before she died. They called to talk to her, and I answered the phone. Nothing unusual about it; they talked every week or so."

"Did you talk to them at all?"

He shook his head. "We never had much to say to each other; the dislike was mutual."

"Where do they live?"

"Nashua area where she grew up."

"What about friends?"

"She had three close friends: Betty Johnson, Ann Blake, and Maggie Tunicci. They golfed together twice a week and generally lunched every week, too, all at the Manchester Country Club over in Bedford."

The Manchester Country Club was an exclusive club, over a hundred years old. I had been to several events there, mostly bar association luncheons, but had no desire to become a member. For one thing, I didn't golf. And I couldn't see joining a club just to have lunch or dinner a few times a week. Truth be told, I wasn't much of a joiner. I also preferred eating at diverse ethnic restaurants rather than going to the same one over and over, though the club's red wine marinated rack of lamb was one of the best I've ever had.

"I need the addresses of these gals."

"I don't know their addresses. You can probably find them at the club."

"Anyone else we should talk to? Acquaintances even."

"Mo had only a few close friends; sure, she met people at the club but that was in passing. When I'd have dinner with her there, she'd introduce me to a bunch of people. I was always amazed how she remembered everyone's name, even if she'd met them only once. She had a real talent for that. But don't ask me any of the names. You might have to go to the club and speak to staff. They might give you some leads."

❁　❁　❁

After leaving the jail, I called Hedges. "Glen, any more info on Ginnie's fans?"

"I've narrowed it down to three or four, but I'm having trouble getting any contact details. It might be worth talking to her coworkers to see if she ever told them anything."

"I'll drive over there now. One more thing." I hated to distract Hedges from trying to find Ginnie, but I needed help with Garcia's case. "I need you on my Garcia case. Mrs. Garcia had a visitor the day of her death. I've got the names of her family and friends at the Manchester Country Club. They might know whether she was seeing anybody, and also about her mental state for a psychological autopsy." I gave him the names Garcia had provided and a description of Mrs. Garcia's visitor.

When he didn't respond, I said, "This work is on the clock."

"You mean I'll actually get paid?"

"Oh, yeah. Garcia can afford it."

❂   ❂   ❂

At the station, I waved at the receptionist and walked right to Cassidy's office. For a Sunday, the place was bustling, people moving to and fro. I guess the news never rests. Cassidy was staring at his computer screen when I opened the door.

"Dutch, what brings you here?" He had a worried look on his face as if I had just caught him looking at porn. He leaned over and gestured for me to sit across from him. But I didn't feel like sitting so I stood close to his desk and stared down at him.

"We're looking at Ginnie's kidnapping from a different angle. We checked out people who had a grudge but we got nowhere. Now we're thinking maybe it was an obsessed fan. Did she ever talk to you about anything like that?"

He shook his head. "She said she got fan mail from time to time, but nothing stands out. Let me think. I don't remember any gifts. Once recently she got flowers but that was from you."

"Flowers?"

"Yeah. A few days before she disappeared. She got two dozen red roses delivered. I assumed they were from you."

I had never sent Ginnie flowers, a realization that immediately made me feel guilty.

"Ginnie tossed the roses in the trash. I thought you two had had a fight. I never imagined they came from someone else."

"Did you tell the police about that?"

Cassidy shrugged and held his hands out by his sides. "It never occurred to me it was important. As I say, I thought the flowers came from you."

"Do you know who delivered them?"

"I don't but check with Dorothy, the receptionist. She would've received the flowers and called Ginnie."

I thanked him and walked to the reception area. Behind the desk was a young woman who was heavily made up with perfectly groomed hair. In my haste to get to Cassidy, I hadn't even glanced at her on my way in. I guessed she would've preferred being in front of the camera rather than answering phones.

I explained who I was.

"I know who you are. I'm sorry about Ms. Turner. I liked her; I really did."

I didn't appreciate her using the past tense while referring to Ginnie but I let it go. "I hear Ginnie received some flowers recently. Any idea who sent them?"

She stared off into space, apparently studying the light fixtures hanging from the ceiling. "There was a card. I know that. It's just . . ."

"What is it, Dorothy?"

She bit her lip and fluttered her eyelashes. She must've been all of twenty-four years old and used to playing the coy damsel. I tried to keep my temper.

"The card had a poem; I thought it showed how much you loved her. It wasn't from you?"

I shook my head.

"I remember it: 'Roses are red, violets are blue. I'd rather be dead than live without you.'"

Shivers ran through my spine. That note showed her admirer to be a loose cannon. Could he be the kidnapper?

"Who delivered the flowers?"

"That's easy. There's only one florist we see here. Pierucci's, they're on Elm Street."

"I've heard of them. Do you know the delivery person?"

She returned her gaze toward the ceiling. "It was a woman, older, thirty maybe. Not white; maybe Asian."

"Maybe?"

"You just can't tell these days," she said, smiling. "Sometimes the Dominicans look Asian to me. The light-skinned ones anyway."

❋   ❋   ❋

Pierucci's had a gold FTB sign with an image of a running Mercury prominently displayed on its front window. I parked in front and noticed right away it was closed. A sign in front said the store was closed on Sundays and opened Monday at 8:00 a.m. I would have to get here at opening tomorrow before heading to Cambridge.

CHAPTER FOURTEEN

THE PROPRIETOR WAS an elderly Italian man who stood behind the counter arranging flowers. I introduced myself and told him I was looking for the person who took the order for Ginnie's flowers.

He cut the stem of a carnation and placed it delicately into a vase along with other carnations. "It's Carla Fernandez you're looking for. She took the order and delivered the flowers too. She made a point to tell me about it because your wife is a bit of a celebrity around here. But I'm afraid I can't help you. Carla quit right after that delivery. Something about wanting to travel with her boyfriend. You ask me, she should dump the loser. Carla's headstrong, wouldn't listen to me anyway."

"Any idea where I can find Carla now?"

He smacked his lips. "If she hasn't left for her trip—New York I think it was."

He walked toward the back of the store and leaned down to open a drawer on a file cabinet. "Just a minute." He pulled out a manila folder. "Here it is: Carla's address. I could probably get in trouble for this, but here you go."

He handed me the file, which had her employment application and home address. I wrote down the address, which was on the northeast side of Manchester.

He resumed cutting flowers, leaning over the vases as he did so. "Thank you, sir," I said, shaking his hand. I knew one thing: when I found Ginnie, one of the first things I'd do is buy her a huge bouquet of flowers from this fine establishment.

As I got back in my car, I called Hedges and filled him in on this latest lead. "I've got to head to Cambridge. Can you stop by Carla Fernandez's place, see what she remembers?"

"I'm at the country club now. I'll stop there as soon as I finish."

"Any luck finding Mo's friends?"

"Far as I can tell, they're playing a round now. I'll catch them at the eighteenth hole."

✺ ✺ ✺

Driving down Route 93, I couldn't help feeling nostalgic for my hometown. I always told myself I had to spend more time in Boston. After all, it was only an hour or so from Manchester. I took the exit for Cambridge and made my way to Massachusetts Avenue and the office of Dr. Marilyn Gumina.

Dr. Gumina had long greyish-black hair, parted in the middle and extending to her mid-back. She was in her early forties, heavyset, about five two. She greeted me with a welcoming smile, extending both her hands to take mine in hers.

"Mr. Francis, so nice to meet you. Please have a seat."

I took the seat across from her desk and glanced at the framed diplomas on the wall and took in the room. There was crimson every-where: a crimson clock on the wall, crimson bobble heads, a crimson pen and pencil set on her desk. She was proud of her Harvard crimson.

"So Judge Garcia's in a bit of trouble, it seems," she said, taking the lead. She spoke with an unusual accent, elongating the last word of each phrase. A bit like George Plimpton or William Buckley. Every word marked her as privileged and well educated. Or perhaps I was pre-judging her, as was my habit due to my origins as a working-class Bostonian.

"He's in jail and the prosecutor seems sure of a conviction."

She leaned back in her chair. "I've done some homework in preparation for our meeting. Googled your client to get background on the case. Found some obscure references, old newspaper articles. Not very flattering."

I was impressed. I hadn't gotten around to doing that yet, a standard procedure for any new client. Ginnie's situation truly did distract me. "And what did you find?"

"He's got a history," she said, hissing the "s" sound.

"What kind of history?" I had to catch myself from imitating her.

"It seems his wife made a few calls to the police."

I didn't like what I was hearing. "I'm waiting."

"Right. The calls were for domestic abuse. It's not clear whether there was physical abuse, but certainly she felt threatened."

"That's not good news."

"Indeed. Does not portray your client in a very favorable light."

"But what does it mean in terms of your potential assignment?"

"The psychological autopsy? Well, I've got to gather as much information as possible; her relationship with her husband is, of course, primary. What were the sources of her stress? Is there a history of alcohol or drug abuse? What other significant relationships did she have? Did she keep a diary? These are the things I need to know, Mr. Francis."

"So are you saying a past history of abuse could've contributed to her decision to commit suicide?"

"It certainly could have, but the converse is also true."

"How do you mean?"

"If your client abused her in the past, that might indicate a propensity to continue to abuse her, perhaps to the point of murder." I didn't like the way she drew out "murder," rolling the "r"s.

I sat back, trying not to look as worried as I felt. "Doctor, I've already got an investigator tracking down Mrs. Garcia's friends and family."

"I'll need to interview them."

"That might be a problem. How can I convince them to talk to you?"

"You're right. But the more information I have, the stronger will be my opinion. If you want the psychological autopsy to persuade a jury, I have to be well armed."

With her hands folded on the desk, she continued. "There are a large number of parameters involved, including details about Maureen's death, family background, social context, life trajectory, social interaction, working conditions, physical and mental health and history, and previous suicidal behavior, if any. In short, I need to know what were the negative elements in her life."

"This is more complicated than I imagined. Let me start by talking to my client. He should know some of these details."

"It would be better, Mr. Francis, if I interviewed your client."

I hesitated, not wanting to expose Judge Garcia to any kind of questioning for fear it would be used against him at trial. Since Dr. Gumina would be testifying as an expert, her conversations with Garcia would be fair game. And there'd be no psychotherapist-patient privilege since Garcia wasn't her patient. "Let me think about that, Doctor."

I moved to stand, figuring this meeting was over, but Dr. Gumina stopped me. "Mr. Francis, any news on your wife?"

"I went on air with the profile. The police are busy following up leads." I told her about our shifting theories about the kidnapping.

"Any ransom demand?"

"No, but I have received some strange mailings." I described the four manila envelopes with Ginnie's body parts.

"Oh my. To me that doesn't indicate someone obsessed with her."

"What does it tell you?"

"He obviously doesn't want to hurt her. Otherwise, he'd be sending more than nails and hair. But why send them to you, especially when there's no ransom demand?"

"He's torturing me."

She remained quiet for a few seconds, thinking. "Maybe that's the point."

"Sorry?"

"Kidnappers can be tormented and sadistic people; they lack empathy. Maybe the kidnapper is not so much obsessed with your wife but is just using her to get at you."

I straightened, my body tensing. I was shaken. The idea that Ginnie was kidnapped to get back at me for some perceived slight hit me to the core. Could I really have been the cause? "What're you saying, that I'm the reason Ginnie was kidnapped?"

"Do you have any enemies like that?"

"I'm a lawyer. I've sued a lot of people over the years. I've defended some bad people. I'm sure there are dozens of people who are pissed off at me."

"I suggest you do an inventory of recent cases, figure out which ones raised the strongest emotions."

I shivered, suddenly feeling cold. "Ginnie was kidnapped just as things were heating up on the Garcia case. The public wanted to lynch him."

"What about Mrs. Garcia's family and friends? They'd certainly be out to get your client. The question is whether they'd go after you in such an extreme way, angry at you for defending him."

"My investigator will be meeting with them. I'll give him a call." I stood up. "Thank you, Dr. Gumina, not only for your help on the Garcia case but also for your insight on my wife's kidnapping. You've given me a lot to think about."

She shook my hand firmly. "I wish you luck."

CHAPTER FIFTEEN

ON THE SHORT drive to Boston, I phoned Hedges. "Just calling for an update."

"Those three ladies are something else. Very high society. Didn't want to give me the time of day."

It sounded like he was driving, too. "So did you charm them?"

"'Course. But I didn't get far. They wouldn't give me details but it was obvious Mrs. Garcia was having an affair. When I gave them the guy's description, you should've heard the stuttering. It was a chorus of stuttering."

"Did you get a name?"

"No, but I'm sure they know him. After I stop by Carla's, I'll hang around the club and look for a guy fitting that description."

I told him what Dr. Gumina had said about my being the cause of Ginnie's kidnapping.

"Jesus, that's heavy. Might be something there, but I say we follow up on the obsessed fan angle first."

"I agree. Call me when something breaks."

❀ ❀ ❀

I met Rodger Dodds at noon at the Union Oyster House, Boston's oldest restaurant. Rodger was dressed in a black suit and red tie, befitting his prominence on the bench. "Dutch, so good to see you." He shook my hand with a strong grip. The maître d' led us to a table in the corner.

"You're looking well." I took my seat. "The bench suits you."

"It's a wonderful job. Don't tell anyone, but I'm having the time of my life. I have more time to consider cases than I ever had in private practice. Government workers, you know what I mean."

He seemed happier than ever. Rodger had been through a lot in the last ten years: the death of his wife from cancer, the stresses of managing a major law firm during difficult financial times, and my divorce from his daughter Sherry and departure from the firm. At first, he was resentful when I left, but I convinced him we could maintain a cordial relationship despite the divorce. I was ready for a change of scenery and made my way north to Manchester.

"So you're working only sixty hours a week," I said, knowing Rodger's workaholic tendencies.

"Hah! I love the law; you know that." He waved to the waiter to take our order. "Sparkling water, please."

The waiter, a fiftyish pudgy man with a salt-and-pepper mustache, nodded and stepped backward. He returned in a few seconds with a bottle, poured our water, twisting the bottle at the end as if he were pouring wine, and recited the specials.

Rodger ordered a Caesar salad with grilled shrimp, an unusual choice for him, while I ordered a cup of clam chowder and pan-seared shrimp and scallops.

"Trying to stay fit," he said, rubbing his belly.

We sipped our water, an awkward silence taking over. Our relationship had become strained over my representation of his niece when he had questioned some of my tactical decisions and I had questioned his forthrightness.

Suddenly, Rodger put down his fork and stared at me. "Just before coming here, I got a call about you."

"From whom?"

"Your mother-in-law."

"Barbara? Why'd she call you?" As far as I knew, the only time Barbara had met Rodger was at my wedding.

He looked at me intently. "She wanted assurance you had nothing to do with Ginnie's disappearance."

"Oh, come on."

"It's the truth. Apparently, she just received some kind of letter saying you were responsible. I told her you're as trustworthy as they come and you love Ginnie."

"I appreciate the good word." I was flabbergasted that my mother-in-law would think I'd harm Ginnie. I thought we'd worked out that issue before. "Did she say what was in the letter?"

"Something about you not being who you seemed. She wanted to talk to me before she called the police."

"She can't be serious."

He took a sip of water. "You're going through a lot, I know. I'm sure nothing will come of it," he assured me, wiping his mouth with the napkin.

"Must've come from the kidnapper."

"Any leads on who it could be?"

I told him about the threats to Ginnie the day of the kidnapping and the investigation into Billy Conti and Curt Bernard. "Also, I received some envelopes with her hair and nail clippings. I don't mind telling you that scared me more than anything. I'm looking into the possibility of an obsessed fan, but the psychiatrist I just met thinks Ginnie might've been kidnapped because of me." I explained Dr. Gumina's theory.

"Does anyone hate you that much?'

Before I could answer, our food arrived and I spread my napkin over my lap. Rodger cut up his lettuce and mixed in the Caesar dressing while I sipped the chowder. I tried to think of how to answer Rodger's question. Aside from perhaps Mo Garcia's brothers, there were only a few people I thought who truly hated me. I would have to check out each of them.

❊   ❊   ❊

On the drive back to Manchester, I placed a call to my mother-in-law. "Barbara, this is Dutch. I just had lunch with Rodger Dodds and he told me about the letter."

"I gave it to that nice Officer Leary."

Just what I needed. More reason for Leary to be suspicious of me. "I hope you don't believe what it said."

"I don't know what to believe anymore, Dutch. I'm so sick with worry."

"Barbara, I assure you the letter came from the kidnapper. I don't know why he sent it except to deflect the police's attention onto me. You have to know I had nothing to do with Ginnie's kidnapping."

"I want to believe that. I really do."

❊   ❊   ❊

It was a little after three o'clock when I arrived in Manchester. I drove straight to the police department and met Delahunty at his desk.

I didn't bother with pleasantries and got right to the point. "I heard about the letter to Barbara Turner."

"Yeah. Typed on a white lined index card in a manila envelope just like the ones you received. Also, no return address. Mailed on

Saturday from Manchester, so that makes five consecutive days of mailings."

"What exactly did it say?"

"Quote: 'Your son-in-law is not what he seems. He's responsible for your daughter's disappearance.' That was the whole letter."

"Great." Nausea swept over me. "What're you going to do about it?"

"Of course I think it's bullshit, but Leary wants to run with it. The department is pushing me to have you take a polygraph."

"Are you shitting me?"

"It's not that unusual when a spouse is kidnapped."

I stared at him, not believing what I was hearing. Here it was, a week after Ginnie's kidnapping, and the Manchester Police Department still considered me a suspect. No wonder they hadn't found Ginnie. At first, I wanted to tell him to shove it but then realized that would only increase the cloud of suspicion over my head.

"Let's do it now."

"Seriously? You're willing to do that?"

"I need your department to change its focus and cross me off as a suspect."

He picked up the phone. "Tell you what, let me see if our polygraph examiner is available."

While he was on the phone, I went to the bathroom. My stomach was cramping. This had been one stressful day. If the kidnapper really were motivated by a desire to punish me, he was certainly succeeding. After washing up, I returned to Delahunty's desk.

"Come with me," he said, standing up.

He led me up a flight of stairs to a small room in the corner. Sitting behind a machine with wires and flashing lights was a dark-skinned man with broad shoulders and a drooping mustache. He must've caught the surprised look on my face as he stood up and extended his hand. "My mother's from southern Italy. Just thought I'd get that out of the way."

"Dutch Francis," Delahunty said, "this is Sergeant Walt Sandberg."

Sandberg pulled out a chair. "Here, take a seat. Do you know much about the polygraph?"

"I know it's of dubious reliability and not admissible in court."

"Well, I happen to think it's very reliable, but we don't need to debate that." He sat back down and fiddled with the machine. "Let's get started. First, I'm going to place electronic sensors on your chest and stomach to record respiratory activity. Lift up your shirt."

I complied then he attached the sensors. "Now let me see your fingers." He placed a strange-looking device on my fingers. "These are disposable adhesive electrodes. They record sweat gland activity. Finally, I'm going to use a blood pressure cuff to record cardiovascular activity."

All hooked up, I got ready to answer his questions.

"I'm going to leave you guys to it," Delahunty said, moving toward the door. "Dutch, stop by my desk when you're finished."

After Delahunty left, Sandberg said, "I'm going to ask you some basic questions, easy stuff, just to get a base level on your responses." He proceeded to ask about my background, education, and work history as if this were a job interview. We chatted some more about mundane subjects then he asked if I had any questions.

"Don't think so."

"Now I'm going to ask about your wife's disappearance. Is Ginnie Turner your wife?"

"Yes."

"Do you know where she is?"

"No."

"Did you harm her in any way?"

"No, I didn't."

"Have you ever abused her, either physically or emotionally?"

I hesitated answering this, pondering whether I had ever said anything to Ginnie that could be considered emotionally abusive. I could think of nothing.

"The answer's 'no.'"

Perhaps it was my imagination, but I thought he gave me a skeptical look.

"Do you know who took your wife?"

"I wish I did."

"Could you answer the question?"

"Again, the answer's 'no.'"

"Do you know why your wife was kidnapped?"

"I have some guesses."

"What are they?"

"Either someone with a grudge because of her reporting, an obsessive fan, or someone trying to punish me."

He raised his eyebrows. "That should do it. Let's take these things off you." He removed the sensors, electrodes, and cuff.

I stood up. "How's it look?"

"I need some time to score and analyze the results."

We shook hands then I walked down the stairs to Delahunty's desk.

"How ya doin'?" he asked.

"I've been better." I told him about the obsessed fan and Dr. Gumina's theory.

"Let us follow up. I'll need a list of any potential enemies."

"Whatever happened with the videos from near the station?"

"We've enhanced them as best we can but still can't make out any license plates. We haven't ruled any of them out as being the kidnapper but right now we've hit a dead end."

"I thought Bernard was our guy, especially when his car was a match."

He shook his head. "Unfortunately, he didn't pan out. I'll call you as soon as I get the polygraph results."

"I'm not worried."

❀　❀　❀

By the time I left the station, it was close to five o'clock. I had shut off my phone during the polygraph exam at Sandberg's request and when I turned it back on there were several missed calls from Hedges. I called him back.

Before I could say anything, he blurted, "Carla came home a little while ago. I'm watching her house."

"I'm on my way."

CHAPTER SIXTEEN

I GOT TO Carla's in less than ten minutes, parked, walked to Hedges' car, and leaned through the driver's-side window. "You should see her," he said. "She's about five eight, a hundred twenty pounds. Built like a brick shithouse."

"Let me see for myself."

He got out of the car and we walked to Carla's front door and rang the doorbell. The door was opened by a young woman wearing a Red Sox shirt tied in front and skintight black pants. My guess was her nationality was Filipina, which might explain why the receptionist couldn't tell if she were Latina or Asian. She looked at us the same way most people had recently: with skepticism and a certain amount of distrust.

"Mr. Pierucci suggested I contact you. My name's Dutch Francis." I handed her my card. "And this is Glen Hedges."

"Strange; Mr. Pierucci never mentioned anything." She stared at the cards as if deciphering a haiku.

"He told me you delivered some flowers to Ginnie Turner at Channel 9. She's my wife and you may have heard she's gone missing."

"Ohmygod! I like remember that so well. A creepy guy ordered them and paid cash."

"That's what we want to know," Hedges said. "Whatever you remember about the guy would be a big help."

She tilted her head and looked at me. "You think he had something to do with your wife's disappearance. That's like so disgusting." She folded her arms and blew out her cheeks. "Let's see: white guy, short, maybe five seven, chubby, with red cheeks."

"Facial hair?" I asked.

"None, though he had longish sideburns."

"What's that mean?"

"They came below the earlobes."

"Hair color?"

"Brownish."

"This is great. You've been a big help. Would you be willing to talk to a police sketch artist?"

She bit her lower lip. "Yeah, like sure."

"I'll get someone right over." I pulled out my cell phone and called Delahunty. "Bill, it's Dutch. Look, I've got a lead on that obsessive fan suspect I mentioned but we need a sketch artist right away."

He hemmed and hawed and said he didn't know if one were available. I got a bit testy. "This is my wife we're talking about here," I reminded him. Finally, he relented and said he'd get the sketch artist over to Carla's within the hour. I hung up and told Carla what he'd said.

"I'll stay here," she said. "And make sure I get the details right."

❖ ❖ ❖

Even though it was late, I couldn't relax so I stopped by the office. Hedges went home, promising to return to the country club in the morning to continue the investigation into Mrs. Garcia's visitor the day of her death.

I wanted to review my case files to see if something would clue me in to a possible kidnapper, someone I had dealt with as an attorney, someone I had humiliated or embarrassed, someone so unhinged he would kidnap my wife to make me suffer. I didn't want to ignore any possibility. If the kidnapper's motive was to make me suffer, then everyone mentioned in those files was a suspect, at least for the cases where my client had prevailed. I pulled down boxes from atop the metal file cabinet and thumbed through each file. I considered each case, recalling depositions I had taken, people I had accused of wrongdoing. At first nothing jumped out at me but then I remembered there was a file missing: the Handford file. Mrs. Handford certainly had a grudge against me as well as Carlos Garcia. Could she have taken Ginnie to punish me, or perhaps distract me from defending Garcia?

I was still thinking this over when my phone rang. It was Delahunty.

"Come by the station," he said. "I've got a pretty good sketch here."

❋   ❋   ❋

Delahunty was sitting at his desk when I arrived. He waved for me to sit down beside him and cleared some papers out of the way. "Here he is," he said. I was amazed at how well the sketch fit Carla's description. Brown hair hanging down over his collar, red chubby cheeks, and long sideburns. I stared at it, fighting my emotions, from anger and hatred to revulsion and disdain. Could this be the man who had kidnapped my wife? Could this be the man who cut off her pubic hair, clipped her nails, sent that awful letter to Barbara Turner? Part of me wanted to act out and punch the sketch as if punching this piece of paper would hurt the actual kidnapper.

I held the sketch up. Had I seen him before? I couldn't tell.

"We'll scan it and send it around the state. See what turns up. You really think this guy might've taken her?"

"You tell me: he was obsessed with her, wrote her a bizarre poem, and sent her flowers. All just before she disappeared. Yeah, I like this guy for it."

He took back the sketch and stared at it. "Jesus, strange looking dude."

"We need to get this on the air now. Hold on."

I called Dennis Cassidy at Channel 9 and explained the situation. "Dennis, this is urgent. Can you show the sketch on the late news?"

He agreed and gave me his email address. Within five minutes, the sketch was on the way to him.

❀ ❀ ❀

At home I opened a bottle of Molson, made a turkey sandwich, and turned on the TV. The news was just starting. The camera zoomed in on Cassidy, his face grim. "The investigation into the kidnapping of our colleague Ginnie Turner continues. The police have identified a potential suspect."

He held up the sketch and waited for the camera to zoom in on it. "The police are looking for this man. If you recognize him, please immediately call the phone number flashing on the screen. This sketch has also been posted on the Channel 9 website. Time is of the essence. Please hurry."

CHAPTER SEVENTEEN

IN THE MORNING, I appeared in court for the judge's decision on the preliminary hearing. Judge Shane strode to the bench as if in a hurry. In the courtroom were me, Garcia, and Tompkins and, arriving just as the judge was taking the bench, was Garcia's brother-in-law Sam Collins.

Judge Shane looked at me then turned toward Tompkins. "Counsel, I have reached a decision."

Garcia shifted beside me. He was nervous, his forehead moist. I put my hand on his shoulder to calm him.

"After reviewing all the evidence," Judge Shane continued, "I have decided that probable cause exists to hold over the defendant for trial on a charge of murder."

Even though the decision was expected, Garcia let out a loud moan.

The judge silenced him with an icy glare. "Judge Garcia, I won't tolerate any more outbursts in my courtroom. You will remain in custody until trial." She turned to me. "Has the defendant reconsidered his insistence on a speedy trial?"

I looked over at Garcia who was staring at his hands folded on the defense table. He shook his head. Then I turned back to the judge. "No, Your Honor."

"That's a shame. Particularly for you, Mr. Francis."

"I agree, Your Honor."

"Very well, we will begin jury selection Thursday morning." She strode off the bench.

As the bailiff escorted Garcia back to jail, I noticed Sam Collins get up and approach the exit. "Mr. Collins? Can I talk to you for a moment?" I needed to test Dr. Gumina's theory, see if Collins could've been the kidnapper.

I never got a chance, though, because without saying a word Collins stopped, flipped me the bird, and stormed out the door.

❊ ❊ ❊

I called Delahunty as I exited the courthouse. "Bill, any feedback on the sketch?"

"Yeah, lots of leads. We've identified one guy in particular and will put him in a lineup. But Carla won't be available until this evening."

"Have you got a tail on him? Can we search his home?" I was nervous about what would happen if this guy really were the kidnapper. If he learned the cops were onto him, he might hurt Ginnie.

"Easy," he said. "I've got a plainclothes on him. We don't have enough yet for a search warrant."

After having previous leads go nowhere, I didn't want to wait around to see if this one panned out. I reminded him of Dr. Gumina's theory. "I've been going through old cases to figure out who might have a grudge against me. There are a ton of people I know I've pissed off, including a woman who blames me for her husband's suicide."

"Doubt she's our kidnapper, but who knows? What else did you find?"

"Nothing definite. There's the obvious: Judge Garcia's brothers-in-law. One of them was in court today and flipped me off. I think you should have someone pay them a visit."

"That will be impossible today. We had a few officers call in sick so we're shorthanded."

"I'll do it myself."

"Dutch, we talked about that. It's not a good idea."

"The brother who shot me the bird and glared at me at the start of the prelim: I've got a bad feeling about him."

"Look, if this lineup doesn't go anywhere, I'll check them out myself tomorrow. Okay?"

"I'll think about it."

"Thanks. Oh, I almost forgot: the polygraph."

"Yeah?"

"You passed with flying colors."

"Now can you get serious about finding Ginnie?"

"Dutch, we have been serious. You know that."

"Sure."

❊   ❊   ❊

At the office, I continued going through case files. After a few hours, Hedges called. "No luck yet locating our bald guy. I'm at the club now and will try the Andrews sisters again, see if they'll give me his name."

"The Andrews sisters?"

"Yeah, that's what I call Mrs. Garcia's friends."

"You're older than I thought." As much as I knew we had to track down this witness soon, I had other priorities. "Let's put that on hold. I want to visit Garcia's in-laws. Can you pick me up?"

❊   ❊   ❊

Despite Delahunty's concerns, I couldn't wait any longer to investigate Garcia's in-laws. I obtained their home addresses from an online search and was soon sitting in Hedges' car on the way to Nashua.

I pulled out my phone and did further internet research on the Collins brothers. Joe's name brought up a few newspaper articles about his arrest, trial, and conviction for possessing methamphetamine with the intent to sell. He had been sentenced to New Hampshire State Prison and had served six years. Best I could tell he was single and had led a tough life.

Sam Collins had much less of an online presence. His name came up on only a few pages. A few years ago, he had been leading a picket line of plumbers in front of a major hotel. He had a high forehead like his brother but was cleanshaven with fat puffy cheeks.

"Let's stop at Joe Collins' place first," I said. "That's closer."

Joe lived in a trailer park on the outskirts of Nashua. There was no answer when we knocked on the door. Hedges walked to the back of the trailer and peered in the windows. "Ginnie!" he yelled. I prayed she would answer but there was nothing but silence. "Ginnie!" A dog began barking a few trailers away, then it seemed like every dog in the park joined in.

"What's going on here?" yelled a man with a full red beard who came from the trailer next door. Behind him was a Doberman pinscher, snarling, as he walked toward us.

"We're looking for Joe," I said.

"What kinda business you got with Joe?"

"That would be a private kinda business," Hedges said. "Any idea where he is?"

Red Beard pulled his shoulders back and faced Hedges. Veins bulged in his neck as he clenched his fists. "None of your goddamn business."

I tried to defuse the situation by putting up my hands. "We just want to talk to him. That's all."

He turned toward me. "I suggest you get off his property before I report you for trespassing."

"You don't look like the type of guy who's anxious to talk to the cops," Hedges said. "My guess is there're a few warrants out there with your name on them."

Red Beard appeared to get flustered as he unclenched his fists. "I don't like the way you look." He pointed at Hedges.

"That makes us even," Hedges said. "I'm not exactly swooning at the sight of you."

A beige station wagon with brown siding pulled up in front of the house and parked. Emerging from the car was a fiftyish guy with a greyish goatee, his high forehead glistening in the midafternoon sun. He reminded me of Whitey Bulger. "What the hell's going on here?" he asked no one in particular.

"These fellas say they got some business with you," Red Beard said.

"Business? Really? Who the hell are you fellas?"

I held out my hand to shake, but he ignored it. "Name's Dutch Francis; this is Glen Hedges."

"Francis? You're the lawyer defending my asshole brother-in-law." I nodded.

"So that makes you an asshole, too."

"Wait a second, pal," Hedges said.

"You wait a second. And get the fuck off my property."

"You want me to move them off, Joe," said Red Beard, taking a step toward me.

Collins put up his palm. "Just get the fuck outa here."

I moved toward Hedges' car but stopped and pointed at Collins. "I find out you've touched my wife, you'll be very sorry."

"Your wife? What the fuck're you talkin' about?"

"You know my wife is Ginnie Turner. Some asshole kidnapped her. That wouldn't be you, would it?"

Collins glanced at Red Beard and shrugged. Without another word, he unlocked his front door and went inside, leaving Red Beard staring at me and Hedges.

❖   ❖   ❖

I had an uneasy feeling about Joe Collins. He had the drawn, emaciated look of a meth addict. A few crude tattoos were visible at the bottom of his neck, clearly extending from his chest. I couldn't make out what they were, strange swirls and markings, probably inked in prison. He was just the kind of slimeball I could imagine kidnapping Ginnie and it made me feel sick. I hated to leave him but he hadn't given me anything to go on.

We stopped by Sam Collins' house, a run-down bungalow in a working-class section of Nashua. I didn't expect him to be any more cooperative than his brother, especially considering he had given me the finger a few hours ago. I knocked on the door and there was no answer. "His brother probably warned him," Hedges said. I pounded on the door, trying to will someone to answer.

Hedges began yelling, "Ginnie! Ginnie!" He walked around back and continued yelling. No sounds came from the house. I stared at the windows, looking for an opening, seriously considering breaking in. But what if Ginnie weren't there? I would be in deep shit. No doubt Sam Collins would press charges. If I had any evidence of Ginnie's presence, I wouldn't hesitate. But all I had was Dr. Gumina's theory so I dismissed the idea.

"Let's get a drink," Hedges said, "and come back in a few hours."

We located O'Brien's Pub in downtown Nashua and stopped by for a drink. I ordered a Guinness and Hedges got Jameson Gold Reserve neat. "I guess you're buying," I said, making note of his expensive drink.

We sat at a booth across from a wide-screen TV showing a soccer match. Hedges held up his glass and I tapped it with my pint. "To finding Ginnie."

"Tell me something." A sense of dread overcame me. "Are we spinning our wheels? Do we have any chance of finding her?"

He sipped the whiskey and wiped his lips with the back of his hand. "What other choice do we have?"

"What I was thinking." I took a long gulp of Guinness. "Something about Joe worries me. Maybe Delahunty could put a tail on him."

"On both of them. But we probably need to give him more to go on."

I sipped the Guinness and stared at the soccer match. I always got a kick out of how easily soccer players fell down after being barely touched. They would drop to the ground, writhe as if in agony, and wait for the ref to blow the whistle. I couldn't help comparing soccer to rugby where players really did get hit hard and usually bounced right back up. I thought of the traditional description of the difference between soccer and rugby: soccer was a sport for gentlemen played by ruffians; rugby was a sport for ruffians played by gentlemen. Although I'd never played soccer, I had to agree that was true. Rugby players beat each other up the whole match then joined together for post-match drinking and singing, acting as if they were the best of friends.

I thought back to my days of playing rugby, remembering how carefree I was then. I had stress from my cases, sure, and relationship difficulties, but the stress was nothing compared to what I was going through now. Losing Ginnie was the worst thing I could imagine. Sometimes I felt like falling to the ground like those soccer players and begging for someone to come to my aid. But I knew I had to keep fighting, keep looking, for I was all Ginnie had.

I had nearly half a pint of Guinness left when Delahunty called. "We're putting together a lineup and Carla's on the way over. Do you want to watch it?"

"I'm in Nashua. Give me half an hour."

"Make it fast."

I asked Hedges to drop me at the police station and I'd take a cab home. "I don't want to miss the opportunity to eyeball the guy who might've kidnapped Ginnie. We'll have to put Sam Collins on the back burner for the time being."

CHAPTER EIGHTEEN

LESS THAN THIRTY minutes later, I was standing in the police station with Delahunty in front of a mirrored window. Carla stood beside us looking over the six men in the lineup. They stood in the adjacent room in front of signs on the wall numbered one through six. All bore some resemblance to the sketch of Carla's flower delivery guy.

"Now take your time," Delahunty told her. "Look them over carefully."

She was taking her time, aligning herself across from each one, staring at each for a full minute before moving to the next one. In the meantime, Delahunty barked orders through the microphone, telling the men to turn this way and that. The men were of varying heights; one was six three, another five seven. All were Caucasian, of course, though a couple had slightly darker complexions than the others. Number three had an obvious scar over his left eye, a two-inch line. Surely if he were the one, Carla would've noticed the scar. Carla's hesitancy was starting to worry Delahunty, who seemed to regret telling her to take her time.

"I would say," Carla said, "that it's number two. Yeah, that's him."

"Are you certain?" Delahunty asked.

"As certain as I can be." She turned to me. "I hope you find your wife soon, Mr. Francis. Like, I really do. Must be terrible."

"It is terrible. Thank you for your concern."

"May I leave now?" she asked Delahunty.

"Your duty is done. We'll call if we need you again."

I followed Delahunty into the lineup room where he dismissed five of the men. The suspect was named Paul Young. Delahunty told him to sit at the table against the far wall. "You'll have to wait outside," he said to me.

"But, Bill . . ."

He shook his head. "Against policy. You can listen in but you can't be here."

I took a seat outside the room as Delahunty began the questioning with a video camera recording everything. I could hear through the intercom system. "Paul, this is your lucky day. Our witness picked you out of the lineup."

"What the hell? What did I do?" He had a high, squeaky voice that didn't really fit his chubby frame and long stringy hair.

"Paul, how old are you? What, twenty-three?"

"Twenty-four."

"Congratulations. Now let's get to the point. About two weeks ago did you buy flowers for Channel 9 newscaster Ginnie Turner?"

Young leaned backward. "You mean that's what this is about. You think I had something to do with her disappearance? That's crazy, man."

"Answer the question."

"It was nothing, man. Just flowers."

"Are you infatuated with the woman?"

"I appreciate good women."

"So you make it a habit to send flowers to public figures. Who else?"

He shook his head. "No one else."

"So if I understand you correctly, the only woman you've sent flowers to wound up disappearing not long after."

"I tell ya, I had nothing to do with that."

It was hard for me to sit back and remain quiet. I wanted to rush into the room, grab him by the shirt, and shake answers out of him. But Delahunty was taking it slow, going by the book, which was smart.

"You tellin' me it was a coincidence that Ms. Turner disappeared shortly after you sent her flowers and a disturbing love note?"

Young got a distressed look on his face as if accepting the seriousness of his situation for the first time. "Exactly what I'm tellin' ya."

"But you know where she is."

Young glanced toward the glass wall, trying to see on the other side, perhaps realizing who I was. "You got it wrong, man."

"Where is she, Paul?"

"I . . . I don't know. Why don't you go find the real kidnapper? Why you bothering me?"

"We know you got a record."

"What kinda record?"

As soon as Young stopped speaking, Delahunty threw his hands in the air. Young pushed his chair a few inches back. "Don't fuck with me!" Delahunty yelled.

"So I got a record. Not for kidnapping though."

"I got you for three burglaries, possession of heroin with intent to sell, a few others. If I were to guess, I'd say you got a drug habit. Let me see your arms."

"Ah, man." Reluctantly he unbuttoned his sleeves and rolled them up. Both forearms were covered with needle tracks. "I got a problem; I'm dealing with it though."

"Oh, you are? How's that?"

"I've been going to the methadone clinic."

"Good for you. Bet your mother is real proud." Delahunty walked around the table and leaned over Young, his face inches from Young's. "Bet you'd like a lock of her hair, wouldn't you?"

"What? I don't know what you're talking about."

"Sure, you'd like her hair, maybe her fingernails and toenails." Delahunty's face came even closer. "Maybe something even more intimate?"

"I . . . I wouldn't hurt her, ever."

Now Delahunty pulled away. "Who said anything about hurting her? Is there something you want to tell me?"

Young shook his head back and forth. "Leave me alone; I didn't do nothing."

"You didn't? How about: 'Roses are red; violets are blue. I'd rather be dead than live without you.' Is that true, Paulie? You'd rather be dead? Or maybe you'd rather *she* be dead if she wouldn't have you?"

Sweat began forming on Young's forehead and he wiped it with his uncovered forearm. "C-can I go now? You got no reason to hold me. All I did was buy her flowers."

"You can go, but I want to search your apartment, make sure you're not holding Ms. Turner. You got a problem with that?"

"Do I have to let you? What about a search warrant?"

"I can get a warrant if that's how you want to play it but I thought you were innocent; all you did was buy her flowers."

"I am innocent." Young looked around the room. "O-okay. You can search my apartment but only to confirm that Ms. Turner is not there."

Delahunty glanced in my direction and nodded. I nodded back, forgetting that Delahunty couldn't see me, realizing this punk was innocent. He wouldn't have agreed to a search if he had Ginnie. "Go on with ya," Delahunty said. "We'll be back in touch."

After Young had left, not daring to look at me, Delahunty approached. "I'm afraid this guy is in the clear. Like everything else in this case, we've hit a dead end."

"I say we move on the Collins brothers." I told him about the confrontation today with Joe Collins. "And Sam wasn't home. Can you put a tail on both of them?"

"Let me do some research first. I'll check DMV records to see what vehicles they own and see if any match ones from the videos. I'm also following up leads from your TV appearance."

"Anything promising?"

"A few, but there are so damn many it's hard to know."

Delahunty put his hand on my shoulder. "Don't give up hope. I'll find her if it's the last thing I do."

CHAPTER NINETEEN

By the time I got home I was overwhelmed with despair. I was no closer to finding Ginnie than I was the night she was taken. Today's mail did not contain any manila envelopes, which, strangely, disappointed me. At least those mailings had been tangible evidence of Ginnie's existence. Now all I had was my hopes, fears, and memories.

Even though it was getting late, I felt wired, unable to sleep. Just for something to do, I turned on my laptop and scanned Maureen Garcia's Facebook page, which was open to the public. There were recent posts from people saying how much they missed her, hoping her husband got what's coming to him. I thought it strange that people would post to a dead woman's Facebook page.

Her page revealed a woman who enjoyed hiking, bicycling, and nature. There were many references to the fresh air, New Hampshire's natural beauty from the White Mountains to the seashore. She seemed to take advantage of all that the state had to offer. Her friends list had 156 names. There was no indication that this was a woman who would take her own life. In fact, there were some photos of her husband and her together, both smiling with their arms around each other. In many of the photos, Maureen wore dark glasses with stripes on the frames. Her profile photo showed her wearing hoop earrings, fully made up with bright red lipstick, her brown hair combed back from her head. One post she had copied said, "Don't underestimate me because I'm quiet."

A recent post also caught my attention. It was from *The Citizen*, a small-town newspaper in Merrimack, about a dozen miles south of Manchester. It said: "Breaking news: Judge Carlos Garcia held over for trial for murdering his wife. Don't worry, Mo, that murdering husband of yours and his scumbag lawyer will take a fall."

I don't think I'd ever read *The Citizen*. I certainly never met any of its reporters or editors so I was puzzled why they called me a scumbag. Was it simply because I was defending an accused murderer? That seemed over the top, but I had bigger things to worry about.

When I finished reading Mo Garcia's page, I moved to Ginnie's. There were hundreds of recent posts, people who claimed to have seen her. Some said they'd caught a glimpse of Ginnie walking in a mall, driving on the freeway, or amidst a crowd at a sporting event. They all seemed unreliable but I decided to tip off Delahunty in the morning.

Just when I was about to shut off the laptop and go to bed, a text message appeared on my screen; it didn't seem to be a normal text message. The box was large and the letters were all caps: *SAW THE WEAK SKETCH ON CHANNEL 9. SERIOUSLY? DO YOU REALLY WANT TO SEE YOUR WIFE AGAIN?*

My heart sank. Could this be the kidnapper? Finally, he had contacted me. It took me a while to figure out how to reply. I wrote: *When can I see her?*

A new text appeared: *NOT SO FAST. GATHER $300,000. I WILL BE IN TOUCH.*

As suddenly as the message had appeared, it now disappeared. I texted back: *How do I know you have Ginnie?* There was no response. I sat staring at the screen for several minutes.

What do I do now? I was frozen. Should I call Delahunty? He was almost certainly asleep. And what could he possibly do at this hour? I put my laptop away and got ready for bed. I knew I wouldn't sleep but I had to let this new development sink in. For a change, I felt hope that Ginnie would soon be home. But where in the world was I going to get $300,000? That amount was way beyond my means.

❊   ❊   ❊

As soon as my clock hit 7:00 a.m., I called Delahunty, who had just arrived at the station. "Bill, there's been a ransom demand."

"Jesus Christ! Finally."

"Yeah, but I have no idea how I'm going to pay it."

"Whoa! We need to talk this through before you pay anything. How did the kidnapper contact you? Another manila envelope?"

"No, a strange text message on my laptop."

"I'll send a techie over to examine your computer. Sit tight until we talk again."

I couldn't sit tight so I called Hedges and filled him in on this development.

"About time something broke. Think it's one of the Collins brothers?"

"Shit, how do I know?"

"Maybe it's a coincidence, but he contacts you soon after we visited them."

"Yeah, but he mentioned seeing the sketch on Channel 9. That didn't look anything like the Collins brothers."

"Maybe the guy got nervous, worried you were close to identifying him."

"Could be. I'm waiting for Delahunty's techie. I'll touch base when I know more."

Delahunty's techie arrived within a half hour. She was young, probably early twenties, with a pink highlight on her long blond hair. "Mr. Francis?" She extended her hand. "I'm from the Manchester PD." I let her in and set her up on the kitchen table with the laptop. I tried not to get in her way but every so often I glanced over her shoulder and saw nothing but unintelligible code. She spent an hour and a half playing with my computer and came up dry. "This guy's good. He's eliminated all traces of his presence."

"Just as I thought."

"If he texts you again, take a photo of the screen with your cell phone. I'm guessing you won't be able to take a screen shot." She removed her wires and packed up her equipment. "Good luck," she said as she was leaving.

I stared at the laptop as if the kidnapper were somewhere inside. Another text appeared: *DON'T CALL IN ANOTHER POLICE FORENSICS EXPERT OR I'M DONE WITH YOU. UNDERSTOOD?*

I swallowed. My God, this guy was good. *Yes*, I typed. I grabbed my cell phone and put it in camera mode. As I held it up to take a screen shot, a message appeared.

WHAT THE HELL ARE YOU DOING?

Stunned, I stared at the screen. It took me a moment to notice the camera light on. Somehow the kidnapper had activated my laptop camera to watch me.

NOW YOU KNOW I CAN SEE YOU. DON'T PULL THAT SHIT AGAIN.

I typed: *Sorry. I didn't realize you could see me.* Damn, I would have to keep the screen closed if I were to have any privacy.

I breathed heavily and waited for his next message. *YOU HAVE UNTIL NEXT WEEK TO GATHER THE MONEY*, he texted.

It will take me longer than that. I don't have that much cash.

NEXT WEEK!
Wait! I want to talk to Ginnie.
MAYBE LATER, AFTER YOU GATHER THE CASH.
How do I know you really have her?
FOR NOW, THAT'S A CHANCE YOU'LL JUST HAVE TO
TAKE.

I waited another half hour and there were no more texts so I closed the screen and called Delahunty. I told him I'd be right over.

❀ ❀ ❀

When I arrived, he was at his desk so I sat beside him. Leary soon appeared and stood next to me, hovering in a way that made me uncomfortable.

"Did you take a photo of the ransom demand?" asked Delahunty.

"No, he told me no photos." I told them about the kidnapper's seeing me through the computer camera and his warning about my taking photos.

"So all we got is your word about a ransom?" asked Leary.

Her tone was accusatory. My nerves were on edge. I turned to her and said, "Why don't you leave this to the adults."

"You ask me," Leary said, looking at Delahunty, "his story doesn't add up."

Delahunty put his hands up. "Marie, we've got no evidence Dutch had anything to do with his wife's disappearance. In fact, the polygraph proved otherwise. Let's focus on this ransom demand."

She frowned, folding her arms across her chest.

"I can't pay the ransom. I don't have that kind of money. If I raided my retirement accounts and all my savings, I could probably come up with a hundred thousand."

"You won't have to. We'll get some cash together, draw him out, and make the arrest just when he grabs the money."

"Won't that put Ginnie at risk?"

"What choice do we have?"

"Let me think about it."

❀   ❀   ❀

Time was wearing heavily on me. I didn't have much time to raise the ransom. For a few hours, I was overwhelmed by the enormousness of the task but gradually my nerves settled and I began to think like a lawyer. There had to be a way to get money quickly. I sat at my kitchen table, writing on a notepad a list of possibilities. First on the list was Citizens Bank.

I wanted to see how much I could mortgage the condo for. It turned out I couldn't even qualify for a mortgage because the condo was in Ginnie's name. It had always been hers and we didn't bother changing that when we got married. Dejected, I returned to the condo, contemplating the possibilities.

Next on my list was Rodger Dodds. He had made a fortune in private practice and did not waste it with a lavish lifestyle. He had told me to let him know if he could help in any way. I punched in the number for the First Circuit Court of Appeals, feeling more nervous than I should have.

"Judge Rodger Dodds, please."

"May I say who's calling?"

"Dutch Francis."

"The judge doesn't usually accept blind calls," he said in a high-pitched voice.

"I'm not blind; I'm . . ." What the hell was I? An ex-partner, ex-son-in-law? "Just tell him it's me; he'll accept my call."

"Well . . ." he said, sounding doubtful. "Okay, I'll ring the judge right away."

After a few moments on hold, I pushed the speaker button and placed the phone on my kitchen table.

"Dutch?" came Rodger's voice through the speaker. "Hold on a second." There was some muffled conversation for a minute or so before Rodger came back on. "My law clerk. I've got to train her on basic legal research, for Christ's sake. Graduated from a terrific school, near the top of her class, but doesn't know Shepard's from Shinola."

"It's all computer research now, Rodger. You know that: Lexis and Westlaw. The trick is to input the right search terms. Shepard's is old school."

"Well, I'm old school and that's what I like. But you weren't calling to discuss my personnel problems."

"Rodger, I hate to ask, but Ginnie's life is at stake. I've run out of options. The kidnapper demanded a ransom, three hundred grand. So far I've raised $100,000, all from savings and retirement accounts."

"After all those years with the firm, that's all you could manage to save?"

"Ahem." I cleared my throat. "Your daughter had something to do with that."

"Still . . ."

"And I'm not the best financial manager around, I admit it. If I can get a hundred grand, Rodger, it would go a long way. I'd much appreciate it."

This was a lot to ask, I knew, of a man who had met Ginnie only one time, at our wedding. But our history went back about two decades, most of that time cordial and friendly. I spent many holidays at Rodger's house, which is how I got to know his daughter Sherry. He was a mentor, a father figure I looked up to and emulated.

"We're going to need collateral."

"Who's 'we'?"

"A manner of speech."

So this was a business transaction like any other. For a moment he had fooled me. I had actually credited him with having human emotions; I had thought he cared.

But I wasn't going to turn my back on any funds. Still, I had no collateral. "The best I can do is a personal guarantee. I've got some cases that should pay off in the next year."

"Hmm."

"You've got the money, Rodger. You can afford it."

"Well . . . I will do my best. For Ginnie. Give me a little time to see what I can spring loose."

I thanked him profusely, still embarrassed for having to ask. Then I geared up for another tough call: to Channel 9. Surely Ginnie's employer would do what it could to save her. The station had been proactive so far, allowing me to go on the air, showing the sketch of the suspect, and regularly appealing to viewers for help finding Ginnie. I got through to her co-anchor, Dennis Cassidy, right away.

"Dennis, there's been a major development. The kidnapper contacted me. He wants three hundred grand ransom. I was hoping the station could kick in a hundred thousand."

"Dutch, that's crazy. The station doesn't have that kind of money." I could hear the distress in his voice. "Is this the guy from the sketch?"

"I don't know. He's been sending me text messages that the police can't trace." I inhaled deeply, seriously debating what to say next. "Can you get the station to make a substantial contribution? I'm a long way from three hundred."

"That's a lot of money, Dutch. We're a small station in a minor market. We just don't have that kind of money."

I was tired of his whining. "For Christ sake, Dennis, this is about Ginnie. How would it look if I went to the *Union Leader* and told them Ginnie's employer refused to help her?"

"You wouldn't do that."

"Dennis, I'll do whatever it takes to get her back."

"Give me a little time. I'll talk to the board. Don't worry. I'll push for the most possible."

"I don't have much time, Dennis."

Cassidy and I didn't always get along. He often was sniffing for a story even when I told him I had to keep some cases private. But he cared for Ginnie; I could see that.

CHAPTER TWENTY

By THREE O'CLOCK I hadn't heard back from either Rodger or Dennis. I was impatient and wanted events to move quickly so I could get Ginnie released. I placed a call to Hedges and left him a voicemail. I was going stir crazy so I made my way over to the jail. Jury selection started tomorrow and I had a lot to discuss with my client. In particular, I had not yet had an opportunity to ask him about the past incidents of domestic abuse.

He was sleeping when Hank opened his cell door. Startled, he sat upright.

"Sorry to bother you."

He rubbed his eyes. "I was wondering if you were going to come by. We don't have much time."

"Yeah, well, I've been dealing with other things." I leaned against the bars, trying to get my mind off Ginnie so I could properly defend my client. I started by telling him what Dr. Gumina had found online.

"What can I say?" He held up his hands.

"For starters, maybe you could tell me why you withheld this information from me."

"You never asked."

I didn't like his flip attitude. "Goddamnit! I can't defend you unless I know everything. Surely you knew the relevance of these incidents."

"It was nothing. Mo was drinking and got out of control."

"Three times?"

He hung his head. "I was never arrested. She got drunk and called 911."

"A wife who drunk-dialed 911. Is that what we're going to tell the jury?"

"These calls shouldn't come into evidence. They're not relevant to whether I murdered her."

"Really? Even you don't believe that. We have no chance of keeping them out."

"I never hit her. Get the 911 tapes. You'll see. Each time I had to stop her from hitting me."

"So why was she mad at you?"

"Oh, it was bullshit really. I had been cold to her, uncommunicative, not affectionate. Our marriage was on the rocks."

"This was before your affair?"

"Before my affair with Arlene."

"There were others?"

"What do you think?"

I didn't like what I was hearing. This information was not giving me confidence in our chances of winning this case. I would have to explore issues of domestic abuse with prospective jurors. I wasn't looking forward to jury selection.

My phone rang. It was Hedges. Because I had a lot more to cover with Garcia, I let the call go to voicemail. I turned back to Garcia.

"Have you met with Dr. Gumina?"

"She came by this morning."

He leaned his head against the wall. It seemed extra dark outside, clouds forming in the patch of sky visible from the small barred window beneath the ceiling.

"I doubt Dr. Gumina will be ready by the time of trial," I said. "She hasn't been able to talk to anyone but you yet. Mo's friends and brothers won't take her calls. She'd get crushed on cross-examination. A psychological autopsy based only on the word of the defendant? You know what'll happen with that."

"Look, I wasn't all that hot on the psych autopsy in the first place. Gumina will have the medical records; that should be enough for her to say whether Mo was suicidal."

I stood up and paced across the cell. I was frustrated but tried not to show it. My client wasn't thinking straight and there was nothing I could do. Our whole defense depended on proving that his wife was suicidal. We needed more proof than a half-assed psychological autopsy.

"There's one more possible lead. I found out from the mail carrier that a guy visited your house the day of her death; he was tall, husky, and bald. You know anyone like that?"

He thought about it for a while, long enough for me to wonder if he was leveling with me. Finally, he shook his head. "No one comes to mind. Might've been a repairman."

"Don't think so. He wasn't driving any kind of truck, just one of those electric cars, a Tesla."

"You think he might've had something to do with Mo's death?"

I shrugged. "What do I know? It's a lead and we have to follow up." I paused. "I got a lot on my plate right now as you know. Last night Ginnie's kidnapper demanded a ransom."

"Dutch . . ." He reached out as if to touch my shoulder, then, thinking better of it, pulled his hand back. "I'm so sorry."

"Sure you are." In view of his past behavior, I had to doubt the sincerity of this statement. "I'm distracted and I hate to go to trial unprepared. I know you want this over. But you're taking a big risk."

"I know, but with you on my side, I feel pretty good." He stared into my eyes, trying to look sincere. "Tell you what I'll do. I'll pay your fee in advance to help you out."

I was dumbfounded. In all the time I had known Carlos Garcia he had seemed like a hard-hearted guy, totally devoid of sentimentality. He had negotiated my fee aggressively, getting me to agree to take half up front, only $50,000. Now he was going to give me the rest of the fee, another $50,000, to help me out. I was starting to get a different impression of my client. Maybe he wasn't such a bad guy after all; maybe he was even innocent.

❈ ❈ ❈

As I walked back to the office, I returned Hedges' call. "Did you get my voicemail?" he asked.

"I didn't listen to it yet."

"Here's the deal: I talked to the Andrews sisters again. Under my withering questioning, they came clean, saying the description sounded familiar. Mr. Baldie is a member. His name is Terry Harris. He's forty-five years old, lives in Bedford, divorced, real estate broker. I did a Google search on him; seems he was a college wrestler."

"Good work. Anyone say whether he was involved with Mo?"

"All three women were coy; wouldn't admit to any hanky-panky."

"We've got to talk to Harris. You know where to find him?"

"I got his work and home addresses. Want to come along?"

"Pick me up at the office."

❈ ❈ ❈

Hedges and I were getting used to this routine: ganging up on unsuspecting witnesses or suspects, trying to squeeze information out of them. Terry Harris was going to be a challenge: he wouldn't be intimidated by either of us. As we drove toward his home, I kept hoping he was a lightweight wrestler, not a heavyweight. At least then Hedges would have a chance if he had to throw his weight around. His home was at the tip of a circular driveway. The house was massive with a three-car garage. There was no doorbell, only a brass door knocker in the shape of a lion's head. I slammed the door knocker a few times and waited.

The door was opened by a stocky bald-headed man standing a bit under six feet. I guessed his weight at one-eighty, about forty pounds lighter than Hedges. Plus, Hedges had a few inches on him. Still, I didn't want to see him and Hedges square off.

"Mr. Harris, sorry to bother you at home but we wondered if we could ask a few questions."

"What's this about?" he asked brusquely, not even pretending to be polite. He clearly communicated that we were invading his personal space and he didn't like it one bit.

"My name's Dutch Francis and this is Glen Hedges. I'm an attorney and I represent Carlos Garcia."

"I got nothing to say to you." He moved to shut the door, but I held up my hand.

"Please don't make me get a subpoena. That would be inconvenient for both of us."

He hesitated. No one likes to be served with a subpoena. They lose all control over the timing of their appearance and are forced to obey it.

"We just want to know about your visit to Maureen Garcia the day she died," Hedges said.

That raised his eyebrows. "How did you know about that?"

"We've done some investigation," I said. "So, shall we talk here or go inside?"

He seemed to soften. "Come in. I'll give you ten minutes."

His home was a showplace, the furniture meticulously arranged. Above the fireplace, below the mantel, was a gold bas relief of Aladdin's lamp. The beveled mirror above the mantel was framed in baroque-style gold. The Oriental carpet was at least an inch thick. We sat down on a wood-framed couch with bright red–flowered upholstering.

"I'd offer you a drink," Harris said, "but I don't want to."

So there, I thought. Playing the tough guy.

"What do you want to know?" he asked.

"What time did you arrive?" Hedges asked.

"About two thirty."

"Mind telling us what you were doing there?" I asked.

"Mo is . . . was . . . my friend. We met at the club. Golfed a few times; had lunch there."

I considered how to ask my next question. "I've got to ask this so pardon my being direct, but were you two having an affair?"

He didn't flinch, stared straight ahead. I thought he blinked a few times, getting emotional. So there was more than a friendship. "What's that got to do with this?"

Bingo. "It might give us some insight into why she took her own life."

"Mo didn't kill herself; that asshole of a husband killed her."

"Perhaps, but it's our job to exhaust all other possibilities."

"She was a wonderful woman; it was her husband's affair that got her down. That's what brought us together; she couldn't handle his cheating and lying."

"So her husband's cheating justified her cheating?" Hedges said, adding fuel to the fire.

Harris said nothing but he tensed up as if wanting to hit Hedges.

"Why were you there?" Hedges asked. "Wasn't it risky for you to go to her house?"

Harris stared at the floor, thinking. "I had to talk to her about something important."

"What was that?"

"None of your goddamn business."

I decided to try a different approach. "So how long were you with her that day?"

"I was there only about half an hour. I had to get to an open house."

"And what was her emotional state when you left?" This was the key question, one that Dr. Gumina would find useful.

He shook his head as if he didn't want to answer, but he opened up. "She was still upset, unsure what to do. I told her I wanted to break things off. I wasn't going to wait around any longer for her if she were going to stay with her husband. We were supposed to have lunch the next day and talk some more. The more we talked, the angrier she got at Carlos. He had humiliated her, flaunting his affair with that floozie in public."

"She's a clinical psychologist," Hedges said, "not a floozie."

"Who gives a shit?"

"You brought it up. Just wanted to set the record straight."

Harris turned toward me. "Are we done here?"

"One other thing: would you mind speaking to an expert I've retained on the case. Her name's Marilyn Gumina. She's a psychiatrist in Cambridge."

"Why would I talk to her?"

"We're trying to do a psychological autopsy of Mrs. Garcia, see if she was in such a state that she'd kill herself. It would be helpful to get your input."

"My, you sure are desperate to get your guy off, aren't you?"

I shrugged. "I don't think he did it."

"Right. Mo didn't kill herself so if you want me to convince your expert of that, I'll give her a few minutes of my time. As well as a piece of my mind."

❊ ❊ ❊

After returning home, I quickly drained two bottles of Molson, then checked emails on my laptop. Within five minutes a message popped up.

HOW'RE YOU COMING ALONG WITH THE RANSOM?

I swallowed. *I need more time.*

FORGET IT. YOU KNOW THE DEADLINE. GET THE MONEY OR ELSE.

How do I know Ginnie's okay? Why did you send me her hair and nails?

There was a long pause. I wondered if he were still there. *I'M NOT GOING TO ANSWER YOUR QUESTIONS. I'M THE ONE WHO ASKS QUESTIONS.*

I didn't care what he said; I wanted answers. *What do you have against Ginnie? She's a good person. You'd better not hurt her. Do you know she's pregnant?*

DON'T WORRY; SHE'S FINE.

Prove it to me.

There was no response. I waited fifteen minutes, but he was gone.

CHAPTER TWENTY-ONE

BEFORE TRIAL THE next day I visited Judge Garcia to fill him in on the meeting with Terry Harris. He had never heard of Harris and acted dismayed that his wife was having an affair. He seemed embarrassed that the affair would become public as if it reflected poorly on him. When I pointed out that his own affair accomplished that purpose by itself, he clammed up. I tried to convince him that the affair helped his case, that Harris' breaking up with Mo on the day of her death would strengthen our suicide defense, but he brushed me off.

I left the jail, thinking that the last thing I wanted to do was pick a jury in Judge Carlos Garcia's case. I wanted to raise money for Ginnie's ransom, or even better, find the kidnapper.

There were a hundred prospective jurors crowded into the courtroom. The bailiff had to bring in folding chairs to seat all of them. For jury selection, the judge allowed the media to stand in the back. No cameras or video were allowed. Standing against the wall amidst the reporters was Sam Collins. I couldn't stand the smug look on his face but there was no way I could confront him. Quickly I texted Delahunty informing him of Collins' presence. While I did so, the clerk called the first twenty prospective jurors to fill the fourteen seats in the jury box and six seats in front of the box.

With Garcia by my side, I scanned the list of juror names, all Hillsborough County residents. Some lawyers have assistants who can run quick Google searches of each name, read their Facebook pages, look at their Instagram photos. I was a solo practitioner with a temporary assistant who worked on an as-needed basis. The truth was, I didn't have enough work for a full-time assistant so I limped along, hiring someone as the cases came in. But with Ginnie's kidnapping and Garcia's speedy trial, I hadn't had a chance to hire anyone. So I called on Hedges to help me out, emailing him the lists while awaiting his research with a reply of thumbs-up or -down.

Judge Shane began the questioning, asking each juror to state name, town or city, occupation, occupations of spouse and adult children, and extent of prior jury service. This information didn't help much unless people were in law enforcement. Then I'd worry that they'd view any defendant as guilty. If the police arrested him and the attorney general charged him, many thought, then the defendant must be guilty of something. Getting them to admit this bias was the trick. I didn't want to use up my fifteen peremptory challenges if I could convince the judge to excuse the juror for cause. There were no limits on the number of for-cause challenges.

Before coming to the courtroom, the prospective jurors had completed questionnaires that were jointly drafted by the defense and prosecution. I read all the questionnaires and highlighted the answers that were troubling or that I needed to ask about. There were many troubling answers, particularly related to the presumption of innocence—or rather, the presumption of guilt as it turned out. Many people also viewed with suspicion a defendant's decision not to testify in his own defense. All the jurors, it seemed, had heard about the case.

Garcia had read the questionnaires as well and had definite opinions about which jurors to challenge. Most I agreed on but there were some I wanted to question first. "Let's check out the demeanor first," I told him. Sometimes a person seems like a terrible juror on paper but comes across as fair when you talk to them.

Barbara Zanobini, a social worker married to a deputy sheriff, seemed like a prosecution juror. Hillsborough County has sheriff's offices in Goffstown and Nashua, and a satellite office in the courthouse in Manchester. Her husband was assigned to Goffstown. Garcia thought she'd be pro-prosecution because of her husband's occupation, but the more I questioned her the more apparent it became that she had definite liberal leanings. She believed in the presumption of innocence and the privilege against self-incrimination, a rarity among the panel. I asked her if she discussed her husband's work with him. She said she did so regularly.

"And does your husband investigate murder cases?"

"He's had a few. We don't have many murders in New Hampshire, as you know."

"Tell me about them."

"There were some drug-related murders of young men in Goffstown a year or two ago. Let's see: a shooting by a deranged boyfriend, and a barroom fight that resulted in a death, but that would be manslaughter, wouldn't it?"

I nodded. "Anything about those cases that would make you biased in this case?"

She thought for a moment. "I don't think so. Your client claims he didn't do it as I understand it."

"Some people think that if the police have arrested someone and the prosecutor has charged him then he is probably guilty. Do you have that viewpoint?"

"Well, you wonder why they'd waste every one's time if the defendant is innocent. But I'm sure there are cases where the police charge people for other reasons."

I paused, wondering where she was going. "Are you familiar with such cases?"

"My husband has told me about some: when a deputy arrests someone because he didn't like the person's attitude or the color of his skin. I know that happens."

I liked what I was hearing. "So you've heard of situations where the cops arrest someone they do not believe is guilty?"

"Yeah, but I don't think it happens a lot."

Uh-oh, did I ask one question too many? I had to get this discussion back on track. "Can you imagine a situation where the police charged someone for political reasons?"

"What do you mean by 'political'?"

"Where, for example, the police were bowing to public pressure to arrest someone. Cases with a lot of publicity."

She hesitated, lowering her head, deep in thought. "I can see that happening," she said, nodding. "Police are like everyone else: there are good ones and bad ones."

"Do you feel the same way about prosecutors?"

"I do." Now she was smiling. "And defense lawyers, too."

I laughed. "Touché."

"How about a situation where the police genuinely believe they've arrested the murderer, but the evidence doesn't support the charge. Are you aware of cases like that?"

She shook her head.

"You have to answer audibly," Judge Shane said.

"I haven't heard of that kind of case."

"Can you imagine that happening?"

"I suppose. As I said, the police aren't perfect. They make mistakes just like the rest of us."

I decided to stop questioning her. Garcia leaned over and wanted me to grill her some more, but I waved my hand, signaling I was finished. He frowned but I didn't care. This was a juror I wanted. I had to hope Tompkins wouldn't bounce her.

As we broke for lunch, I edged my way through all the prospective jurors to the hallway where I found Delahunty and Leary questioning Sam Collins, who was leaning against the wall.

When Delahunty saw me approach, he said, "Mr. Collins admits he hates your guts but denies he took Ginnie. I'm not sure I believe him." He turned toward Collins, whose double chin bounced up and down as he swallowed. He was dark, darker than most Irishmen, with black hair spotted with bits of grey. "If you had nothing to do with Ginnie's kidnapping, you won't mind if we search your house."

"Screw you. Get a warrant."

"Why put us through all that trouble?" Leary asked. "Just call your wife and tell her to let us in."

"Why should I do that?"

I put my hand up. "The way it looks to me, Mr. Collins, is you took Ginnie to punish me for defending Carlos; maybe divert my attention so he'll get convicted. I don't know what sick motivation you may have, but I'll tell you this: if my wife doesn't return home safely, I'll hound you for the rest of my days."

"I'm shaking, I am."

I had had enough. I grabbed him by the overalls near his neck and pushed him against the wall. Then I raised my left fist, getting ready for a hook, before Delahunty grabbed my arm, pushing me back as Leary stepped between us.

"Are we done here?" Collins asked.

"Just know we're watching you," answered Delahunty.

As Collins walked away, Leary said, "That was a bad move, pal. Getting his cooperation was our best chance. No way we got enough for a warrant."

I ignored her and told Delahunty, "The kidnapper contacted me last night. Just to keep the pressure on."

"You thought any more about whether to pay the ransom?"

"I'm raising the money, but we should keep trying to find the kidnapper."

"We've got to be careful to keep things under the radar, or we might put Ginnie in jeopardy."

"I hope I didn't already screw things up by confronting Collins. If he has her, there's no telling what he'd do."

"I checked both Collins brothers' vehicle registrations. None matched the video."

Hearing this, I actually felt relieved. It had been distressing to imagine Ginnie as a prisoner of that asshole. I walked away, shaking my head.

❊   ❊   ❊

In the afternoon Tompkins spent very little time on jury selection, what lawyers call *voir dire* from the French, meaning "to see" and "to say." He acted as if any juror was good enough for him. His questions were mostly directed to the whole panel rather than individual jurors. He asked if anyone had ever been accused of spousal abuse, a good question designed to identify any juror who might identify with Garcia. To my surprise, a woman raised her hand. Her name was Victoria Dominguez; she was about 300 pounds and barely fit into her folding seat.

Tompkins asked, "Can you tell us what happened?"

She sat up straight and her jowls shook. "I married a no-good two-timing SOB who got fired from another job. I was plain worn out from working at the grocery store and taking care of our house while he laid around on the couch watching TV. So one day I got fed up and threw him out."

From her demeanor, I had a feeling what she meant, but Tompkins pushed the issue. "What do you mean?"

"What I mean is I picked his ass up off the couch, whacked him in the head, dragged him to the front door, and threw his ass out. Not my fault he fell on his face. But that pansy filed charges against me and I had to go to court and all."

"What was the result of those charges?"

"I got probation, which is a royal pain in the you-know-what."

Tompkins couldn't let it go. "What happened with your husband?"

"He's back home, lying on the couch, not doing a damned thing with his life."

To my surprise, he left Dominguez on the jury. Before the day was out, we had sixteen jurors, which included four alternates. I liked the ones we wound up with, a mixture of students, housewives, and a few retired men. They weren't perfect but definitely better than some of the prospects. Even Garcia was pleased. "Good job," he said before returning to his cell.

CHAPTER TWENTY-TWO

ON THE WAY home from court, I stopped at Barbara Turner's house. Barbara answered in sweats and a t-shirt that had a photo of Ginnie with the words, "Have you seen this woman?"

She noticed me reading the t-shirt and said, "I had a few dozen made and handed them out at church."

"Anybody respond?"

"Not that I know of." She let me in and directed me to the kitchen table. On top of the table were a dozen red roses.

"From a secret admirer?"

We sat down at the table. "From that nice Officer Leary."

"Leary was here again?"

"A few times." She folded her arms across her chest. "She doesn't like you."

"The feeling's mutual."

"She thinks you did something to Ginnie."

"She's got her head up her ass."

Barbara offered me coffee, which was already brewed. She poured two cups then placed a carton of milk and a sugar bowl in front of me.

"Then there's the letter, of course." She took a long sip of coffee.

I nodded. "I told you that was bullshit. Didn't Leary tell you I passed the polygraph?"

She shook her head and looked away, moisture forming in her eyes.

"Look, Barbara. I don't know how else to say this, but I love Ginnie with all my heart."

She wiped her eyes then sipped the coffee. "It's the ones who love the victim you have to worry about. That's what Officer Leary told me."

I couldn't believe Leary was still pointing the finger at me. "I wanted you to know I received a ransom demand last night."

Her eyes opened wide. "For how much?"

"Three hundred thousand. Do you still think I had something to do with this?"

"Where are you going to get that kind of money?"

"I will raise it. Ginnie will be back next week."

"I wish I could believe that."

In silence we both drank our coffee. With a white paper napkin, she dabbed at the sides of her mouth. Suddenly she stood up and carried the two cups to the sink.

"You'd better go."

"Barbara..."

"Really, please go."

I left, wondering if my relationship with my mother-in-law would ever be the same.

❈ ❈ ❈

Once I arrived home, I turned into a collections attorney, except I was trying to collect money that wasn't owed to me. I tried Rodger's cell phone first. He answered on the first ring.

"I bet you want to know about the ransom money."

"That is kind of on my mind."

"I realize this is killing you but hang in there."

"I'm hanging, Rodger, though I feel like I'm strangling."

He cleared his throat. "Understand that this is a loan. I'm not saying anyone's going to chase you to collect, but that's how it's got to be structured."

"I'm listening."

"I can free up $50,000."

I swallowed. That brought me to $200,000. If Channel 9 came through with a hundred, I would have enough for the ransom. "I appreciate that, Rodger. I'm still a hundred short but I've got one other possibility. If that doesn't pan out, are you open to kicking in a little more? I won't ask unless it's absolutely necessary."

He paused and exhaled into the phone. "That's really pushing it, Dutch."

"I wouldn't ask, Rodger, if I weren't desperate."

"Let's see what happens. In the meantime, I'll wire you the fifty. Give me your bank info." After I had given him the information, he paused. "I'll need you to sign a promissory note."

"Really? You don't trust me to pay you back?"

This was bullshit, but what choice did I have. I needed the money fast. "Okay. I'll email it to you."

I then called Cassidy at the station.

"Dutch, I'm getting ready for the newscast so I don't have much time."

"Just checking on the ransom money."

"The board's meeting tomorrow. I'll let you know then."

I could sense the impatience in his voice but I couldn't let him go right then. "I'm almost there, Dennis, but I'm a hundred short."

The line went silent. "I told you that's not going to happen."

"I get it. I'll find other sources. Thanks for all your help." I had no idea what those sources would be, but I'd have to figure that out pretty damn soon.

CHAPTER TWENTY-THREE

THE HILLSBOROUGH COUNTY Courthouse was crowded at a few minutes before nine. There were dozens of people waiting to go through the metal detector. The line went all the way down the walkway. I noticed a few of my jurors in line, which gave me some relief since I wouldn't be the only who was late.

I entered the courtroom at 9:01 and Judge Shane was on the bench. Three juror seats were empty. "Morning," I said to no one in particular. Tompkins looked over and nodded. Garcia asked how things were going. I told him there was some hope; I'd know more tonight.

I took several deep breaths, trying to focus my mind on the moment. I had to put aside the distractions of Ginnie's kidnapping and give my full attention to Garcia's case. After a few minutes, the three missing jurors arrived. The panel had a mix of jurors who looked either weary from a poor night's sleep or wired from too much coffee.

Tompkins stood behind the podium where he placed his notes. I was surprised to see that his notes were handwritten. Most lawyers type their notes so they won't have any problem reading them. I tended to type just a few notes in twenty-point font so I could read them at a glance.

Tompkins began with Garcia's affair. "This murder case begins as many do: with a cheating husband who decided to get rid of the wife who stood between him and his mistress. While he was cheating on his wife with Arlene Downey, he was promising Ms. Downey he would leave his wife. Maureen Garcia—her friends called her 'Mo'—did not want a divorce. Despite her husband's philandering she wanted to make the marriage work. Of course, the defendant could've gotten a divorce even if his wife did not agree, but he didn't want to be troubled so he took the easy way out. He killed her. He killed her in a most clever way. She had a prescription for hydrocodone, also known as Vicodin, a powerful narcotic prescribed for severe pain, because of a back injury. She was supposed to take one or two as needed. But her husband had other ideas. He knew from his research that an overdose of Vicodin can have fatal consequences. He also knew that the effects of Vicodin would increase if you ground it up. So he ground up the entire bottle of Vicodin—some twenty-five tablets—and laced her Thai noodles with it."

Now Tompkins raised his voice, emphasizing each word. "He laced her food with poison! He knew this would kill her and he succeeded. Mo Garcia died on the night of April 21. The only person to have access to her Vicodin was her husband. He was with her when she died. He called the police, pretending ignorance as to what had happened. He will do the same with you; don't you fall for it! Don't cut the defendant any slack just because he's a judge. Don't let him get away with murder.

"You will also hear from the 911 operator who received calls from Mo Garcia that she was being abused and threatened by her husband. So when you think of defendant, think abuser, not judge.

"I submit to you that the evidence will show that the defendant is guilty of murder in the first degree. When the evidence is concluded, I will ask you to bring in a verdict of guilty. Thank you for your attention."

Tompkins' opening statement was more argumentative than I expected. I decided to let it slide, not wanting to alienate the jury with objections so early in the case. But now it was my turn. I had tried to prepare last night though my mind wandered frequently. I had managed to put together only a one-page outline. That would have to suffice. Garcia knew what he was getting, but I would give it my best shot.

I stood in front of the jury and fixed my gaze on a man in the back row, a fireman who wrote short stories in his spare time. He had come across as my toughest challenge, a hard nut with a grim appearance. If I could only show him there was reasonable doubt about Garcia's guilt—or better yet prove Garcia was innocent—then we had a chance. He would be my touchstone, the one I would try to reach, hoping he would bring the others along with him.

"Ladies and gentlemen, the prosecutor has asked you not to cut my client any slack merely because he's a judge. I mimic that remark. Judge Garcia is not looking for any favors because of his position. By the same token, you shouldn't evaluate him any more harshly. He's entitled to the same reasoned analysis you would give to any other defendant. Nothing more and nothing less.

"The prosecutor will have you believe that Judge Garcia wanted his wife dead, yet he gives no compelling reason why that would be so. He didn't need her okay to file for divorce. True, he was having an affair with Arlene Downey and his wife learned of the affair. They fought about it as you might expect. It's also true that in the past his wife had even called the police a few times, drunk and upset. Although she claimed emotional abuse, there was never a suggestion to the police on these three occasions that Judge Garcia physically abused his wife in any way. Their fights were always verbal. Those are key facts here.

"I expect the evidence to show that for most of his marriage Judge Garcia was a kind and caring husband. Like many marriages, however, the couple drew apart and he sought companionship outside the marriage. He was torn about whether to get a divorce; he was in love with Ms. Downey but reluctant to leave his wife alone.

"Is this really motive for murder, ladies and gentlemen? The evidence will show that it is not. Judge Garcia had no motive to kill his wife. He was distraught when he found her unresponsive in her bedroom. He did everything he could to save her life.

"The evidence will show that Ms. Garcia took her own life. She could not accept the fact that her husband wanted a divorce. In fact, she herself was having an affair with a man she met at the country club. The day she killed herself that man told her he wanted to break up. So she researched how to kill herself, using opiates she had been prescribed by her doctor. This is one subject on which the prosecution and the defense agree: Ms. Garcia died from an overdose of Vicodin. The question you will have to decide was who put the ground-up pills in her dinner. Was it my client, who had no motive to kill his wife, or was it his wife herself?

"The totality of the evidence, you will see, will show that Mrs. Garcia took her own life. At the close of the evidence, I will be asking you to bring a verdict of not guilty. Thank you."

❁   ❁   ❁

For his first witness, as he had at the preliminary hearing, Tompkins called Officer Richard Sambuchino, who related the same story about responding to the 911 call.

I flipped through a pile of documents the prosecution had provided me. I had conducted discovery and obtained Sambuchino's personnel file, which contained a lot of useful information. I decided to put it to good use.

"Officer Sambuchino, you were the officer responsible for deciding to arrest my client, correct?"

He turned toward the jury as if purposely avoiding me. "I wouldn't say that. It was a team decision."

"And who was on that team?" I was hoping he'd name some other officers whose files I had obtained.

"Me, the detectives, and the sergeant."

"That would be Sergeant Walsh, your direct supervisor?"

"Correct."

That's what I was hoping he'd say. "You and Sergeant Walsh have made some mistaken arrests in the past, true?"

"What do you mean?"

"I mean" —and I held up a manila file full of paper— "that you two were accused of the false arrest of a man named Doug Ackerman last year."

"'Accused' being the key word." Sambuchino was getting testy. I liked that.

"The City of Manchester agreed to pay Mr. Ackerman four hundred and sixty-five thousand dollars in that case, true?"

"So I've heard. Ridiculous is what I think. Waste of taxpayers' money."

"And you and Sergeant Walsh were suspended for a week because of that arrest?"

"We agreed to that as part of the settlement."

He was waffling. Now I went for the kill. "You arrested Mr. Ackerman for spousal abuse, isn't that true?"

He nodded. "True."

"And it turned out that Mrs. Ackerman actually was abused by her boyfriend, not her husband, right?"

"As it turned out," he said sarcastically, "but we had no reason to suspect him at the time."

"Yet, Officer Sambuchino, you arrested Mr. Ackerman simply because he was the husband of the victim?"

He stiffened, finally realizing where I was going with this line of questioning. "Not true. We arrested him because the evidence seemed to point toward him."

"Just like the evidence pointed to my client Judge Garcia?"

"Right," he said, pointing his index finger at me. "Exactly right."

"Yet you have no evidence my client put the drugs into her food, isn't that right?"

"His fingerprints were on the prescription bottle. I'd say that's pretty good evidence."

"The prescription bottle was in his medicine cabinet, was it not?" Now I was getting testy.

"It was."

"So he had reason to touch it if, for example, it was in the way of his toothpaste?"

He looked away. "I suppose, but that's not how I saw it."

"That's not how you saw it because you were prepared to charge the husband, isn't that right?"

He stared at me but didn't answer. I didn't care; I had made my point.

Next was Sergeant Walsh, who testified to essentially the same facts as Sambuchino. I could've objected as cumulative, but I let it go because I could reinforce my theme that the police had rushed to judgment against the husband.

Once Tompkins had finished, I stood up and asked, "Sergeant, in cases of this sort, where a wife is killed, isn't it true that you look first at the husband as a suspect?"

"Usually that's the obvious place to look." He smiled and nodded to the jury, thinking I had just stepped on myself.

"Would you agree that an investigation can be colored by the theory that is attached to it?"

"I have no idea what you're talking about."

This time I smiled for I knew he was playing with me. "Soon after a crime occurs, the police develop a theory of what happened. True?"

"Generally. After we examine the evidence."

"Whatever theory is first attached to a crime is hard to shake, isn't it?"

"Depends on the evidence, as I said."

It was clear he was going to stick to his "evidence" mantra so I would have to adjust. "In this case, the police developed an initial theory that my client was responsible for his wife's death?"

"That was our first theory based on the evidence."

"The evidence being that he was present when she died, right?"

"That's one piece of the evidence."

"The other was that his fingerprints were on the prescription bottle? Officer Sambuchino told us that."

"Yes."

"What other evidence connected my client to this death?"

He seemed taken aback by the question, as if he'd never thought of that issue before. "That's enough, isn't it?"

"To show murder beyond a reasonable doubt?"

Tompkins was on his feet. "Objection, Mr. Francis is arguing with the witness."

Judge Shane was quick to sustain the objection. I thought of arguing but decided to let it go. I would have plenty of opportunity during closing argument to argue that the prosecution hadn't proven their case beyond a reasonable doubt.

❊ ❊ ❊

As soon as I got to my office, I called Dr. Gumina. To my surprise, she answered right away.

"Just checking on the status of your work."

"Let's see: I've reviewed Mrs. Garcia's medical records. Lot of references to depression and anxiety. No question her relationship with your client had an impact on her."

"Okay, what else?"

"I also talked to her boyfriend. He doesn't care for your client, but his breaking up with her so close to her death certainly helps our case."

"Do you think she committed suicide?"

"That's hard to say. I wish we had more data."

This was not the answer I was hoping for. More data would not be forthcoming since the Collins brothers and Mo's friends would not talk to her. "What about your meeting with Carlos?"

"Well . . . We should talk."

"You're on the stand next week. Could we meet on Sunday to go over everything?"

"I think that would be a good idea."

I was nervous about Dr. Gumina's testimony. She really didn't have much to work with, but maybe I could finesse it, see what would fly.

What concerned me more, of course, was finding Ginnie. There were a few missed calls on my cell phone from Delahunty, but no voicemails. I called him back.

"What's going on?" I asked, trying to keep the impatience out of my voice.

"There's a guy whose name keeps popping up as a potential suspect. A few people have called in his name to the hotline from your TV appearance."

"Have you talked to him?"

"Not yet. It's too soon. Besides, I don't want to upset your ransom payment if that's the way you want to go."

I was still weighing my course of action: just pay the ransom outright and hope for the best, or let the cops set a trap for him. "I've got to get back to court. Can we talk tonight?"

"I've got something going tonight. How about in the morning?"

"Sure."

"Why don't you stop by the station."

❊   ❊   ❊

For his first witness in the afternoon, Tompkins called Tad Chaiprasit. He was the kid who had delivered the drunken noodles the night of Mo's death. Hedges had interviewed him so I knew what he'd say.

Tompkins stood behind the podium as the witness was sworn. Tad sat down and played with his faint mustache then, apparently realizing there was nothing to play with, started on his long stringy hair.

Softly, Tompkins began his questioning. "Mr. Chaiprasit, where do you work?"

"At the Bangkok Palace Restaurant." He spoke in a high-pitched voice.

"What do you do there?"

"I bus tables and make deliveries."

"And how long have you had this job?"

"Long time. At least ten months."

"I see," Tompkins said, rubbing his bald head. "Were you working the evening of April 21st?"

"Let's see." He glanced at the ceiling. "Was that a Friday?"

"Yes, it was."

"So, yeah, I was working."

"Do you remember making a delivery to River Road in Manchester?"

He thought for a moment as if surprised at the question, which of course was ridiculous because Tompkins must have prepared him to testify.

He nodded. "I do. The judge's house."

"How do you know it was the judge's house?"

"That's what my boss told me before I left the restaurant."

"So when you got to the judge's house, who answered the door?"

"The judge did."

"Do you see that person in the courtroom?"

He pointed at Garcia. "He's right there, beside the guy with the beard."

I couldn't help it; I started rubbing my beard then glanced at Garcia as did all the jurors.

Tompkins turned to Judge Shane. "May the record reflect that the witness has identified the defendant?"

"The record will so reflect," the judge said.

Tompkins returned his attention to the witness. "Did the judge say anything when you delivered the food?"

"All he said was, 'Thanks,' and gave me a five-dollar tip."

"About what time was it that you delivered the noodles?"

Chaiprasit scratched his head. "Best guess is seven o'clock."

Tompkins moved toward his seat then stopped, as if remembering one more question. "Mr. Chaiprasit, when you first saw the judge, did he appear angry?"

My instinct took over and I was on my feet. "Objection, that's speculation."

"Sustained," said Judge Shane.

"But, Judge," Tompkins said, "the witness should be allowed to describe the defendant's demeanor."

"That's not the question you asked, Mr. Tompkins."

Tompkins cleared his throat and directed his attention to the witness. "While you were delivering the food, did you happen to notice Judge Garcia's demeanor?"

"His what?"

"The expression on his face."

Chaiprasit shook his head.

"You have to answer out loud, sir," the judge said.

"I didn't notice," he said.

The judge turned toward the prosecutor. "Any further questions, Mr. Tompkins?"

"No, Your Honor."

"Cross-examination?"

"Yes, Your Honor." I stood at the table since I didn't expect to take much time.

"Mr. Chaiprasit, when my client opened the door, were you able to see inside the house?"

"I could, a little."

"Did you see a woman there?"

"I did."

"Can you describe her?"

"She was short, maybe five four, with grey and black hair down to her shoulders."

"Did you believe her to be Judge Garcia's wife?"

"That's what it seemed to me."

"Did she happen to say anything while you were standing there at the door?"

Again, he shook his head.

"You have to answer audibly, Mr. Chaiprasit," said Judge Shane.

"No, she didn't *say* anything."

"Did you happen to observe anything unusual about her?"

"I guess."

"Tell the jury what you observed." I turned toward the jury.

"She was sobbing, really crying, and her cheeks were all red."

I had what I needed. "Thank you, sir. Nothing further."

The final witness for the day was police IT specialist Victor Gaspari, who testified to what he had found on my client's laptop. As at the prelim, I established that both Carlos and Mo used the laptop and either one could have accessed the websites regarding Vicodin poisoning.

❊　❊　❊

I got home just as my cell phone rang. It was Dennis Cassidy. "Dutch, the board met today and approved a $50,000 payment. It took a lot of arm-twisting, but everyone wanted to convey how highly they think of Ginnie."

"I appreciate that, Dennis. If I can get another fifty thousand, I'll be home free."

"I pray you get it." He sounded worried.

"I'll get it."

"Has he given you any proof he actually has Ginnie?"

"I've asked. He says once I gather the cash, he'll provide proof."

"Let me know. I'll be praying for you."

"You said that already, Dennis."

"Yeah, well. This situation merits lots of prayer."

After hanging up, I placed a call to Hedges just to check in.

I told him about the money I'd raised. "I'm almost there."

"Sure wish I could contribute. I feel bad about that."

"Don't sweat it. I know how much, or really how little, you make."

"If it's any consolation, I've been working on finding her. I paid a visit to Sam Collins' house today. I wanted to talk to his wife, see if she would reveal anything useful."

"He was in court again today. Still glaring at me."

"His wife Meg's a beaut! Grey hair with the front strands dyed blue, a tattoo on her neck in the shape of a pearl necklace. She wasn't that big, but she had a presence that made even me nervous."

"Did you charm your way in?"

"Fat chance. Sam told her the cops think he had something to do with that missing newscaster. But you're not going to like what she said next."

I didn't like anything to do with the Collins brothers, but I wasn't prepared for what Hedges was about to report.

"'Her husband's Carlos' lawyer, right?' she says. I go, 'That's right.' So she says, 'Carlos is a worm. I've no doubt he killed her,' and she smirks at me."

"Seems the whole Collins family is good at the dirty looks."

"Oh yeah. Then she mentions Ginnie and says, 'You ask me, she found a better man than Dutch Francis. He won't find her until she wants to be found.'"

My body tensed. I felt like smashing my fist against the wall, but controlled myself. I let a few seconds pass. "Any chance Ginnie was there?"

"I doubt it. I yelled her name loudly. If she were there, she would've yelled back."

"So what do you think? Do we rule out the Collins brothers as suspects?"

"Unless you've got a more likely one, I think I'll keep an eye on them. Maybe they have Ginnie somewhere else. I'll drop by their houses from time to time."

"Glen, you really don't have to do all this."

"I know I don't, but I'm not resting until Ginnie's safe."

CHAPTER TWENTY-FOUR

THE FIRST ORDER of business on Saturday morning was to meet with Delahunty and figure out if he had any viable suspects. I was getting disheartened with all the dead ends. Maybe this would be the real one; maybe I actually would get Ginnie back.

We met in the conference room, the same one with the orange plastic chairs where we met the day after Ginnie's kidnapping. It had now been a week and a half since she was taken; in that time, I had lost eight pounds and my blood pressure had soared. Delahunty dispensed with hand-shaking and took a seat across from me. I was glad Leary wasn't there; she really got on my nerves.

"So here's what we've come up with." He placed a two-inch pile of paper on the table in front of him. "There's a fella who says you're a slimeball for defending Garcia and you got what you deserved when Ginnie was kidnapped."

"Probably not a unique perspective."

"True, but this guy seems more intense than the others. Maybe you know him: Nicholas Wolfe?"

The name sounded familiar but I couldn't place it. "Why this guy?"

"He fits the profile. To a T. He failed to show up for work without any notice, has been acting strangely, and is obsessed with the case. We got more tips on Wolfe than any others by far."

"Sounds promising." After so many disappointing leads, I was trying hard not to get my hopes up.

"I did an online search of him. He's editor of a small town weekly, the *Merrimack Citizen*."

"Wait a minute. I read a Facebook post by that guy. It was on Mrs. Garcia's page. If I recall, he called me a scumbag for defending Garcia."

"That's consistent anyway. Here are some of his columns I printed." He pulled a few pages from the top of his pile and handed them to me.

The first was published right after Garcia's arrest, arguing that the death penalty was too good for him, but not mentioning that New Hampshire had banned the death penalty long ago. There were several more similarly vitriolic articles as the case progressed.

"Why so much hostility toward Garcia?"

"I wondered that, too. Seems Garcia ruled against him in a defamation case and awarded over a million dollars to the plaintiff. Wolfe had to close down his newspaper, the *Merrimack Guardian*, and file bankruptcy. It took him a few years, but he managed to raise enough funds to launch the *Citizen*."

"So he's looking to get his revenge on Garcia and anyone associated with him?"

"Seems that way. I did some research on him and read his columns espousing far right ideals. He's an ardent supporter of the National Rifle Association and the death penalty, of course. Take a look at this." He handed me a few pages from Wolfe's Facebook account.

Wolfe was fifty-four years old, Republican, single, lived alone, and had a well-publicized bout with prostate cancer, which he survived due to radiological implants. The photo on his home page showed a man with a goatee and light thinning hair.

"This is even closer to home." Delahunty pulled a handful of pages from the bottom of the pile and slid them over to me.

I read through them. The first was published a few days after Ginnie's kidnapping and asserted, "Police have no leads on who might have taken the Channel 9 newscaster." A column a few days ago repeated that statement but took a swipe at me: "Ms. Turner's husband, attorney Dutch Francis, who currently represents the accused wife-killer Judge Carlos Garcia, has reportedly been given a polygraph exam. The results are not yet known. Could he have done something to his wife? That's still an open question."

"How would he know about the polygraph?"

"I'm afraid we have a leak somewhere. We're still investigating."

"I'd bet on Leary. Has she been questioned?"

"I can't comment on an open investigation."

"At least he didn't mention the letter to Barbara Turner."

"I doubt he knows about it. Only a handful of officers have seen it. If it were leaked, we'd have a short list of suspects."

I flipped through the pile of columns. "Looks like he's been busy writing regularly. When has he missed work?"

"According to the staff, he didn't report to the office for two days after the kidnapping. And he talks about Ginnie incessantly."

"That checks a few boxes on Dr. Gumina's list." I didn't want to get my hopes up. Even though there was nothing about Nicholas Wolfe that I liked, that didn't mean he took Ginnie. "Where do we go from here?"

"I have a plainclothes officer checking up on him. We'll keep him on our radar."

"Does he have any particular expertise in computers?"

"Not that we've discovered yet." He retrieved his papers, straightening the pile. "That brings me to the ransom. Have you made a decision on how to handle the drop?"

"I need just fifty thousand more. I'm thinking of paying so I can get Ginnie back."

"How about this: we hide some marked bills in the bag with a GPS tracker. We'll stay a safe distance away from him but close enough to go to Ginnie's aid if necessary."

This was the best idea I'd heard yet from the Manchester Police Department. "I like it."

He reached across the table and grabbed my arm. "I feel like we're getting close to getting her back. Hang in there."

❋   ❋   ❋

After leaving the station, I called Hedges and filled him in on what I'd learned. "Delahunty says he's checking him out."

"Why don't I keep an eye on him, too, boss?"

"I was thinking that was the way to go. If he's got Ginnie, we'll need to move quickly. And before I forget, let's check out Grace Handford. She's the widow of a client who committed suicide and she blames me for her husband's death." I gave him all the contact information I had on her. "I doubt she had anything to do with this, but we've got to cover all our bases."

"I'll get right on it." He paused. "I don't mind telling you I'm getting worried. The longer this goes, the worse it looks."

"I hear you."

❋   ❋   ❋

I spent Saturday afternoon at the bank withdrawing all the funds that had been wired into my account. I was amazed at how difficult it was to cash out a few hundred thousand dollars. The teller decided the transaction was outside her pay range and called in the branch manager who wanted two forms of identification. By the time I was finished, nearly two hours later, I had $250,000 in cash. I stuffed

250 one-thousand-dollar bills into a gym bag and walked guardedly back to my car, looking all around me for any sign of a robber. I had run out of ideas for obtaining the remaining $50,000. Maybe the kidnapper would be satisfied with what I had. If not, I didn't know what I'd do.

In the evening I went to the Green Radish to meet Tim Murray, one of my poker buddies and a former rugby teammate. We ordered a couple of pints of Guinness and put some quarters into the pool table. I racked up the balls and took the first shot. On the break, the cue ball bounced off the rack and rolled into the left corner pocket.

"Nice shot," said Murray. "The first game's mine. Rack 'em up."

Murray was a wiseass, a ball-busting insurance defense attorney without pretensions. He became a lawyer to make money and that's just what he did, becoming a billing machine. He once billed 230 hours in a month, securing his promotion to partner.

He was just what I needed. I had spent enough time by myself trying to deal with Ginnie's kidnapping. It got to the point that I was afraid to go home for fear of what the mail would bring. It felt almost like PTSD; I would have nightmares of the mailman walking to my front door, mail in hand, only to have the mail explode in my face as soon as he handed it to me. And I hated asking people for money, which was something that always turned me off about politics, but I had no choice.

I finished racking the balls and Murray broke. He had better luck than I, hitting a solid and a striped ball in the hole. "I'll go with solid." He then proceeded to run four balls.

"Thanks for giving me a turn."

"Do your best; you don't have a chance."

I hit some tough shots and missed some easy ones. There was one truth about my pool game: the only consistency was my inconsistency. After the game, we sipped our stouts and leaned against the shelf lining the wall near the pool table.

"Anything new on Ginnie?" I had talked to him periodically since the kidnapping. Several times he had offered to help in any way he could.

"Yeah, got a ransom demand."

"No shit. That's good, no?"

"At least there's an end in sight. But I don't have enough money." I told him what I had. "I'm fifty grand short."

He looked me in the eye. "Dutch, I told you I'd help if I could. I've made a lot of money as a lawyer; my expenses are manageable since I don't have a wife or kids. So it's a no-brainer; I'll kick in the fifty grand."

I was flabbergasted. "You'd really do that?"

"You'd better believe it."

I touched my glass against his, lifting it to my lips. "One thing I've realized since this thing started."

"Yeah, what's that?"

"Ginnie. I love her so much it hurts."

❀ ❀ ❀

When I got home, I opened my laptop to check emails and a message popped up.

DO YOU HAVE MY MONEY YET?

I'll have it soon. Don't worry.

SHOW ME WHAT YOU HAVE.

I grabbed the gym bag from my bedroom closet, unzipped it, and showed him the cash.

It's fifty grand short, but the rest is on the way.

YOU DON'T HAVE MUCH TIME. GET THE MONEY OR ELSE.

Are you threatening to hurt my wife?

YOU KNOW EXACTLY WHAT I MEAN. I'M NOT FOOLING AROUND.

I understand. Now can I talk to Ginnie?

I TOLD YOU WE WOULD DEAL WITH THAT LATER, AFTER YOU GATHER ALL THE MONEY.

Can you at least let me hear her voice?

He didn't respond, apparently satisfied that his threat had its intended effect. It did.

CHAPTER TWENTY-FIVE

Traffic to Cambridge was light on Sunday morning and I had no trouble finding a parking space on the street. When Dr. Gumina answered the door, dressed casually in jeans and a crimson polo shirt, I asked how she was feeling.

"I'm nervous. I've testified dozens of times, but every time I get butterflies."

"I know what you mean. Same thing happens to me before a trial." She tugged on my elbow. "This is not a clear-cut one, you know." Was she getting doubts about her testimony? "Is it ever?"

"Sometimes, yes."

"Well, let's rehearse your testimony and tease out the weak points. If you don't mind, I'm going to stand up because that's how it is at trial." I stood up and placed my hands on the back of the chair.

"Dr. Gumina, what is your occupation?"

"I'm a forensic psychiatrist."

"Can you explain to the jury what you do as a forensic psychiatrist?" I looked to the side, pretending the jury was there.

"First let me explain what a psychiatrist does, though most of the jurors will undoubtedly know this. To become a psychiatrist, I had to graduate medical school then complete an internship for another year in general medicine and a two-year residency in psychiatry. As a psychiatrist, unlike a psychologist, I can prescribe drugs to help the patient. Typically, we treat patients with depression and anxiety though it could run the gamut from schizophrenia to neuroses."

That was probably more information than was needed but I pressed on. "What's the 'forensic' part of your practice?"

"'Forensic' means related to court proceedings like this one. For many years I was a clinical psychiatrist, which means I would see patients in my office and treat them either through psychotherapy or medication or both. The goal in clinical psychiatry is to get the client better. Then I became interested in forensic psychiatry and so took special courses designed to train me in that discipline. Forensic psychiatrists handle the examination and evaluation of criminal defendants to determine whether they're insane or incompetent to stand trial. We also do the same sort of work in civil cases to determine the nature and extent of a plaintiff's mental illness."

Dr. Gumina was more long-winded than I anticipated. She really must've been nervous. I was afraid we'd lose the jury with all this information so I cut to the chase. "Dr. Gumina, were you retained by me to work on this case?"

"Yes, I was."

"And have you been paid for your time?" I've found it's better to take the wind out of the other side's sails by getting the expert's payment right on the table.

"Of course. I don't work for free."

"What is the rate for an hour of your time?"

"I charge $750 an hour, but for court testimony I charge a flat rate of $6,000 a day."

It was always a tense moment speaking about an expert's fees. Experts, especially physicians, get paid far more than the typical juror so there was always a risk the jury would look askance at the testimony of a high-priced expert. Most jurors would be lucky to earn $6,000 a month, never mind a day.

"What was your assignment in this case?"

"You asked me to perform a psychological autopsy to determine whether the deceased committed suicide."

"Dr. Gumina, please explain to the jury what a psychological autopsy is."

"A psychological autopsy is a process designed to assess the behavior, thoughts, feelings, and relationships of the deceased."

She turned to the side while speaking, pretending to address the jury, which pleased me. It showed she knew what she was doing and was feeling more comfortable.

"In your practice, have you performed other psychological autopsies?"

"I have. This is the fourteenth or fifteenth that I've performed. Not all resulted in court testimony though."

"How many times have you testified as an expert witness regarding a psychological autopsy?"

"About half that number. So, seven or eight."

Not a huge number, but more than most psychiatrists. "And how do you, as a forensic psychiatrist, go about performing a psychological autopsy?"

"First, I review any available medical records then I talk to family members, coworkers, and friends about issues that may have been present in the decedent's life just prior to the death. I also look for social media postings and other writings by the decedent. My goal is to reconstitute the psychosocial environment of the decedent and thus understand better the circumstances of her death."

Now I was getting to the tough part of her testimony. "Were you able to perform a psychological autopsy of the decedent, Maureen Garcia?"

"I was."

"What did you do in this case in order to conduct a psychological autopsy?"

"I reviewed her medical records from her primary care provider. There were no mental health records available. My understanding is Mrs. Garcia did not seek any mental health treatment. I also spoke with her husband, Judge Garcia, and Terry Harris, the man she was seeing, and did a search of Facebook, Twitter, and other social media."

I swallowed, knowing how this answer left her exposed. I would have to cross-examine her aggressively. "And, Dr. Gumina, as a result of conducting a psychological autopsy on Mrs. Garcia, have you reached any opinions regarding her death?"

"I have."

"What are your opinions?"

"Based on all the information I had, I believe it is more likely than not that Mrs. Garcia took her own life."

"What evidence in particular supports that conclusion?"

She inhaled deeply, knowing she was skating on thin ice. "Mrs. Garcia reported to her primary care provider that she was feeling depressed about her husband's affair. It was clear she knew about the affair and was upset about it. Terry Harris confirmed that he was having an affair with Mrs. Garcia in the months before her death. The day of her death he had told her he wanted to break things off. Finally, Judge Garcia told me he had spoken to his wife about divorce and she reacted strongly, saying she did not want one. So I see a woman who is in the midst of great conflict leading to extreme stress. On the one hand, she's upset at Mr. Harris, who rejected her. On the other hand, she's been rejected by her husband. This double rejection culminated, unfortunately, in her decision to poison herself with Vicodin."

"Thank you, Dr. Gumina, I have no further questions." I sat down, sweating, knowing Tompkins would have a field day at trial.

CHAPTER TWENTY-SIX

BEFORE PREPARING FOR cross-examination, we took a lunch break and walked to a deli down the street. Dr. Gumina turned toward me. "So what's the latest on your wife?"

I told her about the obsessed fan Paul Young and the Collins brothers. "The police are looking at one other suspect, a newspaper editor who has it out for Judge Garcia and perhaps for me as well. But there have been two major developments since we last met: first, my mother-in-law got a letter claiming I did something to Ginnie."

"Oh my. That's consistent with the kidnapper wanting to torture you. What was the second one?"

"A ransom demand. Three hundred thousand dollars, which I've barely managed to raise."

We stood just inside the entrance to the deli. She stopped to read the chalk menu board above the counter. "I'm surprised. After those mailings, it seemed clear the kidnapper wanted to punish you. A ransom doesn't fit that pattern."

"I know, but I have to admit I was glad to get one."

"Got your hopes up?"

"Certainly, though I'd still like to catch the bastard before paying the ransom."

The proprietor asked if we wanted to order. I ordered an Italian cold cut sandwich; Dr. Gumina opted for tuna.

"Has he provided proof he really has Ginnie?"

"I've asked. He says not until I have all the money, which should be tomorrow."

"My suggestion is you don't pay without proof."

I don't think she intended to dash my hopes, but that's what happened. She read the look on my face. "I don't mean to be so negative, but you should prepare for that possibility."

She paused, staring at the proprietor making the sandwiches. "Despite the ransom demand, I still think those mailings were meant to cause you pain. Have you identified any potential enemies?"

"There are so many it's hard to narrow down. Then there's Grace Handford, who probably has the biggest gripe against me, as well as Judge Garcia." I summarized the Handford case and the tragic aftermath. "But I don't see her as the kidnapper."

"Why not?"

I paid for the sandwiches and thought about her question as we walked back toward her office. "I guess I never thought a woman could be capable of such cruelty."

"Though it's not typical, I wouldn't rule it out. Women have been known to do worse. And when was it you met with her?"

"She picked up the file about two weeks ago." I reached for the door to her building and froze. "Wait a minute; it was the day of Ginnie's kidnapping. My God, could she be the one?"

"It's worth checking out." We went inside and took the elevator to her office. I was feeling out of sorts. Dr. Gumina had increased my anxiety, both about the ransom demand and Mrs. Handford. I suspect I took it out on her while playing the role of the prosecutor cross-examining her. I knew I had an edge to my voice but couldn't help myself. After we finished the sandwiches, I launched into the cross-examination.

"Dr. Gumina, you've testified in other cases about psychological autopsies, have you not?"

"Yes. As I said, seven or eight times."

"Have you ever testified in a case where you had less support for your opinions than this one?"

"I'm not sure what you mean?"

I was just warming up. "Well, let me explain what I mean. You talked to a total of two people in performing your psychological autopsy, correct?"

"Yes, Judge Garcia and Mr. Harris."

"You're aware, are you not, that Mrs. Garcia is survived by two brothers, Samuel and Joseph Collins?"

"I am."

"You did not talk to either of her brothers, did you?"

"They refused to talk to me."

"So the answer is you didn't talk to them?"

"That's correct."

"You would agree that Mrs. Garcia's blood relatives would have useful information about her mental state?"

"They might; I don't know since I couldn't talk to them."

So far Dr. Gumina was doing fine; she admitted what she had to admit and had not become too combative.

"You're also aware that Mrs. Garcia was a member of the Manchester Country Club?"

"Yes."

"Yet other than Mr. Harris, you spoke to none of her friends from the club."

"I'm afraid they refused to speak to me also."

"Would you agree her closest friends would have useful information about her mental state?"

"Again, they might."

I took a step back. "As far as social media goes, you did review postings by Mrs. Garcia?"

"I did. She posted sporadically but there were some."

"In any of her postings, did Mrs. Garcia so much as hint that she was contemplating suicide?"

"She did not."

"So it would be fair to say that her postings on social media do not support your opinion?"

"Well . . . they don't disprove my opinion either."

I raised the volume. "That's not what I asked you."

Dr. Gumina frowned. "No, her social media postings do not support my opinion." She paused, then added, "Or disprove it."

"So let's put aside the Facebook page. The sum total of what you base your opinion on is your interview of her husband, who has a motive to lie, your interview of Mr. Harris, and your review of Mrs. Garcia's medical records. Is that correct?"

"There was another piece of information I neglected to mention. I'm informed that Mrs. Garcia's fingerprints were found on a bottle of St. John's Wort. That would support my conclusion she was suffering from depression."

I frowned and looked toward the ceiling. "St. John's Wort? Is that the best you can do?"

She stared at me without answering. Perhaps I had crossed the line. "Allow me to get back to my original question, Dr. Gumina. Have you ever testified about a psychological autopsy where you had less information?"

"Typically, I'm able to interview friends and family members. And some people have extensive online postings or other writings such as a diary."

I knew Tompkins would not let the issue go, so I pressed her. "So what is the answer to my question?"

Dr. Gumina inhaled deeply, turned briefly toward the window as if looking for help, and said, "I would say you are correct. This is the least amount of information I have had."

I paused and let silence fill the room. "Thank you, Doctor. Let's turn to one of those pieces of information: the medical records. You would agree that medical records are important sources of information of mental health history?"

"Yes, they usually are."

"And you've testified that Mrs. Garcia reported feeling depressed to her primary care physician?"

"I did."

"Let's review those notes. Now, do you see at the bottom of the page referring to depression, there is a note by the doctor?"

"I see that."

"Please read for the jury what that notes states."

She looked up. "Really, you want me to read now?"

"Let's do it as if we were in the courtroom. So, yes, read the note."

"The handwriting's a bit difficult but it appears to say, 'Patient declines medication or psychotherapy.'"

I knew I was scoring prosecution points so I piled it on. "That's an important piece of information, isn't it?"

"It is."

"It's important because people with major depression would seek help, wouldn't they?"

"Some would but not everyone."

"Come now, Doctor. If someone like Mrs. Garcia were truly hurting inside, it just makes sense that she would seek some treatment. Would you agree?"

"Not entirely. Most people would but some people—and I don't know if Mrs. Garcia falls into this category—do not trust psychiatrists or psychotropic medication. Besides, Mrs. Garcia was taking St. John's Wort, which some people believe treats depression."

"Can we agree, Doctor, that there's nothing in the medical records to suggest Mrs. Garcia would commit suicide?"

"You are right; not in the records themselves."

"If she had told her doctor she was thinking of taking her own life, good medical practice would have required the doctor to note that in her chart?"

"Of course."

"The chart would say 'suicidal ideation.' True?"

"It should, yes."

"So we can conclude from the absence of any such record that Mrs. Garcia did not tell her doctor she was contemplating suicide?"

"That's fair."

"Now if you didn't rely on the medical records themselves to conclude Mrs. Garcia was suicidal, that leaves your interviews of Mr. Harris and the defendant. Correct?"

"Well, and my years of training and experience."

"Of course, we can't discount that. But in terms of evidence you considered in this case, is my statement correct?"

"Except for the St. John's Wort, I believe it is."

I grinned at her as if we were sharing an inside joke. "And Mr. Harris said he had spoken with Mrs. Garcia on the day of her death, informing her he wanted to break off their relationship."

"That's true."

"So from that evidence, you concluded Mrs. Garcia committed suicide?"

"Not that alone; I also spoke to her husband."

"Let's talk about that. Did the defendant tell you his wife threatened suicide?"

"No. He didn't say that."

I don't know if Tompkins would have asked the next question because he didn't know what I knew. But I couldn't resist. "In fact, did you ask the defendant if he believed his wife committed suicide?"

"I did ask that."

"Well, what was his answer?" I knew the answer well enough but I had to hear her say it.

"He said he didn't believe she would do that."

I sat down in the chair. "I'm sorry. What was your answer?"

"Judge Garcia didn't believe his wife would kill herself."

Opening my arms wide, I went in for the kill. "So you want this jury"—again I turned to the side, as if glancing toward the jury— "to believe something even the defendant himself does not believe?"

Dr. Gumina looked at me, obviously helpless, and hesitated. "I guess, I guess you're right."

We looked at each other, without speaking, for several seconds. She shook her head. "I knew this would be a mistake."

"No, no," I lied. "You did fine."

"I don't think so."

"I'll call you in a few days."

"Will you let me know what happens with your wife?"

"I will. I appreciate all your insight."

❊   ❊   ❊

On the drive home, I called Hedges and asked, "Learn anything about Wolfe?"

"Went by his house. Shithole with peeling paint. Followed him as he drove across town to visit someone. I kept out of sight but didn't see any sign of Ginnie."

"Okay. How about Mrs. Handford?"

"Stopped by her house too, but no one answered."

"Dr. Gumina advised me not to discount her. She picked up the case file the day Ginnie was kidnapped. It contained my revisions to her husband's bombastic letter. That might've convinced her I actually was responsible for the letter."

"No worries. I'll follow up."

CHAPTER TWENTY-SEVEN

TO START OFF the week, Tompkins called the medical examiner, Marie McAulley. As she took the stand, she glanced sideways at me. I wondered if she'd learned anything from my cross-examination of her at the preliminary hearing. Tompkins went over her qualifications slowly, emphasizing the number of bodies she'd examined and the number of times she'd testified as an expert witness.

Dr. McAulley testified to the time of death as ten p.m. and the cause as crushed hydrocodone tablets mixed with food. No surprises there.

"A witness has testified that he delivered the drunken noodles about seven p.m.," Tompkins said. "Does that change your opinion at all regarding time of death?"

"Not at all. That is entirely consistent with an overdose. In that first hour there would've been many signs of distress including blue lips and fingernails, cold and clammy skin, coughing, increased sweating, irregular breathing, and unusual drowsiness."

"Are those signs you would expect someone, such as the defendant, to notice?"

"Absolutely. Anyone who was with the victim would've noticed them."

I knew what was coming next but I had no way to stop it.

"In your review of all the police reports, do you see any indication that the defendant contacted police or medical personnel, anyone at all, to report his wife's symptoms?"

"There was none. Though he did call when she died."

"In your professional opinion, if Mrs. Garcia had been seen by medical personnel in the hour or so before she died, could her life have been saved?"

"That's entirely possible, though there are so many variables that it's hard to say for sure."

"Thank you, Doctor." Tompkins sat down. Nothing about the defendant putting the drug into her food and nothing about red wine masking the taste of the drug. I looked at Garcia. There was nothing to ask her, I thought, so I shook my head no. He didn't object.

"No questions," I said.

For the rest of the day, Tompkins called a succession of police witnesses, seemingly every cop who had anything to do with the case. They droned on and on. I really didn't pay much attention and didn't ask many questions. It was a down day for me. I almost felt bad for my client, but he was the reason I wasn't out looking for Ginnie. Screw him; I had given him fair warning.

❊ ❊ ❊

I called Hedges right after getting home. "Just checking in."

"I stopped by Mrs. Handford's house last night. Nice part of Manchester I never knew about. There were some lights on, but when I rang the bell, no one answered. And her car was in the driveway. I got a creepy vibe, like she was watching me."

"What kind of car?"

"A grey Audi SUV."

"Let me run it by Delahunty, see if there's anything in the video." I wasn't sure about Mrs. Handford as a viable suspect, but I needed to follow up. "What about Wolfe?"

"I planned to go back this evening. Want to join me?"

❄   ❄   ❄

A half hour later, we sat in Hedges' car a few doors down from Nicholas Wolfe's house. Hedges was right: it did look like crap.

The sun was sinking, casting shadows from the houses onto the street. "Why don't I ring the bell, see if he's home?" Hedges asked.

I nodded. "I'll wait here."

Hedges climbed the concrete steps and rang the bell. When there was no answer, he knocked on the door. Still not getting an answer, he waved me over. "No one's home. Let's take a look around."

I got out of the car and walked over to him. The last thing I needed was to get arrested for trespassing, but it was worth the risk, I decided, to know whether Ginnie was there. We took a concrete path to the backyard, acting as if we belonged there. The shrieks of young children came from neighboring backyards. We looked in a few windows, hoping for a sign of Ginnie, but not seeing anything of note. Then on the side of the house we looked into a window to a back bedroom.

The shrieks of the children had died down. No one was in the room, but I was shocked at what I saw.

The wall on the left was lined with whips and chains. Some kind of mechanical device stretched the width of the room. Ropes, pulleys, and assorted sexual devices adorned the machine.

"What's that?" Hedges pointed to the floor.

There was an irregular stain, crimson in color. "Could that be blood?"

"Damn!" Hedges grimaced. "Think so. Let's get out of here."

On the drive back to Manchester, I called Delahunty and told him what we'd seen in Wolfe's bedroom. He wasn't happy with me.

"You were trespassing. Not good."

"What am I supposed to do? Ginnie's been missing for two weeks. I can't leave any stone unturned. Which reminds me: we're looking into another potential suspect who has a beef against me. I mentioned her a few days ago. Her name's Grace Handford. Hedges went by last night and saw a grey Audi SUV in the driveway. Any of those on the videos?"

"Dutch, we can't go chasing anyone who drives a car similar to the ones on the videos."

"This isn't 'anyone.' She holds me responsible for her husband's death after Garcia dismissed his case."

He exhaled heavily. "I'll check my list and look into it. How's the ransom going?"

"I'll have the full three hundred tomorrow. I have a feeling something will happen soon."

※ ※ ※

I was uneasy about what we'd seen in Wolfe's bedroom. I tried not to imagine what would have happened to Ginnie if Wolfe had kidnapped her. I wanted this over with. I would just pay the ransom and get Ginnie back. That seemed like the best course of action. We hadn't gotten anywhere with our investigation.

I opened my laptop, hoping the kidnapper would contact me. He didn't disappoint. A text message soon appeared.

GATHER ALL THE MONEY AND GET READY TO DELIVER IT TOMORROW NIGHT. I WILL SEND YOU FURTHER INSTRUCTIONS RIGHT BEFORE THE DROP SO KEEP YOUR LAPTOP OPEN.

Wait. I need proof Ginnie is alive.
WHAT KIND OF PROOF?
Let me talk to her.
NO.
Then I won't deliver the money. I had to take a stand. If Ginnie were still alive, then he should be able to produce proof.
SHE'LL LEAVE A MESSAGE ON YOUR CELL PHONE AT 8 AM TOMORROW. DON'T ANSWER THE PHONE.

❀   ❀   ❀

It was the longest night of my life. Of course I didn't sleep at all. At seven, I showered and waited for Delahunty to come by. He soon arrived with a dolly of state-of-the-art recording and tracking equipment that he unpacked in my living room. "This is my StingRay," he said, lifting a rectangular box with wires coming from several outlets onto the kitchen table. "With this baby we can intercept the cell signal and track the location of the cell phone." He ran some tests of his equipment and announced he was ready to go.

At 8:00 a.m. sharp my phone rang. It took all the control I had not to answer. Reluctantly, I let voicemail pick up. I had recorded a special greeting for Ginnie saying how much I loved her and would do everything I could to get her back. We waited several minutes for Ginnie's message to record.

Delahunty had recorded the message and played it back over his speakers. "This is Ginnie," the message said. Her voice was strangely calm, wooden, her words disjointed and slow. "I miss you so much. Please pay the man and come get me." That was it. I was disappointed; I wanted more from her, some indication of how she'd been treated, some hint of where she was.

Delahunty stared at his equipment. "We've located the origin of the call; it's in the local area. It will take some time to get a more definite location."

"Do you think you'll find her?" Hearing her voice after so much time had passed made me long for her even more. Ginnie was alive; I was grateful for that.

"Too soon to tell."

As Delahunty gathered his equipment, I opened my laptop, careful not to point the camera anywhere near Delahunty or his equipment. A message soon popped up. *SATISFIED?*

Where is she? I typed.

He ignored my question. *10 PM BRING THE MONEY TO THE BACK OF POLK ELEMENTARY SCHOOL. DROP THE BAG IN THE FAR END OF THE PARKING LOT THEN LEAVE. IF I SEE ANYONE ELSE THERE, YOUR WIFE WILL DIE!*

What if a stranger is there? I can't control that.

NOT MY PROBLEM. MAKE SURE NO ONE ELSE IS THERE. BUT FIRST SHOW ME THE MONEY AGAIN.

I walked to my bedroom closet and pulled out the gym bag where I had stored the cash along with the marked bills. The GPS tracker Delahunty had brought over was sewn into the bottom. Once back in front of the laptop, I unzipped the bag and pulled out the piles of bills, feeling like a drug dealer showing off his ill-gotten gains.

It's all there.

GOOD WORK. YOUR WIFE WILL APPRECIATE IT. AFTER I COUNT THE MONEY I WILL LET HER GO.

That was it; he was gone. I looked at Delahunty.

"We'll cover streets leading to the school in unmarked vehicles," he said. "Call me as soon as you drop the money."

"Don't move on him until I give the okay. I don't want to put Ginnie at any risk."

CHAPTER TWENTY-EIGHT

I WAS SLEEPWALKING as I entered the courtroom and pulled my notes from my briefcase. Since I hadn't slept last night, I had plenty of time to prepare to cross-examine the prosecution's star witness, Chief Criminologist Christopher Bentham. My outline took on a distinct blurry appearance as I tried to read it. This was not going to be easy.

Tompkins began with Bentham's background. With a bachelor's degree in psychology and a master's degree in sociology, Bentham would've been sufficiently qualified to offer expert opinions. But he also had a doctorate degree in criminology, which meant that I would have to call him "Dr. Bentham."

"Please tell the jury what evidence you've examined in this case," Tompkins said.

"May I look at my report?"

"If it would refresh your recollection. Let the record reflect that your report was provided in discovery to the defense."

Bentham pulled out a manila folder from his briefcase and flipped it open. He searched through the papers before finding what he wanted. "Here it is." Bentham had a high-pitched voice that belied his rough-looking appearance with a full beard, deep-set dark eyes, and stocky build. He looked more like a linebacker than a criminologist.

"I've listened to the 911 recordings, the statement the defendant gave to the police, and reviewed the police report, medical examiner's report, medical records of the victim, and photos of the murder scene."

I jumped up, still a bit wobbly. "Object to the term 'murder' scene. Speculation."

Tompkins was quick to respond. "This is a murder case, Your Honor, so the characterization is accurate."

"Gentlemen," Judge Shane said, "let's refrain from prejudging the evidence. We all know what the witness is referring to. The objection is sustained." She then turned toward Bentham. "You can refer to the scene where the body was found, the victim's home, or any other term that is less prejudicial."

"Very well, Your Honor."

"Have you completed your list of materials reviewed?" Tompkins asked.

Bentham checked the paper in front of him. "I also visited the scene. I examined a prescription bottle of Vicodin as well as the fingerprint analysis of the bottle."

"Thank you. Could you tell the jury what a forensic criminologist does?"

"Certainly." He put down the paper and faced the jury. "We study crime prevention, the causes of crime, criminal behavior, and society's response to crime. The forensic part of my work involves testifying in court before judges and juries, as in this case, and offering opinions on how a crime occurred. The goal is to assist the finder of fact in analyzing the evidence and rendering a decision."

Tompkins put down his notes and walked toward the back area of the jury box. "Based on your training and experience and the materials you've reviewed in connection with this case, Dr. Bentham, have you reached any opinions on this matter?'

"I have."

"What opinions have you reached?"

"Objection," I said, again struggling to my feet. "No foundation that this witness is qualified to render such opinions."

Tompkins responded. "That's absurd, Your Honor. Dr. Bentham is a respected criminologist whose opinion has been offered in countless cases."

Shane gave me an exasperated look. She knew I was right, but it was a problem Tompkins could easily resolve. "Mr. Tompkins," Judge Shane said, "I believe Mr. Francis is correct. You should lay more foundation for the witness's testimony."

Tompkins glared at me for breaking up his rhythm. "Very well." Then he turned toward the witness. "Dr. Bentham, have you testified as an expert forensic criminologist in other cases?"

"Yes, I have. Many times."

"Please tell the jury how many times."

"At least three dozen."

"And in what courts?"

"In most of the counties in New Hampshire as well as the United States District Court."

Tompkins nodded, satisfied. Still, he pressed on. "In what kinds of cases have you testified as an expert witness?" I could tell that Tompkins was going to keep using the word "expert" to plant that idea in the jury's mind. Very clever of him.

"It runs the gamut. From rape to burglary, robbery, murder."

"What was your assignment in this case?"

"To review the materials I mentioned and formulate opinions about what happened to Maureen Garcia."

"And"—Tompkins glanced at me—"have you formulated such opinions?"

"I have."

"Please tell the jury what opinions you have reached."

Again, Bentham turned toward the jury. "I believe she was purposely poisoned and that the person most likely responsible is her husband, the defendant Carlos Garcia."

"On what do you base your opinion that the defendant poisoned his wife?"

"From the materials I reviewed, it's clear that the defendant handled the bottle of Vicodin. No one else's fingerprints were on the bottle besides the defendant's and the victim's. The defendant is the only person who had contact with the victim for several hours leading up to her death. The defendant had a motive to kill his wife since he was having an extramarital affair and by all accounts was no longer in love with his wife. Finally, the defendant's tone of voice on the 911 call was not what one would expect from finding a spouse dead. It was flat, matter-of-fact, no emotion, almost as if he weren't surprised to find her that way."

I considered objecting but decided to let it go. By now I was fully awake and itching to get at Bentham. But Tompkins had one more question.

"The defense has proffered a theory that Mrs. Garcia took her own life. Have you considered that possibility?"

"I have."

"And what conclusions have you reached in that regard?"

"I don't believe she committed suicide. There is nothing in her medical records, her Facebook page, or anywhere else to indicate she was contemplating suicide. No doubt she was unhappy with her husband's affair, but her condition had not reached the level of clinical depression. She was not prescribed any anti-depressants or even anti-anxiety medications. Moreover, it doesn't make sense that she would sprinkle the drug into her food. If she were going to kill herself, why not just take an overdose of pills? So I think it highly unlikely that Maureen Garcia took her own life."

Tompkins straightened his papers on the podium. "Thank you, Dr. Bentham. That's all I have."

I stood up and walked to the podium, nearly brushing Tompkins as we passed each other.

"Dr. Bentham, you mentioned testifying in murder cases before. In how many such cases have you testified?"

He shook his head back and forth. "I don't know the exact number."

"Come, Dr. Bentham. Give us your best estimate."

He looked down as if counting in his head. "Best estimate would be about fifteen, though I could be off by a few either way."

I stepped from the podium and raised my arms. "Of that number, whether it's fifteen or higher or lower, how many of those cases involved poisoning?"

Bentham shot a glance at Tompkins. "None," he said softly.

"Sorry?"

"I said 'none.'"

"So this case is the first time you've testified as an expert criminologist in a case involving poisoning?"

"That's correct."

"Well, you must've investigated other cases that did not involve courtroom testimony. Am I right?"

"You are."

"How many cases fall into that category?"

"Oh, I don't know. Lots."

"Hundreds?"

"Sure."

"Thousands?" I prodded him.

"No, not that many."

"Can you estimate how many hundreds?"

"Probably three to four hundred."

"I see. And of that number, how many involved a suspicion, no matter how small, of poisoning?"

Again, he looked down, as if doing an internal inventory of his cases. "None I can think of."

"So this is the first such case you ever investigated?"

"That would be true."

I glanced at my notes. "Would you agree, Dr. Bentham, that criminology is a subjective science?"

"How do you mean?"

"Well, two equally competent criminologists could review the same materials and come up with contradictory opinions. Do you agree with that?"

"I suppose that's true."

"Is it also true that you have been trained to analyze evidence using skepticism?"

"I'm always skeptical of evidence until I verify its accuracy."

I wasn't sure my points were clear enough so I tried again. "In other words, do you view evidence, no matter how accurate, from the perspective of both the police and the defendant?"

"I try to do that. Sure."

"Let's turn to the evidence in this case. The prescription bottle is the only evidence tying my client to the Vicodin. True?"

"I'm not sure anything more is needed."

"Could you answer my question, please?"

"It's true that the prescription bottle ties your client to the Vicodin."

"The bottle also ties the victim to the Vicodin. True?"

"Yes."

"Can you tell by analyzing fingerprints on the bottle which fingerprints were there the longest?"

"You mean who was the last person to touch the bottle?"

"Exactly."

"No. There's no way to know that."

"That would be important to know, wouldn't it?"

"It would."

"If Mrs. Garcia had been the last person to touch the bottle, then your opinion would change, wouldn't it?"

He thought about his answer for a moment. "It might."

"You'd agree that if she last touched the bottle that she likely placed the Vicodin in the food herself?"

"That's probably true."

"That's a big hole in your theory, isn't it?"

Tompkins got to his feet. "Objection, that's argumentative."

"It is, Mr. Francis," Judge Shane said. "Save the argument for closing."

"Very well, Your Honor. I have only a few minutes left. Dr. Bentham, you testified that Mrs. Garcia was not depressed."

"I didn't say that," he interrupted. "I'm not qualified to make that assessment."

"Well, you did say you did not believe she committed suicide?"

"Correct."

I pulled out the police report, which had an inventory of all items taken from the Garcias' medicine cabinet. "You did review the police inventory?"

"I did."

"Did you note that the police found St. John's Wort in the cabinet?"

"I did."

"St. John's Wort is a common over-the-counter herb used to treat depression, isn't it?"

"I believe that's true."

"Whose fingerprints were found on the bottle of St. John's Wort?"

"The victim's."

"My client's were not on the bottle?"

"That's correct."

"So do you conclude, then, that Mrs. Garcia was taking the St. John's Wort?"

"That's a reasonable conclusion."

I didn't like that answer. I pushed him. "I know it's a reasonable conclusion. Is it your conclusion?"

"That would be my conclusion."

"So would it be fair to say that the fact that Mrs. Garcia was taking an herb used to treat depression tends to support the defense position that she committed suicide?"

"I suppose but . . . I don't believe that's the case."

"Thank you, Dr. Bentham. You told us what you believe. Let's change subjects. You testified that based on all the materials you reviewed, my client likely killed his wife. Is that your testimony?"

"Yes, it is."

"You're aware this is a criminal case with a burden of proof beyond a reasonable doubt?"

"I am aware of that."

"And you would agree that 'more likely than not' is a lesser burden than 'beyond a reasonable doubt'?"

He exhaled deeply. "I do agree."

"So the jury could believe every word of your testimony and still bring in a verdict of not guilty?"

"Objection," Tompkins shouted. "Mr. Francis is again arguing with the witness."

"Sustained. Anything else, Mr. Francis."

I tried to suppress a smile, believing that Bentham's worth as a witness had been reduced to nothing. "No, Your Honor."

❖ ❖ ❖

At lunch I called Delahunty. "Any update on our kidnapper?"

"We've narrowed the area to a couple of blocks in Hooksett. I have officers going door-to-door."

"Hookset? Have you ruled out Merrimack where Wolfe lives, or Manchester near Handford's house?"

"Definitely not either place, though I did want to let you know there's an Audi SUV on the videos."

"So Handford's a viable suspect?"

"I wouldn't say that. We need a lot more evidence."

"What kind of evidence?"

"Dutch, we have nothing on Mrs. Handford. At least with Wolfe we know he hates your client and you both."

"Handford hates us, too; I assure you."

"Let's play it out in Hookset. If nothing turns up, we'll consider other possibilities."

❋ ❋ ❋

For the afternoon session, Tompkins called several witnesses, starting with Arlene Downey. Her testimony was consistent to what she had said at the prelim except Tompkins didn't ask about any discussions concerning life insurance. The jury seemed transfixed by her testimony. She looked even more striking than before, wearing a light grey skirt suit, her hair perfectly in place. I asked her just a few questions about whether Carlos had ever mentioned wanting to hurt his wife and she didn't hesitate to say, "Never."

Next was Beverly Branson, the waitress at Fat Tuesday's who had served Downey and Garcia the evening of Mo's death. Her testimony was brief with no surprises. She said Carlos had mentioned divorcing the "bitch" and was crying. I barely asked her anything.

Tompkins saved his most effective witness, the one I dreaded most, for last. Smirking in my direction, he stood and said, "The People call their last witness, Mary Silberg."

Silberg slowly made her way to the witness stand. She must've been mid-sixties and walked as if she had hip problems. When she raised her right hand, the ring and little finger were bent forward. She couldn't straighten them.

"Mrs. Silberg, are you currently retired?"

"Yes. Happily."

"And what was your occupation before you retired?"

"I was a 911 dispatcher for the Manchester Police Department."

Tompkins glanced at the jury to make sure they were paying attention. I tried to keep this evidence out on a motion in limine—away from the jury—but the judge ruled against me, saying the calls showed a motive for the defendant to harm his wife. Although I disagreed with her, and objected loudly, she of course won in the end.

"Mrs. Silberg, did you happen to receive any 911 calls from the deceased, Maureen Garcia?"

"I did, three times in the last ten years."

"How is it that you remember these calls?"

"She mentioned on the first call that her husband was a local judge. So that stuck in my mind." She paused. "And, of course, I read the transcripts recently to remind myself of the calls."

"Let's take these calls in order. When was the first one?"

"As I said, ten years ago."

Tompkins went to counsel table and switched on his CD player. "Please confirm that this was the first call."

There were several short beeps then a long beep before a voice came on, Maureen Garcia:

Help, it's my husband.

Ma'am, what seems to be the problem?

He's screaming and throwing things. I'm afraid of him.

Tell me your name and address.

It's Maureen Garcia. My husband's a judge. He has a terrible temper.

And your address?

1600 River Road, Manchester.

I'll send officers right out there. Stay on the line.

There were several seconds of silence while Silberg was calling the officers.

Mrs. Garcia, has he hurt you?

Not yet, but I'm afraid he will. He's so angry at me. I don't know what I did.

Where is he now?

He's in the bedroom. He slammed the door shut. That's when I called you. Oh, there's a knock on the door. That must be the police. It is; I see the flashing lights.

Tompkins shut off the CD player. The sound of Mo Garcia's voice had filled the courtroom: scared, teary, in obvious distress. I could do nothing but sit there. The jury hardly moved. Tompkins then proceeded to play the next two calls, which bore an eerie similarity to the first one: Mrs. Garcia complaining about her husband's anger, his throwing things, knocking over tables. The whole time Carlos sat still, looking at the floor.

When Tompkins finished, I stood up, unsure what to ask. There was only one thing I could do.

"Mrs. Silberg, in any of the calls from Maureen Garcia, did she ever say her husband had hit her?"

"She was certainly afraid he would. You heard that yourself."

"Thank you, ma'am. My question is a simple one: did she ever say her husband had hit her?"

"No, she didn't."

I sat down, satisfied that I could get nothing else from her.

CHAPTER TWENTY-NINE

AFTER COURT, I felt exhausted but excited at the prospect of getting Ginnie back. Delahunty had left me a voicemail message that his officers were still canvassing a four-block area of Hookset but hadn't been able to find the kidnapper. I stared at the television, not paying attention to what I was watching, my mind drifting. At 9:30 I gathered the money bag, counted it for the fifth time, and prepared to go to the drop. As I was getting ready to leave, Delahunty called.

"Dutch, we've done further analysis on Ginnie's voicemail message. Bad news."

"What're you talking about?"

"The recording was spliced from other recordings. It wasn't a live call. My best guess is the kidnapper used Ginnie's news broadcasts and pulled out the words he needed for the message. You know what that means?"

"Of course I know what that means. Damn! So we don't know if Ginnie is alive, after all. Mother of God!"

I hung up and reassessed the situation. This changed everything, including whether I wanted to take the risk of confronting the kidnapper. I immediately called Hedges who agreed to come right over.

❋ ❋ ❋

At 9:55 the sky was dark with only a quarter moon. I put on a baseball cap and drove toward the school with Hedges slouching down in the front passenger seat. He was also wearing a baseball cap and had folded his ponytail under the cap. I found the school easily and drove through the parking lot down a mild slope toward the back. There wasn't a soul in sight. As I got out of the car with the gym bag full of cash—three hundred thousand dollars—I listened intently. There were no sounds except for the chirping of crickets. I placed the bag on the ground where the kidnapper would find it then returned to the car.

I had disabled the door lights so the interior did not light up when the door opened. I pretended to enter the car from the driver's side but instead crawled on my belly under the car. Hedges then slid across the front seat to the driver's seat and shut the door. The kidnapper might notice the baseball cap but would have no idea we had switched drivers. I squeezed my way beyond the car and rolled onto the grass adjacent to the parking lot. I was in clear sight of the bag but the kidnapper would never see me. Hedges then drove away.

I found myself breathing heavily as I lay on my stomach. The stress of the situation was catching up to me. I was deeply troubled by Delahunty's call. Why had the kidnapper pretended to have Ginnie call me? I feared the worst but had to focus on the present.

I contemplated different scenarios, plotting my best course of action. But my adrenaline was flowing and all my muscles were tense. Whoever this kidnapper was would be one sorry hombre.

By 10:30 no one had appeared, and I was starting to worry he wouldn't show. My breathing had slowed a bit, but I was besieged by mosquitoes and soon had bites on my face and arms. One time I slapped a mosquito that was chewing on my forehead and when I pulled my hand away, I could feel the slick texture of my own blood.

After another ten minutes, a car appeared at the top of the hill. It descended slowly, as if the driver were looking in all directions. I pushed myself closer to the ground to ensure he wouldn't see me. He drove through the parking lot and stopped adjacent to the bag. He opened his driver's-side door and the light shone on the lot with a bit on me. He appeared to be a large man with a double chin, perhaps in his late thirties.

Without getting out of his car, he reached down to grab the bag with his left hand. Because he was looking down, he didn't notice me get to my feet and run toward his door. Crouching low, I slammed my shoulder into the door. The door smacked into his arm, causing him to drop the bag and scream. His arm was now wedged between the door and the car and he couldn't move. I pushed harder on the door and he screamed some more. He tried to drive the car with his right hand on the wheel and managed to move it a few feet but he hit the curb. Then he pressed on the gas pedal and jumped the curb, knocking me to the ground. But I got up quickly and grabbed hold of the door before he could close it. His left arm was probably not functioning well so he had a hard time keeping the door closed. I yanked it open and was face-to-face with the kidnapper. He had thick brown hair and was clean-shaven with fat round cheeks.

All the plans I had made to deal with this rationally, all of the steps I had envisioned, went out of my mind. I relied solely on instinct and hit him in the mouth with a straight right. His head snapped back then I hit him again, this time with a left hook. He was screaming for me to leave him alone, that I was mistaken. He hadn't done anything. I grabbed hold of his shirt and pulled him toward me. I was surprised at my strength. He must've weighed 250 pounds, but I managed to drag him out of the car onto the pavement.

He held up a hand to ward me off. "Don't hit me again," he pleaded.

I looked toward the car and noticed it was empty. "Where is she?"

He whimpered like an oversized baby. "You keep the money. It's all yours."

"I said, 'Where is she?'" I hit him again.

"Please!" He folded his arms across his face. "I . . . I don't have her."

"What?"

"I was putting you on." He buried his head in his arms. "Pretending to be the kidnapper so I could collect the ransom. I'm a computer geek, that's all."

"You son-of-a-bitch." I pulled his arms away from his face and punched him again. His head snapped back. Blood seeped from his lips and nose.

"I'm sorry but I don't have your wife."

I reached inside the car and pulled out the keys from the ignition. "Don't fuckin' move," I told him as I walked to the back. I opened the trunk just to be sure. It was full of computer parts, wires, and keyboards but no Ginnie.

I called Delahunty who arrived within minutes. "You should've let us handle this," he said, looking at the bloody and bruised computer geek.

"Please." I filled him in on what had happened.

I looked at the asshole, thinking about punching him again. Quickly I made a call to Hedges who said he'd be right here.

Delahunty put handcuffs on the pretend kidnapper. "You're under arrest for extortion." He pulled the guy's wallet from his back pocket and opened it. "His name is Ronald Baker. Thirty-seven years old, lives in Hooksett. We were on track with the cell phone trace. We'll get someone out to search his place right away."

Hedges arrived as Delahunty was placing Baker in the back seat of his cruiser. As I filled him in, I rubbed my knuckles, which were hurting; they were swollen and bleeding.

"So we're back to square one?" Hedges said.

"Looks that way."

"So the real kidnapper hasn't asked for a ransom."

I shook my head. "Nothing, just the envelopes and the letter to Ginnie's mother. That's the only contact we've had."

My head was spinning. I didn't know what to do. Delahunty had left with Baker while Hedges and I stood around in the dark, brooding. All my hopes had been dashed. I'd run into nothing but dead ends. Where was my wife? I was feeling desperate.

I put the bag of cash in the trunk of my car and drove home. My mood was at an all-time low when I got there. I was furious at Baker. How dare he give me hope I would see Ginnie again. What a despicable character! Delahunty called to say that the search of Baker's house had yielded nothing except to show that he appeared to be a hoarder with magazines and newspapers piled to the ceiling. So in addition to the extortion charge, he was also charged with violating the fire code. Big deal. Ginnie wasn't there. That's what counted. We truly were at square one. I had allowed myself to be so hopeful with the ransom demand. Now all I had were envelopes with Ginnie's hair and nails. Would that be all I ever had of my wife?

CHAPTER THIRTY

THE NEXT DAY I was thrilled to learn that a juror had called in sick. So I was free to continue the search for Ginnie's kidnapper. As if I knew what I was doing.

I stopped by the jail to speak to my client. I hadn't talked to him much in recent days since I was overwhelmed with the ransom demand. I told him about the fake kidnapper and asked if I could keep the fifty K as an advance on my fee.

"Jeez, I'm sorry to hear that. Of course, keep the money." He seemed stuck for what to say next, then launched right into his case, putting aside any concerns for Ginnie. "I like how the trial is going. We've got them on the run. I see reasonable doubt all over this case."

"You're forgetting that our best chance of success is to convince the jury Mo committed suicide. Relying on the jury to find reasonable doubt is a tricky proposition."

"I've seen a lot of murder trials and I know reasonable doubt when I see it."

"Carlos, you're a bit too close to this case, don't you think?"

He looked away, pondering how to answer. Then he turned back to me, fire in his eyes. "Of course I'm close to it; this is my life. But if I don't stay positive, I can't endure this trial. It's just too much. I can't sleep; my head aches all the time; I'm a mess."

"I didn't know the case was having that kind of effect on you. You hide it well."

"That's how I was trained: Stone-faced. Never show your emotions. But between you and me, I think we should approach Tompkins with a settlement proposal."

"Settlement? I thought you were determined to let the jury decide?"

"I am."

"I don't get it. What happened to your optimism about reasonable doubt?"

"I do think things are going well."

"Then what the hell?"

"Look, I've seen it happen countless times. The prosecutor gets an inkling the case might settle so he lets up on trial prep. I think we play with Tompkins."

"Forget it. I don't practice like that."

He approached me and put his right hand on my left shoulder. He held it there for several seconds before saying, "I'm the client and I'm directing you as my lawyer to determine if there's any interest in settlement. That's all I ask."

❊   ❊   ❊

I caught Tompkins just as he was leaving his office. "Fancy seeing you here," he said.

"I've come to talk settlement."

"No kidding." We walked together toward the elevator.

"Things aren't going well for you. You've got to admit that."

He sped up the pace. "That's not how I see it. Your guy had motive, opportunity, and means. Your suicide theory is a joke."

I put my hand on his shoulder, slowing him down. "Wayne, I know you don't believe that. This case has reasonable doubt written all over it."

"Please," he said as he pushed the elevator button. We stood quietly for a moment and then entered the crowded elevator. Neither of us spoke until we exited.

"What's your client got in mind?" Tompkins asked, trying to sound bored.

"I think I can get him to plead to manslaughter, credit for time served." I knew this was a non-starter, that Tompkins wouldn't even consider it.

Tompkins stopped before the courtroom door and laughed. "What the hell's he ingesting? No way my office will go for that."

"Give it a try, Wayne. Might be the best deal you'll get."

❊ ❊ ❊

Afterwards, I carried the bag of cash to the bank. I didn't want to waste any time returning the money. It took a lot of phone calls to get all the bank wiring information. When I presented the bag to the teller and told her I wanted to wire the money, her eyes bugged out. She asked me to wait while she got her supervisor who then brought in the bank manager. I returned money to my retirement accounts. I would have to deal with the penalties later. I deposited the Garcia advance in my client trust account and returned the marked funds and GPS tracker to the police department. It was several hours before everything was finalized.

As I was doing all that, I wondered if I had acted too quickly. What if the real kidnapper eventually asked for ransom? Then where would I be? But all the evidence pointed to the kidnapper being motivated by something other than money. And all I had left at this point were Nicholas Wolfe and Grace Handford. Hedges had left me a message that he had followed Handford to a house in Peterborough, not far from Nashua, from where two of the letters were mailed. Three young children had run out to her car as if they hadn't seen her in a while. He suspected Handford's parents lived there.

I had nothing better to do so I drove to Merrimack and parked near Wolfe's house. A Merrimack police car approached from the opposite direction, passing in front of the house without stopping. Five minutes later, long minutes, a van parked in front of Wolfe's house. A man got out and approached the front door. He was tall, about six three, and wearing a Red Sox cap backwards.

He stepped inside but the door remained open. Then the tall guy came back outside followed by Wolfe. I called Delahunty and told him what I was doing.

"Don't go anywhere near the house. I'm on my way."

"It looks like they're driving somewhere. I'll follow them and keep you posted."

As they drove down the street, I started my car and followed from half a block's distance. They drove through town, being careful to make a full stop at every stop sign, then headed toward the lake. By now the sun was low in the sky, casting long shadows. I was feeling sick, thinking about the blood on the bedroom floor and all the S&M devices. If Wolfe had used those on Ginnie, I would lose it entirely.

They stopped in front of a small white cottage behind a couple of enormous oak trees. A light shined from inside the cottage. As they walked toward the cottage and unlocked the front door, I called Delahunty and gave him the address. Could this be where they were hiding Ginnie?

Delahunty pulled up a few minutes later, parked, and opened my passenger door. He let himself in and closed the door quietly. He shook his head. "You know this is insane, don't you?"

"I don't care. I've got to find Ginnie."

"Last night was tough on you; I get that. But shit, we've got nothing but speculation connecting Wolfe to the kidnapping."

"Let's make sure. Come on, we'll knock on the door." Without waiting for his response, I got out of the car. Delahunty quickly followed. He was dressed in plainclothes with an MPD badge pinned to the lapel of his sports jacket.

He held up his hand. "I'll talk to them. That's it. Unless we see something obvious, we'll be on our way."

To the left of the front door was a window covered by a French blind that didn't quite touch the sill. As Delahunty rang the bell, I looked under the blind. Wolfe and the tall guy were sitting across from each other at a dining room table, glasses of red wine in front of them. They looked up suddenly at the ringing of the bell.

Wolfe came to the door. As soon as he opened it, Delahunty held out his badge. "Sergeant Delahunty, Manchester Police Department. Mind if we come in?"

Wolfe glanced at me then over his shoulder at Tall Guy. "What's this about?"

"If you let us in, we'll tell you everything."

Wolfe pointed at me. "Who's this guy?"

"His name's Dutch Francis. He's a lawyer."

"Yeah, I know that name. He's defending that dirtball murderer Carlos Garcia."

I made a strong effort to keep my mouth shut, realizing nothing good would happen if I went off on this guy. Soon, Tall Guy joined us at the door. He had thick blond hair and a chiseled face with a large jutting jaw. "Rather than stand here in view of all the neighbors," he said, looking at Wolfe, "why not let them in?"

Wolfe leaned his head in the direction of the dining room and stepped aside for us to enter. I slipped on a throw rug in the vestibule but struggled to balance myself. They directed us to sit at the table.

"Is this about my stories on Judge Garcia?"

"Actually," Delahunty said, "we're investigating a kidnapping."

Wolfe and Tall Guy briefly exchanged glances. "I get it now," Wolfe said, turning toward me. "You think we had something to do with your wife's disappearance."

"You wrote some nasty things about her." I struggled to keep the venom out of my voice.

"That doesn't mean I took her."

Delahunty leaned forward. "Here's the thing: we received a lot of tips about you and we've got to follow up. You've shown quite a bit of interest in Ms. Turner's disappearance."

"Hasn't everyone? She's well known in these parts."

"True. So I imagine you wouldn't mind if I looked around?"

"I would mind," said Tall Guy.

"What's your name?" asked Delahunty.

"Sheldon Lally. Nick and I are old friends."

"If you won't let us look around, I've got to ask some direct questions." He looked from Wolfe to Lally, letting a few quiet seconds pass, increasing the tension.

"We've got nothing to hide," said Wolfe.

"Let's start with Monday night, June 1st. What were you guys doing?"

"I don't remember," Lally said, "but if you let me look at my phone, I could tell you."

Delahunty nodded. Lally pulled out his phone and tapped a few times. "According to my calendar we were together at the greyhound track?"

"What track?"

"Lakes Region Casino in Belmont," said Wolfe.

"Did you bet with cash or credit card?" I asked.

"Cash," said Lally.

"Anyone else see you there?" Delahunty asked.

Each shrugged as if on cue.

"What about betting slips? Did you keep any of those?"

Both shook their heads. Damn! We weren't getting anywhere.

Delahunty must've sensed my frustration and decided to raise the temperature a bit. He stood up and looked down at both Wolfe and Lally. "That's the best you can do—an alibi that only the two of you can vouch for? I'd say that's pretty damn slim."

"Are we done here?" Wolfe asked, also getting to his feet.

Lally joined him. "Yes, I think we're done. Gentlemen, let me show you to the door."

I had a hard time accepting that we'd run into another dead end. I took a few steps toward the door, being careful of the throw rug, then stopped in front of Wolfe. "Tell me about the blood in your bedroom. How do you explain that?"

Wolfe took a step back and turned toward Lally. "So it was you who was snooping around my property. You were trespassing."

"The blood?" I insisted.

"What I do in the privacy of my own bedroom is none of your goddamn business! Isn't that right, Sheldon?"

Delahunty grabbed my shoulder and nudged me out the door. When we got to the sidewalk, he said, "Don't be surprised if he sues your ass or even presses charges."

"What am I supposed to do, Bill? Every time I think we've got the kidnapper, we get nowhere. I'm close to the boiling point."

"I haven't ruled out Wolfe just yet. I'll do some more digging. And we still have Mrs. Handford to check out."

"I can't believe the investigation's come down to a widow with three small kids. Fucking unbelievable!"

CHAPTER THIRTY-ONE

THE SICK JUROR recovered quickly so we resumed trial the next morning. The courtroom was crowded with media types anticipating the defendant's testimony. When they confronted me after court earlier in the week, I hadn't committed either way, preferring to keep the prosecution guessing. As a result, the headline of yesterday's *Union Leader* was rather bland: "Judge Garcia Case Nearing Conclusion." Garcia welcomed me with a big smile. God, was he cocky. Sitting in the midst of the media was Garcia's brother-in-law Sam Collins, his lips pursed, as he continued glaring in our direction.

Judge Shane asked the prosecutor if the People had any more witnesses. Tompkins stood up. "Your Honor, the People rest."

Judge Shane turned toward me. "Does the defense have any witnesses?"

"Yes, Your Honor. The defense calls Terry Harris."

Harris entered the courtroom, the subpoena we had served on him clutched firmly in his hand. He walked toward the witness box with a smug look on his face, as if all these people—the lawyers, the jury, the media—had gathered here just to listen to him speak. Harris was dressed in a tweed grey sport coat, a bit warm for our summer weather, black pants and a white dress shirt with the top unbuttoned.

Just going to the country club for a cocktail, his appearance seemed to say.

I began my questioning by establishing that Harris was a hostile witness. "Mr. Harris, you are here pursuant to a subpoena that my office served on you. Is that right?"

"I'm not here because I like your company, Mr. Francis." The jury laughed and Harris turned to them and smiled.

I tried to get things back on track. "Could you answer my question, please?"

"Yes, I am here because of the subpoena."

"You have no desire to assist Judge Garcia in defending this case, do you?"

"No, I don't. He can rot in hell for all I care."

Judge Shane leaned toward Harris. "Mr. Harris, please answer the question only and refrain from those types of comments. The jury is instructed to disregard the last comment by the witness."

Harris was proving to be a harder witness to control than I had anticipated. I gathered my notes and took a deep breath. "Mr. Harris, did you know the deceased, Maureen Garcia?"

"Yes, I did."

"Please explain to the jury how you two became acquainted."

Harris hesitated then turned toward the jury as if he were used to testifying in a murder trial. "I'm a member of the Manchester Country Club and so was Mo. That's what she liked to be called. We were introduced there."

Now I had to get to sensitive subjects. My hope was to give the jury a reason to believe Mo had killed herself or, failing that, perhaps even to suspect Harris of killing her. "Did you two develop a personal relationship?"

"We did."

"Would you describe it as a close relationship?"

"That's fair."

"You knew she was married?"

"Judge Garcia is a well-known member of our community. So, yes, I knew."

I glanced toward Garcia, hoping he wouldn't react to my next set of questions. "Did your relationship with Mrs. Garcia eventually develop into a sexual one?"

That got the jury's attention as all eyes were riveted on the witness. Harris must've sensed their looks because he focused his gaze on me.

"Eventually, yes, it did."

"Please describe to the jury the extent of your sexual relationship?"

"How do you mean? You want details?"

"I mean how frequently did you two have liaisons?"

"We started some time in February and we would usually get together a couple of times a week until she was killed."

I hated to object to my own witness's testimony but I had no choice. "Your Honor, I object to the witness's last statement that Mrs. Garcia was killed. The witness does not have personal knowledge to make such a statement."

"That objection is sustained." Judge Shane didn't bother looking up from her computer screen.

"Move to strike."

"Granted. The jury is instructed to disregard the witness's last statement. Please proceed, Mr. Francis."

"Mr. Harris, did Mrs. Garcia speak to you of her relationship with her husband?"

Now it was Tompkins' turn to get on his feet. "Objection. Hearsay."

"Mr. Francis?" Judge Shane looked at me.

"State of mind exception, Your Honor. It is the defense position that Mrs. Garcia committed suicide so her feelings about her relationship with her husband are relevant."

To my relief, Judge Shane overruled the objection.

"Should I answer?" Harris asked the judge.

"Yes, please answer."

"Mo was very upset her husband was having an affair. In fact, she told me she did not feel guilty about our affair because of that."

I needed more. "When you say she was upset, how did that manifest itself."

"What do you mean?"

"Did she show in any way how upset she was?"

"She teared up speaking about his affair, said she felt betrayed and humiliated. As I say, she was upset about it."

It looked like that was the best I could do so I switched subjects. "Let me turn to the day of Mrs. Garcia's death, April 21st. Did you see her that day?"

"I did. I stopped by her house in the afternoon."

"Was it typical for you to go to her home?"

"No," he said, shaking his head. "That was my first time there. I knew her husband was at work so it would be safe."

"Why did you go there?"

"I wanted to speak to her in person. I felt our relationship was going too fast and I wanted to end it."

"Did you tell her that?"

"I did."

"How did she react?"

"She cried, said she thought she had fallen in love with me. That it felt like another betrayal."

"What was she like when you left that day?"

"Still crying, upset. I felt bad."

I turned toward the judge. "No further questions, Your Honor."

"Mr. Tompkins?" the judge said.

"I have just a few." He stood up and approached the podium, not bothering to take his notes. "Were you aware during your relationship with Mrs. Garcia that she was taking Vicodin?"

Harris shook his head back and forth. "I was not; she never mentioned it."

"During the months you were together, you got to know Mrs. Garcia quite well. Would you agree?"

"I would."

"You were close?"

"We were."

"You shared private matters with each other? You told her private matters about yourself and she did the same?"

"True."

Tompkins was ready to go in for the kill. "During the entire time you two were together, while you shared private matters with each other, did Mrs. Garcia ever mention wanting to kill herself?"

"She did not." Harris was emphatic.

"Not once?"

"No, and I don't believe she would ever do such a thing."

"Objection," I shouted. "The witness's lay opinion is irrelevant."

Judge Shane stared at me over her glasses. She hesitated before saying, "The objection is overruled. The witness's answer will stand."

Tompkins was pleased with how things had gone. "Thank you, Your Honor," he said. "I have no further questions."

As Harris left the stand, the judge said, "Mr. Francis, does the defense have any other witnesses?"

Originally, I had planned on calling Dr. Gumina and then resting. After last Sunday's rehearsal, however, I realized that would be a huge mistake. She was vulnerable to attack from several angles, as my mock cross-examination had shown, so I had decided not to call her to the stand. It turned out she had reached the same conclusion and left me a voicemail message last night informing me. I respected her integrity. Not all expert witnesses would pass on a $6,000 payday.

But before resting, I had to check with my client one last time to confirm the decision not to testify.

"May I have a moment, Your Honor?"

"Of course."

I leaned over toward Garcia and whispered, "Are you still on board with not testifying?"

"Without Dr. Gumina, how're you going to prove suicide?"

"I don't need to prove it. All I need is reasonable doubt."

"I thought you considered that approach too risky."

"I'm afraid that's where we are now."

"If I testify, I could provide more than reasonable doubt. The jury will like me. I have a lot of credibility; I'm a judge, after all."

He was agitated. Perhaps the stress of trial really was taking its toll on him. "You *were* a judge."

"Okay, I'm not anymore, but that's only because of this bogus murder charge. After the jury heard those 911 calls, they're bound to think the worst of me."

I straightened up, leaving Garcia staring at me. I may have already lost my wife; I'd be damned if I was going to lose this case too. "We've been over all this. You'd be making a big mistake."

I thought he wasn't going to budge, but he surprised me. "I hired you for a reason so I'll follow your advice."

I turned toward Judge Shane. "Your Honor, the defense rests." A collective groan arose from the audience, who were no doubt hoping to hear from the defendant.

"Very well. We will begin closing arguments tomorrow morning."

❃   ❃   ❃

That night an online edition of the *Merrimack Citizen* was posted, detailing my visit to Wolfe's house and his friend Sheldon's cottage. Wolfe slammed me pretty well, making me seem like an out-of-control jerk, which I supposed had some truth to it. He also slammed me for defending Judge Garcia, characterizing him as a "wife-killer." Now I had to worry about Wolfe making a formal complaint with the police.

My sense of helplessness was growing, as was my anxiety. I had tried everything I could think of to find Ginnie and nothing had panned out. I had made a fool of myself searching—with Hedges' help—men's homes and trespassing on a man's property. So many men seemed to fit my ever-shifting profile of Ginnie's kidnapper—Conti, Bernard, the Collins brothers, Young, Wolfe—but in the end there was no evidence linking them to the kidnapping. Maybe Dr. Gumina was right; maybe I shouldn't have overlooked Grace Handford because of her sex.

I grabbed a bottle of Molson and called Hedges. He answered after several rings. "You probably heard," I said, "that we got nowhere with Wolfe."

"Yeah, Delahunty told me. I was going to call you. I've contacted Handford's parents in Peterborough. Nice people. They're still upset at their son-in-law's suicide. When I mentioned I was working for you, they got visibly upset. Somehow you became the fall guy for the suicide."

"What about Ginnie? Do they know anything about her?"

He spoke softly. "They know about her disappearance, of course, and even volunteered that their daughter had been acting quite strange lately. She had dropped her three kids off around the time Ginnie was taken and has visited them periodically since then. But she seemed distracted and, get this, obsessively interested in Ginnie's disappearance."

"Weren't they curious why you were questioning them in the first place?"

"Sure. I made up a bullshit story about you doing a follow-up on former clients to get feedback."

"What about the daughter? Where is she now?"

"Back in Manchester. I told Delahunty to stop by her house. He just reported back that she wouldn't let him in. She looked like 'shit'—his word—and practically slammed the door on him."

"So what's he going to do now?"

"He's stationed a plainclothes officer near her house and instructed him to report anything unusual."

"Why the hell doesn't he just force his way in?"

"Dutch, you know there's not enough for a warrant."

"Fuck! By the time we get enough for a warrant, it might be too late."

"I hear you."

Again, sleep eluded me. Around three a.m., I got up and dressed. Without thinking I got into my car and drove to the Handford home, which was a short distance away within the Manchester city limits. I arrived there in a few minutes. The house was on an acre of land backed by tall pine trees. Looking at the trees silhouetted by the moonlit sky, I wondered which was the one where Robert Handford had met his end. What a horrible shock for the wife to walk out the back door and see her husband hanging in the wind. The children fortunately were in school or day care at the time of their father's death.

There was an unmarked sedan nearby with a man in the driver's seat. His head was leaning back and he seemed to be asleep. I noticed the Handford house was dark. In hindsight, it probably wasn't the smartest thing to do, but I leaned on the horn and the guy jumped. I waved and kept driving.

CHAPTER THIRTY-TWO

WHEN I ARRIVED at court there were media vans lining Chestnut Street. Channel 9 was there along with several Boston television stations. I maneuvered my way past a crowd of reporters through the entrance. Most asked, "What're you going to tell the jury?" My answer was a standard one: "That my client is innocent. What else?"

In the courtroom I awaited Garcia's entrance, jotting down a few notes and going over my closing. I generally liked to write out the first sentence or two of my closing just until the jitters went away. Then I wrote out bullet points only, each designed to remind me of a subject to discuss. The sequence of these bullet points was important. Each had to build on the last one and hopefully reach a climax, as a result persuading the jury of my client's innocence.

Garcia leaned into me before taking his seat. "Go get 'em, Dutch. I have every confidence in you."

"Thanks, Carlos." I wondered why he felt the need to build me up.

Because the prosecution had the burden of proof, Tompkins got to make his closing argument first. He had proved to be an able opponent during the trial, and I had no doubt he would give a compelling closing. He began by standing in front of the jury box, eschewing the podium. Without the benefit of notes, he said, "Ladies and gentlemen of the jury, you have heard evidence that shows beyond a reasonable doubt that the defendant, Carlos Garcia, murdered his wife, Maureen. He took her prescription Vicodin pills from the medicine cabinet, removed most of them, and then proceeded to grind them into a fine powder. We don't know—and couldn't know—exactly how the defendant ground up the pills but it's safe to assume he used a standard utensil such as the back of a spoon. When he finished grinding the pills, he then sprinkled the powder onto her dinner. We know he handled the dinner because the man who delivered the noodles told you that the defendant answered the door. The defendant paid the man then took the noodles into the house. Perhaps while Mo Garcia was in another room or not paying attention, the defendant then took the opportunity to sprinkle the powder.

"That's what the evidence indicates. Although the State does not have to prove motive—you could find the defendant guilty even without any evidence of motive—we have proven several potential motives. The defendant was involved in an extramarital affair and was contemplating divorce. The defendant wanted to avoid the bad publicity that would no doubt tarnish his reputation throughout the state. He found himself in an untenable situation. He wanted a divorce but wanted to do so quietly, maintaining his reputation. The solution must've come to him while he was watching his wife take her pills one day. It was a simple solution.

"We found a search history on the defendant's computer from several days before the murder that showed he was researching the lethal effects of an overdose of Vicodin. These web pages clearly spelled out the dangers to the central nervous system from the consumption of Vicodin in powder form rather than tablet. They also detailed the additive effects of Vicodin and alcohol in depressing the central nervous system. Combined, they create a dangerous result that could stop breathing altogether. And we know the defendant served alcohol to his wife that night."

Tompkins now paced back and forth in front of the jury, building to a crescendo. "Then we come to the evidence of the 911 calls, which you heard. Mo Garcia called 911 not once but three times to report her husband's abuse. It may not have been physical abuse, but it was abuse all the same. He was yelling and throwing things. She was scared he would get violent. You heard the fear in her voice. Is it too far a stretch to conclude that a man who drove his wife to call 911 three times would murder her? I think not.

"In the face of this evidence, the defendant had to come up with an alternative story. And that's when we get to this bogus suicide theory. The defendant—or rather, his lawyer—would have you believe that his wife was so distraught over his affair and desire for a divorce that she took her own life. Yet where is the evidence supporting this theory? Not one witness testified that Maureen Garcia ever attempted to kill herself. Not one witness testified that she even threatened to take her own life. There's not even any evidence of Mo consulting a psychiatrist or psychologist. In fact, she rejected her treating doctor's suggestion of anti-depressants or therapy. If she were so depressed, so low, wouldn't she have sought treatment? There simply is no evidence that she committed suicide. That theory is garbage. Mo Garcia did not commit suicide. She was murdered by her husband.

"I submit to you that the evidence requires one conclusion: that the defendant is guilty of murder beyond a reasonable doubt. Thank you for your attention."

My mind wandered during Tompkins' closing since I knew he had valid points. I should've been energized to begin my closing argument but I felt down, uninspired. I had to snap out of it.

I inhaled deeply, gathered my notes, and approached the podium. In other trials I had given closing argument with just a quick glance at my notes, but in this case, at this time, I needed the crutch of my notes. I moved the podium closer to the jury and looked at them, pausing for a moment before speaking.

"Ladies and gentlemen of the jury, you have just heard an impassioned closing argument from the prosecutor. Mr. Tompkins claims the evidence shows beyond a reasonable doubt that my client is guilty. I submit to you that the evidence shows no such thing. Instead, the evidence—and more specifically the absence of evidence—shows that the State's case is full of holes. Although not directly stated in closing argument, the prosecutor is hoping you succumb to a prejudice common in cases of this type. When a married woman is suspected of being murdered, the prime suspect tends to be the husband. That is so before any evidence is gathered, before witnesses are interviewed, and even before an autopsy is performed. Our society simply has a built-in bias against husbands in these circumstances. The result is that husbands are forced to prove their innocence contrary to our country's well-established presumption of innocence. I'm sure it felt that way during this trial, that Judge Garcia had to prove he was innocent.

"But let's be clear: he does not have to prove his innocence. The State has to prove him guilty beyond a reasonable doubt. That means if you have any reasonable doubt about whether Judge Garcia intentionally killed his wife, you must find him not guilty. And what does 'beyond a reasonable doubt' mean? It means that you must have an abiding conviction that the defendant is guilty. If you don't have this long-lasting conviction, you must find Judge Garcia not guilty. You may not believe Judge Garcia to be innocent but if your belief contains any reasonable doubt, you must acquit."

I coughed a few times, my throat feeling constricted, and reached to counsel table for my water cup. I took a sip then checked my notes.

"The prosecution has not presented one witness to testify that Judge Garcia made any incriminating statement at any time. Not one.

You would think that someone plotting murder in this way would have one slipup, say something incriminating to someone. Even the police at the scene, who claim they didn't consider him a suspect at first, had nothing to offer you by way of any admission. Judge Garcia's demeanor was what you would expect of a husband who had just lost his wife. You heard the 911 recording the night of her death. I submit to you that's the sound of a distressed man, not a man who had just killed his wife.

"You heard from the person closest to him—Arlene Downey— that Judge Garcia always spoke about his wife in the kindest terms. He was hesitant to file for divorce because he was concerned with upsetting her. Does that sound like a man who's plotting to murder his wife?

"Although we did not have to do so, we proffered evidence suggesting that Mo Garcia may have died by means that had nothing to do with her husband. Terry Harris had an extramarital relationship with Mrs. Garcia and had just met with her to end their relationship. We don't know how Mrs. Garcia responded to this news other than what Mr. Harris has said. Is it not conceivable that the couple argued, perhaps tempers were lost, and Mrs. Garcia became so distraught that she decided to kill herself? We do know when the Thai noodles were delivered, she was distraught, sobbing and crying.

"Let's look at the evidence suggesting that Mo Garcia killed herself. Her fingerprints were found on the Vicodin bottle; she of course had access to the family laptop and likely was the person who researched the deadly effects of Vicodin overdose herself. She had the opportunity to sprinkle the powder onto the food. Moreover, we know she was distraught from the deterioration of her marriage. Her doctor noted in her medical record that she reported feeling depressed and sad. She was taking St. John's Wort. Not every suicidal person announces the intent to kill herself. Not every suicidal person seeks mental health treatment. Some simply kill themselves. The signs are there; the evidence suggests that's what happened in this case.

"Finally, let me address an issue that may be on your minds. My client was a judge of the New Hampshire Superior Court. As I said to you in opening statement, he is entitled to the same treatment as any other criminal defendant. He should not be treated more leniently; nor should he be treated more harshly. He is a man just like any other man. He deserves the presumption of innocence; he deserves the right to trial by jury; he deserves the requirement of proof beyond a reasonable doubt.

"In this case, especially, he deserves a verdict of not guilty."

I sat down, drained, and closed my eyes. I felt like I had given as good a closing as I could under the circumstances; however, I didn't think it was the best closing I'd ever given. It was more disjointed than I would have liked, not as smooth. Well, there was nothing I could do about it now. Garcia took some of the worry away when he squeezed my upper arm and nodded, giving his approval.

❀ ❀ ❀

On the way out of court, Tompkins stopped me. He asked me to step to the side, away from the media. "I know the jury's going out, but I wanted to respond to your plea offer."

"Why now?"

"You know how it is; bureaucracy moves at its own speed."

I was skeptical. "What's the deal?"

"Ten years, manslaughter. Credit for time served."

"I'll talk to my client and get back to you after lunch."

I walked down to the jail. Hank Lerner was on duty. He asked, "Any word on the wife?"

I nearly blew it and told him about the fake kidnapper but held my tongue. "Still nothing but I appreciate your asking."

"Your wife's good people. Everyone knows that."

What he didn't say was that he was surprised she ever married me. But I could tell that's exactly what he was thinking.

"Francis, kills me to say so, but you looked good that time on TV."

"Why thank you, Hank. I do believe that's the first time you've ever complimented me."

"And it'll be the last," he said, chewing on a pencil. "You can bet on that."

Garcia was pacing his cell. I sat down on the bench. "Tompkins finally got back to me with an offer. You might want to sit down."

He did as I suggested. I turned to face him. "He wants you to plead to manslaughter and serve ten years, credit for time served."

Garcia laughed. "Tompkins is nervous. We've got them on the run."

"You sure you don't want to consider it? Who knows what the jury will do? You could get sentenced to life."

He paced the cell, shaking his head.

"The jury's been out just over an hour so chances are they won't have a verdict today."

He stood across from me and leaned his back against the bars. Since the trial had begun, he seemed to age, each passing day creating more wrinkles on his face. Now the wrinkles seemed deeper. They were darker, too; he hadn't shaved today. He looked less confident than usual, vulnerable even. Or perhaps just older.

"I can't do time. If I get convicted, I'll kill myself."

"Carlos!"

He crossed his arms. "I've given it a lot of thought. I won't go to state prison. They'll crucify me there."

"So you'd rather give up? I took you for being stronger than that. Would you really take the same path as Mo?"

He glanced at me sideways then looked away. "Tell Tompkins I reject his plea offer."

I stood up and inhaled deeply. "You're sure?"

He nodded. But from the moisture in his eyes, it wasn't clear how sure he was.

"Any counter?"

He shook his head. "Let the jury decide."

❈ ❈ ❈

I went to Tompkins' office and told him Garcia's response. He seemed surprised. "The good judge is playing with fire."

"He's confident he'll be found innocent."

With his right hand, he rubbed the top of his bald head. "No skin off my nose. I don't see this jury acquitting him. I admit it's possible you might get one or two on your side for a mistrial."

"To me, that would be a win."

"Great. Then we can try this whole thing over again."

CHAPTER THIRTY-THREE

THE JURY RETIRED for the day without reaching a verdict. I arrived home to a pile of mail on the floor. It had been some time since the last delivery of a manila envelope. There were four to me right after the kidnapping and one to my mother-in-law last week. I almost felt disappointed I hadn't received more. At least the mailings were visible proof that Ginnie was still out there somewhere, which is why I felt a bit of hope when I saw it. My heart beat quickly as I picked it up without thinking and noted it was flat. So it didn't contain a finger or toe.

I put the envelope on the kitchen table and called Delahunty. He didn't answer so I left a message. "Bill, I got another envelope. Get over to my house right away."

Ten minutes went by with no return call. I paced from one end of the condo to the other. Every time I passed the kitchen table, I considered tearing the envelope open. The anticipation was killing me. Finally, Delahunty called. He was in a hurry: "I'm on the way over now with the techie. Sit tight."

They arrived in record time. The techie was the same woman with the rat tail who had steamed open the envelope containing Ginnie's clipped toenails. She pulled out her steam machine and opened the envelope in minutes. The envelope contained a lined index card on which was written a chilling note in bold uppercase type:

BY 10 P.M. FRIDAY A WOMAN WILL BE FOUND IN A
SMALL LOCKED ROOM. SHE WILL BE HANGING BY
THE NECK FROM A ROPE, STRANGLED, WITH AN
OPEN COOLER OF WATER AT HER FEET. NOTHING
ELSE WILL BE IN HER ROOM.

"Oh my God!" I yelled. "No, God, no."

This was the first direct threat I had received from the kidnapper.
Only a few hours to find Ginnie or she'd be dead. This screw job was
really playing with me now. Who could I have angered so much that
he'd do something like this?

I backed away from the letter as if it were radioactive. I didn't even
want to look at it. Delahunty approached and put his hand on my
shoulder. "Oldest riddle in the book. She's standing on a block of
ice. It'll take a day or so to melt. So that's how he plans to kill her. He
must've tied the noose around her neck last night and then stood her
on the ice. We've got to stop him."

"Yeah, but how?"

I thought about what the kidnapper had planned. This was a particularly cruel method of killing. Ginnie would be standing on a cold
block of ice that slowly melted, pulling the rope more tightly around
her neck. She would have to stand on her tiptoes to take the pressure
off the rope. Her death would come slowly, painfully, and she'd be
fully aware what was happening. Her only hope was that we found
her before the ice melted too much.

It suddenly dawned on me. Death by hanging. Of course. It could
only be one person. "Bill, I know who has Ginnie."

"I've heard that before, so forgive me for not jumping in anticipation."

"It has to be Grace Handford. I warned you about her."

"I've got a man watching her now but tell me more about why you
suspect her."

"Her husband was working as an investment advisor for a large financial services company when he received a bonus that was lower than he expected. He consulted me to see if there were any claims he could make."

"What did you tell him?"

"There was nothing I could do. The employer had complete discretion on how much bonus to award. But he was bitter and wanted to write a letter of complaint. I advised against doing that since he was an at-will employee and could be fired for any reason or no reason. But he ignored my advice. He wrote a letter and reluctantly I helped him edit it."

I paused, remembering my frustration when the client did that. "Then the inevitable happened: he got fired."

"So was that the end of it?"

"Not quite. Again, against my advice, Handford wanted to file a wrongful termination suit. It didn't last long and was dismissed. By Carlos Garcia."

"No shit."

"Robert was so distraught that he walked to a wooded area near his house and . . ." I swallowed and chills ran up my spine. "Bill, for Christ's sake, he climbed a tree, tied a rope around his neck, attached the other end to a limb, then jumped."

"He hanged himself?"

I nodded.

"The wife came to me just before Ginnie was taken. She wanted the case file and blamed me for her husband getting fired, and presumably for his death."

We remained quiet for several seconds.

"At first, I ignored all the signs pointing to her, thinking a woman incapable of such cruelty, then Dr. Gumina told me to reconsider."

I sat down at the kitchen table and laid my head on my arms, breathing heavily, on the verge of hyperventilating. "What a fool I've been. It's just as Dr. Gumina said. Mrs. Handford was punishing me with those mailings, making me distraught over losing my wife. At the same time, she was distracting me from Garcia's case, hoping he would get convicted. Now she's going to hang Ginnie. She wants Ginnie to die just as her husband died, but even more slowly and painfully. Bill, we've got to move on this now."

Delahunty breathed heavily. "Finally, I think we've got enough for a search warrant. I'll get to work drafting the warrant and affidavit and present it to a judge. I'm hoping we can move on this tonight but it could take a few hours."

I jumped to my feet. "We can't wait. Ginnie's got a noose around her neck right now." I looked at my watch. It was six o'clock. I was frantic. I wanted to go to Handford's house immediately.

"I understand the urgency but I can't search without a warrant." He motioned for the techie to follow him as he hurried out the front door.

❊ ❊ ❊

As I awaited Delahunty's call, I tried watching television and listening to music but again wound up pacing. Before long, my body began shaking. I had a sensation of being surrounded by blocks of ice. As the ice melted slowly, the cold water flowed to every inch of my body, bringing a chill with each contact. I was freezing.

Still shivering after half an hour, I jumped when my phone rang. It was Delahunty. "Good news, Dutch. The judge signed the search warrant. We're going to execute it now."

"I'm on my way."

CHAPTER THIRTY-FOUR

I CALLED HEDGES on the way to Handford's house and arrived just before him. We had only a few hours before Ginnie would be dead. There must've been six patrol cars parked near the house. Delahunty was leading a group of officers down the front path toward the house. He held a megaphone in one hand. Another officer held a battering ram. Hedges and I crouched behind one of the patrol vehicles, trying to discern any movement from within the house. There was none.

A dozen yards from the front door, Delahunty stopped and brought the megaphone to his mouth. "Mrs. Handford, this is the Manchester Police Department. We have a warrant to search your house. Please open the front door."

There was no response. After thirty seconds, Delahunty instructed his men to batter down the door. Two male officers, both tall and bulky, gripped each end of the battering ram and prepared to charge the house. They stopped suddenly, however, when a shot rang out from an upper window. With a sharp ping, the bullet struck the path between the door and the officers with the battering ram. Officers scattered for cover, some hiding behind trees in the front yard, others scampering back to the safety of their patrol cars.

"Go away!" a woman yelled from an upstairs window of the house. "I'll shoot the lot of ya."

Delahunty retreated to the vehicle where Hedges and I were crouching behind. "Stay out of the way," he said. "The last thing we need is civilian casualties." He got no argument from us.

Leaning low, Delahunty opened the back door and removed a rifle. He cocked the rifle and aimed it at the upstairs window.

"Bill," I whispered, "what if you hit Ginnie? We don't know if she's with Mrs. Handford."

He lowered the rifle. "You're right; it's too risky."

He picked up the megaphone and said, "Officers, hold your fire and maintain your position. Mrs. Handford, you don't need to do this. Put down your gun and we'll talk."

"I've nothing to say to you. I don't care what you do to me."

"Where's Ginnie Turner? There's no reason to harm her."

There was no response. Delahunty turned toward me. "She may want to commit suicide by cop. We've got to be careful."

I wasn't really concerned with her wanting to kill herself; my concern was with Ginnie. If Handford wanted to kill herself, though, she wouldn't hesitate to take Ginnie with her. I couldn't risk that happening. "I'm going around back," I said. "I can't wait here."

"It's too dangerous," Delahunty said.

"I don't care."

Hedges touched my shoulder. "Let's approach the rear from opposite directions. I'll go first and draw her fire. You go the other way."

Before I could object, he took off running toward the left side of the house. A shot rang out almost immediately. I ran in the opposite direction. Handford began shooting at both of us, alternating her target. It was obvious she was caught off guard and was shooting without taking serious aim. I made it to the right side of the house and raced around back. Hedges arrived a moment later. In the background I could hear Delahunty pleading with Handford to come out of the house.

The back door was at the top of four steps. The screen door to the porch opened, but the solid wooden door to the house was locked. I tried kicking it and Hedges put his shoulder to it but nothing worked. Finally, Hedges took out his pistol and shot the lock. The door then opened easily into the kitchen. Inside, Handford began screaming from upstairs.

"I'll kill both of ya. Get the hell out of my house."

I noticed a door across the kitchen and guessed it led to the basement. "You distract her," I said to Hedges, "while I check out the basement."

But before I could get to the door, bullets rang from above us. Handford was shooting into her floor, trying to pick us off. I scampered under the kitchen table for cover. At a pause in the shooting, I sprinted for the door and made my way into the basement. It took me a moment to find the light switch and when I got to the bottom of the stairs, I was shocked at what I saw. Ginnie was hanging from a rope, her shod feet barely touching a melting block of ice in a large cooler. I ran toward her and lifted her up. Her body was cold but her eyes were moving. I tried untying the knot but it wouldn't give way. Then I tried easing the noose over her chin but it was too tight.

"Hedges!" I yelled. "Get down here. Bring a knife."

He appeared a moment later holding a long-bladed kitchen knife. "Oh my God." He cut the rope. Ginnie collapsed in my arms. I felt for a pulse and there was a faint one. She looked terrible: pale, drawn, emaciated.

I held her tightly against my chest, trying to warm her body with mine. Before I could get any response, a voice—angry and bitter— cried out. "She was going to get what my Robby got. Now I've got to finish all of you off." She was standing at the bottom of the stairs, pointing her gun at me, then at Hedges. She was wearing long white pants with threads at the bottom and a blue top. She emitted hatred, dark narrow eyes below a high forehead and tightly clenched teeth. I moved Ginnie behind me so I was shielding her with my body. "That won't save her," Handford said.

"You didn't have to do this," I said. "If it was me you wanted, you should've come after me, not my wife."

"Oh yeah? Well, how'd you like it when your wife went missing? How'd you like it when you got pieces of her in the mail? Not so good, I bet. And what about knowing she would hang to death?"

"You knew I'd be tormented; that's just what you wanted."

Ginnie had started slipping, and I pulled her up. Her eyes fluttered. "Not so beautiful now," Handford said, "is she?"

"You're vicious."

"It was because of you I lost my Robby. How could you advise him to send such a nasty letter? You knew he'd get fired!"

"I told you I advised him not to send the letter. He wouldn't listen to me. It was his own fault he got fired."

"Bullshit! He took his own life because of you. It's your fault." She pointed the gun at my chest and, with a look of utter hatred, pulled the trigger.

I staggered back, expecting to be hit, but the gun clicked and did not fire. She was out of bullets. In the next second Hedges rushed forward and tackled her, slamming her head against the wall as he put his shoulder into her gut. She lay on the floor, unconscious, as Delahunty and several other officers ran down the stairs.

❊ ❊ ❊

In the ICU at Catholic Memorial Hospital, I sat by Ginnie's side, holding her hand in mine. Tubes came from her nose and mouth and wires seemed to emanate from everywhere else. She hadn't said a word since I'd found her. The doctors said she was badly undernourished but they were guardedly optimistic she would pull through. I stared at my wife.

I thought of all she had been through in past weeks. She had suffered greatly, both physically and mentally. I hated to think of the residual harm this experience had caused. I vowed to assist her in any way I could on the road to recovery. Looking at her now, I was so grateful she was alive. Sadly, the doctors had determined that she had miscarried during her ordeal so Handford had already claimed one life. I felt sick to learn we had lost our child.

I still had a hard time understanding how a woman could've acted so cruelly, both to Ginnie and me. She was a vicious, sick person and would deserve everything she got.

Staff had set up a cot in Ginnie's room so I could stay with her. I slept there all weekend, leaving only to visit the cafeteria for meals. Ginnie remained unconscious, being fed through a tube. Nurses snugly wrapped warm blankets around her legs and feet. I barely slept, unable to keep my eyes off my wife, hoping, praying that she would pull through.

At around ten o'clock on Monday morning, after the mouth tube had been removed, Ginnie opened her eyes and a flood of relief overcame me. She tried to speak and I moved toward her. "I-I knew you'd come," she whispered, a faint smile forming on her chapped lips. "But what the hell took you so long?"

I kissed her gently and stroked her hair. "I can't imagine what you've gone through." She closed her eyes and fell asleep again. I rested my head on her stomach and closed my eyes, hoping to get some sleep myself, when my phone rang.

It was the judge's clerk. "We've got a jury question and the judge wants you here." I explained what I'd been through during the weekend and told him I couldn't leave my wife's side. "Let me talk to the judge," he said.

A few minutes later he called back to say I could handle the jury question by telephone and he put me on speaker. "Mr. Francis," Judge Shane said, "I'm in the courtroom with Mr. Tompkins. The defendant is also present. The jury is not. We're on the record. Please state your appearances." After we'd done so, the judge said, "Let the record reflect that Mr. Francis is appearing by telephone with the court's consent. How is your wife, Mr. Francis?"

"The good news is she's expected to survive and has even spoken a few words but she's in a bad way."

"Our prayers are with her."

"Thank you."

"The jury question reads as follows: 'The jury is deadlocked and there appears no way we can reach agreement. May we be excused?'"

My heart skipped a beat. This was good news for the defense. If the jury deadlocked, there would be a mistrial. Then the State would have to decide whether to retry the case.

"Mr. Tompkins, let's start with you," the judge said. "How do you propose the court answer this question?"

"Your Honor, the jury's been in deliberation just under a full day. I suggest the court give them the deadlock instruction."

"Mr. Francis?"

"If the jury's deadlocked this early in deliberations, then I believe they should be excused. They wouldn't ask this question unless some jurors have taken hard and fast positions."

There were a few moments of silence before the judge said, "That may be so, Mr. Francis, but I think Mr. Tompkins is correct. I will give the deadlock instruction." There was then the sound of papers being shuffled. "Here it is," Judge Shane said. "My clerk is handing out copies to Mr. Tompkins as well as the defendant. For your benefit, Mr. Francis, I will read the instruction. Let me know if there is any objection to the language. 'Members of the jury, you have advised the court that you have been unable to agree upon a verdict in this case. I have decided to suggest a few thoughts to you. As jurors, you have a duty to discuss the case with one another and to deliberate in an effort to reach a unanimous verdict if each of you can do so without violating your individual judgment and conscience. Each of you must decide the case for yourself, but only after you consider the evidence impartially with your fellow jurors. During your deliberations, you should not hesitate to reexamine your own views and change your opinion if you become persuaded that it is wrong. However, you should not change an honest belief as to the weight or effect of the evidence solely because of the opinions of your fellow jurors or for the mere purpose of returning a verdict.

"'All of you are equally honest and conscientious jurors who have heard the same evidence. All of you share an equal desire to arrive at a verdict. Each of you should ask yourself whether you should question the correctness of your present position.'

"Is that agreeable, gentlemen?"

"Yes, Your Honor," both of us said at the same time.

"Keep your cell phone on, Mr. Francis," the judge said.

"Will do."

I hung up, happy to turn my attention back to Ginnie.

CHAPTER THIRTY-FIVE

THE NEXT FEW days went by slowly. I kept my vigil at Ginnie's side as she gradually recovered. At my request, Hedges came by the hospital with a huge bouquet of flowers from Pierucci's Florist. As soon as he saw Ginnie, tears formed in his eyes.

"Thank you, Glen," she said. "And thanks for helping Dutch find me."

Hedges wiped his eyes. "We did everything we could."

"I know you did." She patted his hand.

Ginnie's feet hurt terribly and were nearly frostbitten from contact with the ice. Although Handford at least had enough compassion to allow Ginnie to keep wearing her shoes, flats with a thin sole, the cold still came through. We held hands without talking and soon I was nodding off.

After the weekend, Ginnie's mother insisted on staying in the room with us. She couldn't stand being away from Ginnie any longer. I stood back as Barbara rubbed Ginnie's head and told her how much she loved her. I hadn't kept her as informed as I should have during the search for Ginnie, and she was still annoyed at me, though she confessed to feeling guilty for suspecting me.

"I didn't want to get your hopes up," I told her. "We were chasing a lot of dead ends."

"All this time I was worrying myself sick."

"Me too."

She turned to face me. "Dutch, you're a good man. Thank you for saving my daughter."

"You don't blame me for her kidnapping?"

"After getting the letter and hearing from Officer Leary, I thought you'd done something to Ginnie. I'm so sorry." She looked at the floor. "I hope you'll forgive me. I had some terrible thoughts then. I'm sorry I doubted you."

"Apology accepted. Of course, it turns out you were somewhat right to be suspicious of me. If I had done a better job with Robert Handford's case, he wouldn't have killed himself and then all the rest wouldn't have happened."

❁   ❁   ❁

The Garcia jury continued deliberating. The judge's instruction must have spurred further discussion. Garcia was getting more anxious as time went by, convinced he'd be convicted. I tried to relieve his anxieties by going over the evidence in our favor, a summary of my closing argument. But he remained anxious, sweating constantly, his stomach aching. I suggested we call in a doctor but he was resistant, insisting he'd be all right.

At the end of the afternoon on Wednesday, the jury foreperson sent another note saying she'd like to speak to the judge. This time I appeared personally in Judge Shane's courtroom.

"Counsel," she said after Tompkins had appeared, "the foreperson has sent the following note: 'Your Honor, we are still hopelessly deadlocked and there is no chance we will reach a verdict. May we be excused?'"

Shane handed the note to her clerk who showed it to Tompkins and me. "Does anyone have any suggestions?" the judge asked.

"I think this jury has been put through enough," I said. "I would ask the court to declare a mistrial."

"Mr. Tompkins?"

"I'm afraid at this point I have to agree."

"Very well, let's call the jury in and I will confirm they are deadlocked."

The bailiff left to retrieve the jury while Garcia leaned toward me. "I hate to go through this again. What can we do to convince Tompkins not to retry the case?"

"Let's wait and see the split."

The jury entered the courtroom quietly, most appearing somber and not looking at either me or Tompkins. They had just spent several days together and must have been disappointed that their efforts would be wasted. I was hopeful that the vote would be in Garcia's favor and would convince Tompkins there was no reason to retry the case.

After the jury was seated, Judge Shane said, "Ladies and gentlemen of the jury, I understand you are deadlocked. Is that correct?"

The foreperson, a middle-aged schoolteacher with a no-nonsense look, stood up. "Yes, Your Honor. We've tried very hard to follow the court's instructions but simply have a difference of opinion."

"Do you believe further deliberations would be fruitful?"

"I do not, Your Honor."

"Is there anyone on the jury who believes further deliberations would be fruitful? Raise your hand." She paused. "I see no hands. What I'm going to do now is poll the jury. I will ask each of you to state your verdict, either guilty or not guilty. Juror number one, Mr. Seeger, what is your verdict?"

Seeger shot a glance at Garcia and said, "Guilty, Your Honor."

Oh shit, I thought. That wasn't good. Garcia shook noticeably, his hands slapping the table. He stared straight down, not moving his eyes.

"Juror number two, Ms. Cole," Judge Shane continued. "What is your verdict?"

Cole was a young college student, a member of her college debating society. Unlike Seeger, she stood up and, turning slightly toward Seeger, said, "Not guilty."

I breathed a sigh of relief. Judge Shane went through the entire jury using the same routine. Some jurors answered with their heads lowered, mumbling their verdict. Others shouted it out for all to hear, proud of their decision. In the end, it turned out well: seven to five for not guilty. But it was not even enough for a verdict in a civil case so I didn't know if the prosecution would refile the charges.

Judge Shane dismissed the jury, stating, "On behalf of the parties—the people of the State of New Hampshire as well as the defendant Carlos Garcia—I want to thank you for your service. You have been a conscientious jury and have served your civic duty well. Even though you did not reach a verdict, your efforts may not be fruitless."

From the jury box, Ms. Cole was raising her hand. "Yes, Ms. Cole," Judge Shane asked. "Do you have a question?"

"I was wondering what happens next. Does the defendant get released from custody? Is there a retrial?"

"Those are very good questions but I'm afraid I can't give you definitive answers. It is up to the prosecution whether there will be a retrial. If Mr. Tompkins' office decides to retry the case, then I suspect the defendant will remain in custody. Mr. Tompkins, I know there are many people you have to consult, but when do you expect a decision on retrial will be made?"

"Your Honor, if I might have until tomorrow morning, I should have a decision."

"Very well, let's reconvene tomorrow morning at nine a.m. As for the jury, you are free to go at this time. The lawyers may want to speak to you. The admonition I have been giving to you throughout the trial about not speaking to anyone regarding the case is now dissolved. You may speak to the lawyers if you wish. But you do not have to speak to them. That's entirely up to you." She paused, glancing at counsel table. "I want to thank you for your service. As some of you may know, the United States of America is one of the few countries on Earth to grant its citizens the right to trial by jury. It is a hallmark of our Constitution. Your participation is vital to ensuring that our Constitutional rights are preserved. You have performed your duty and are now excused."

As Judge Shane left the bench, I announced to the jury: "On behalf of Judge Garcia, I would appreciate a moment of your time to get an understanding of your votes." Some of the jurors put their heads down and walked toward the exit. A handful hung around. The bailiff led Garcia back to his cell, leaving me to talk to the jurors. Ms. Cole was the first to speak. She waited until the door had closed on Garcia.

"I want to make one thing clear. My vote for not guilty was not because I believed your client was innocent. I'm unsure whether or not your client killed his wife."

If this was one of the jurors who had voted in our favor, then the defense was in trouble. Tompkins was listening intently, no doubt preparing to make a full report to his superiors.

"Why then did you vote to acquit?" I asked Ms. Cole.

"Simple. I don't think the prosecution proved your client's guilt beyond a reasonable doubt. I'm not convinced his wife committed suicide, but I can't say your client killed her."

Other jurors nodded in agreement. I asked Seeger why he had voted to convict.

"No way did Mrs. Garcia kill herself. If it wasn't suicide, that left your client as the guilty one."

This was hard to hear. I asked some of the other jurors for their perspectives and found that the guilty votes agreed with Seeger and the not-guilty votes with Cole. It was by no means a full acquittal but was based on the prosecution's failure to meet its high burden of proof by a reasonable doubt. Seven jurors did not have an abiding conviction in his guilt. Garcia had been lucky to get seven votes. Perhaps, I thought, Tompkins would realize he didn't have enough evidence ever to convict and would dismiss the charges. We would find out tomorrow morning.

CHAPTER THIRTY-SIX

I RETURNED TO the hospital and told Ginnie about the mistrial.

"How did you concentrate on trial while I was missing?"

I stroked her hair. "It wasn't easy."

"You're amazing."

"If you'd seen me crying at night, you wouldn't say I was so amazing."

"Crying? Over me?"

I kissed her gently on the lips. "Who else?"

"I'm so proud of you. You searched for me while trying a difficult murder case. I think that's amazing."

"I wouldn't say I was so successful searching for you. A lot of dead ends."

"But who would've guessed that my kidnapper was a crazy woman. No one suspects women."

"I know." I thought of my early contacts with Delahunty and Leary. "At first I was the prime suspect."

"You? Why?"

"I'm your husband. He's always the first suspect. Everyone thinks obsessive love leads to violence. That was the problem with Garcia's case. We were both victims of the same perception that husbands are guilty."

"But with Garcia, wasn't there evidence of prior abuse? You've never abused me."

"Well, Garcia had been accused of emotional abuse, but nothing physical." I stroked her hair. "And I would never abuse you, physically or emotionally."

"Seems both you and the police were motivated by gender bias. You assumed the kidnapper was a man; the police locked onto the husband. No one was thinking outside the box."

"Guilty."

"I can't say I really blame you. Not many people would suspect a widowed mother of three."

"How did she treat you?"

Ginnie closed her eyes for several seconds. "Could've been worse. In some ways I was lucky. She fed me once a day, let me exercise by walking back and forth in the basement, and even took off the handcuffs on occasion. I found it strange she wanted to cut off a lock of my hair and give me a manicure and pedicure, but I played along. But on the fourth or fifth day of captivity, when she ordered me to drop my underwear, I pushed back. We got into a pretty good wrestling match, but she overpowered me and rendered me unconscious. That woman is strong."

"She's a former weightlifting champion."

"I believe it. She wrapped her arm around my neck, squeezed for over a minute, and I went out."

"Jesus, that must've been frightening."

"When I came to, my pants were askew, and I knew she had cut my pubic hair. I felt intense cramping. I pulled my pants up and limped to the toilet where I . . . I lost the baby."

She put her hand over her mouth and sobbed, loud and despairing. "I wanted to keep it; I did. You have to believe me."

I grabbed a pile of tissue and wiped her tears. She reached out to me and we hugged. Before long I was crying as loudly as she was.

She continued telling me what happened. "I dared not look down and screamed bloody murder and I flushed it. I didn't know what else to do. I bled for days afterwards. It was horrible. When I told that bitch she had killed my baby, she seemed pleased with herself. At least she gave me sanitary napkins."

I hugged Ginnie again, holding her tightly, trying to squeeze out the pain, the terrible memories. I was afraid to let go.

"That was by far the worst day. For the first few days, I thought long and hard about the baby and realized how foolish and selfish I was to put my career ahead of us, of our family. I hope you'll forgive me."

I caressed her hair and again wiped away her tears. Just having Ginnie back was relief enough for me; it would take some time for her to recover from this trauma. Although I was devastated by all she'd been through and disappointed at her miscarriage, I hoped we could have another baby. That was a discussion for later, much later.

She had more to tell me. "After the miscarriage, I screamed at her continuously. I was beside myself. Before then, I don't think she had planned out the ending. She was just acting on impulse. She would rant about your causing her husband's death and Judge Garcia throwing out his case. She relished torturing you, not only for pure sadistic joy but also because she wanted to undermine your defense of Judge Garcia. She thought she could score a double win: ruining both your lives."

"But wasn't she worried she'd be caught, especially after sending me the letter about hanging you?"

"She read that letter to me. I knew she was serious. She said you were too stupid to realize she sent the letter. Besides, after I died, she was going to drive my body to the White Mountains and dump it in the woods. She thought it would be weeks before anyone found me, and no one would ever suspect a poor distressed widow.

"It was then that I fully realized how insane she is. I lost all hope when she brought in the cooler of ice. It was so heavy she had to slide it down the stairs. With each thump on a step, my heart beat faster. I just knew I was about to die when she tied the rope around pipes on the ceiling, then formed a noose. I yelled 'help' as loud as I could but, of course, no one could hear me."

"I can't imagine how awful that was for you."

"Then she squeezed me unconscious again. When I came to, I was hanging by the noose with my feet on top of the ice. She had tied my feet and hands together so I was trapped, unable to move. I tried lifting my feet off the ice but that only made me choke more. When the ice began melting after the first day, I knew it was just a matter of time. She abandoned me: no food, no ability to use the toilet. I peed in my undies, the urine dripping down my legs, puddling on top of the ice. I willed myself not to defecate." She wiped her eyes. "It was horrible."

I leaned over and again took her in my arms, holding her tightly. I joined her on the bed and, with our bodies wrapped snugly around each other, we both dozed off.

❁ ❁ ❁

At the court hearing the next morning, Tompkins appeared with his boss, the attorney general himself, Dalton Bellas. After the lawyers had stated their appearances, Judge Shane looked at Bellas.

"Have the People decided whether to retry this case?"

"Your Honor, if I might, we have given this matter a great deal of thought."

Garcia grabbed hold of my elbow as if clutching onto me for support. The next few moments would determine Garcia's immediate future: either he would remain behind bars or would walk out of this courtroom a free man.

Bellas paused as if he were still deciding what to do. He was a big man, perhaps six five, with a thick head of wavy white hair, which looked like a toupee. A distinguished former congressman, he had served three terms before deciding he preferred the law to politics.

Finally, Bellas got to the point. "The People do not believe the defendant is innocent. There simply is too much evidence linking him to his wife's murder." This didn't sound good and Garcia's grip on my elbow tightened. "However, we are mindful that seven of twelve jurors found him not guilty. The People believe they have put on the strongest case possible and do not believe a retrial will serve the interests of justice. Therefore, the People have decided to dismiss the charges against Carlos Garcia."

Garcia nearly jumped out of his chair. Judge Shane remained stone-faced, nodding. It was hard to tell whether she agreed with Bellas' opinion. A good jurist, neutral to the end. "Will the defendant please rise," Judge Shane said. "You are indeed fortunate. Since the charges against you are hereby dismissed, you are free to go. The bailiff will see that your personal effects are returned to you. I wish you luck in your future endeavors."

With that, she closed the hearing and left the bench. Tompkins then approached me with his hand outstretched. "Nice job, Francis," he said. "How you got seven jurors to side with you, I'll never understand."

"I appreciate it," I said, squeezing his hand. "I'm disappointed we didn't get five more." I smiled as Bellas joined us.

"From what I hear, Mr. Francis, you tried a helluva case, particularly in view of your personal circumstances. How is your wife?"

"Thanks for asking. She's doing much better. It'll take a while for the trauma to heal, but she should be discharged from the hospital any day now."

"I'm sorry we had to proceed to trial in view of your situation. As you know, my office would've accommodated you."

"You know what they say: if it weren't for clients the practice of law would be a lot easier."

I started to walk away then thought of something. "On behalf of my client, I want to thank you and Mr. Tompkins for making what I'm sure was a tough decision to dismiss this case. That took courage."

"Courage?" Bellas said as a contemplative look came over his face. "I appreciate the sentiment, but that's an overused word these days. No, what we did was not courage. Let's save that word for more appropriate individuals, like your wife." Then he winked at me before he and Tompkins left the courtroom.

❀ ❀ ❀

After the hearing, Garcia and I went to the Green Radish to celebrate. I was exhilarated, deeply satisfied that this time justice had been done. An innocent man had been set free. That didn't change the tragedy of Mo Garcia's death. But saving someone from a lifetime in prison was certainly worth celebrating. I ordered a draft Molson and Garcia a shot of Johnnie Walker's Blue Label whisky. When our drinks arrived, he raised his glass to toast. "To our jury system. Despite its faults, the best damn system in the world."

We were sitting in a booth across from the bar. For the afternoon the Green Radish was fairly crowded with packs of young women at the end of the bar and young men lingering around the edges, pretending to watch sports on the many television screens.

"You know," Garcia said, staring at his drink, "you had me worried for a little while. I wasn't sure the jury would buy the suicide theory."

"I know you never believed Mo committed suicide. You said you could testify to some other reason for her death. My guess is you didn't disclose that reason to me to avoid putting me in an ethical quandary. Am I right about that?"

He spread his hands, palms out. "Exactly. If I told you, then you couldn't pursue a suicide defense and would have to rely on my testimony only. But you made it clear I shouldn't testify, that the risk was too great and the jury would focus on my credibility and not on whether Mo committed suicide. So I didn't tell you what I knew."

"A lawyer hates to hear a client say, 'I didn't tell you something.' I understand why, but it still makes me uncomfortable."

"It's not as bad as you think. Fact is, Mo tried to poison me."

"What're you saying?"

"She served the noodles that night. Typically, she gave me a little more than her since I had a bigger appetite. She put the plates on the table then turned around to pour drinks. But I wasn't hungry so I switched the plates, giving her the one intended for me. So, you see, she had intended to poison me and it was pure luck that I escaped."

My breathing quickened as I considered his story, which I had a hard time believing. Could Mo really have tried to kill him? There was nothing in her history to indicate a propensity for violence; there was no evidence of threats. Of course, the same could be said of Carlos, except for the three reports of emotional abuse.

I finished my beer and ordered another. I had a sudden desire to get drunk, a feeling I hadn't had in some time, probably since my divorce from Sherry. "Carlos, tell me something and tell me straight: Did you suspect Mo had poisoned the food before you switched plates?"

He looked away, staring at the television, and said nothing.

CHAPTER THIRTY-SEVEN

Upon Ginnie's release from the hospital, she remained home in bed for a week. I took leave from my practice and played nurse, serving her coffee in bed in the morning, then a sandwich at lunch. For dinner I ordered takeout from a variety of local restaurants. Although I loved Thai food, I refrained from ordering any, the taste of the Garcia case still in my mouth. When Ginnie felt better, she limped around the condo, at first taking slow steps then gradually increasing the pace. Her feet still hurt but had healed well. She was fortunate not to lose any toes.

In a few weeks she was ready to go back on the air. The station planned a party to welcome her back but first she wanted to speak to viewers. It was important to her to show that she had recovered, that the kidnapping had not sapped her energy or skills. So at the end of the six o'clock news, I stood in the studio watching as the cameras focused on her. Her eyes sparkled as before and her smile stole my heart. Looking at her then, one would never have guessed the trauma she had only recently undergone. Before going on the air, Ginnie had surprised everyone by rejecting the stylist's assistance. "If there's one thing I learned," she said, "it's not to worry about trivial things such as hair or makeup. Life is too short."

The camera light came on. "To my loyal viewers and supporters," she began, "I offer my heartfelt thanks. I wish I could return the love and warmth you showed me. Channel 9 viewers will remain a part of me, a part I will cherish forever.

"I would be remiss if I did not mention one person in particular who never wavered in his search for me. That would be my husband, the famous trial lawyer Dutch Francis. If it weren't for Dutch, I would never have survived my ordeal. He turned over every stone looking for me. He called on his friends to contribute to my ransom fund and they answered his call, including my employer, this station."

At this point her eyes filled with moisture and I was struck with an urge to go to her, to hold her in my arms and comfort her. But she regained her composure and continued.

"I hope none of you ever has to suffer through a fraction of what I did. But I believe I have come out of it a better person. I appreciate so much more the special people in my life. I appreciate the generosity of all of you. From the bottom of my heart, thank you. Thank you."

❧ ❧ ❧

The party was crowded with people. The station apparently had sent out a general invitation to all past and present employees. I was pleased to see so many people supporting Ginnie. Waitstaff mingled with the crowd, offering asparagus sticks, beef on toast, fried prawns, and other appetizers. I found Dennis Cassidy and thanked him again for the station's donation to Ginnie's ransom fund and expressed my pleasure that it had been returned, unused.

"I would've given more for Ginnie," he said.

I put my hand on his shoulder. "I know you would've; I'm sorry I pushed you so hard."

He looked at my hand as if it had stained his suit. "You love her, that much is clear. You did what you had to do." Then Cassidy waved to someone across the room. "I have to chat someone up."

As I watched him walk across the room, I noticed someone enter wearing an expensive pinstripe suit. To my surprise, it was Judge Rodger Dodds. I waved him over.

"Rodger, I didn't think you'd make it." I shook his hand.

"When I got the invite, I was pleased you included me. I'm so happy Ginnie's better."

"Here she comes now. Ginnie, you remember Rodger."

"Of course." Rodger reached out to shake her hand, but Ginnie leaned in to hug him. "Thank you, Rodger, for helping with the ransom. I'll be forever grateful."

"My dear," he said in his most imperious voice, "I would do whatever I could to ensure your safety."

Yeah, I thought, only if I signed a promissory note.

Suddenly Ginnie's mother appeared. She was dressed in a tight-fitting red dress, a string of pearls accenting her cleavage. Although she was still too thin, she looked glamorous for a widow in her fifties. In her hand, almost ruining the look, was an unlit cigarette.

"Rodger," I said, "I'd like you to meet Ginnie's mother, Barbara Turner. You might remember her from the wedding."

"A pleasure to see you again."

"Oh, the pleasure's all mine." Barbara waved her cigarette in the air. "I'm so sorry I was in such a state last time we spoke. I was desperate, as you know."

"Indeed. Was I right about Dutch?" He smiled, a rare full-mouthed smile, and actually winked.

"You were," Barbara said, stroking my arm. "He's the best son-in-law a mother could ask for."

Rodger unbuttoned his jacket and leaned toward Barbara. "Perhaps, my dear, we could get ourselves drinks. And a light for that cigarette."

Barbara beamed, glad to have the attention. "I would like that very much." She smiled while she took Rodger's arm. Ignoring Ginnie and me, she and Rodger walked toward the bar.

I looked at Ginnie and said, "That's an interesting pair. Just think, Rodger Dodds could be your stepfather."

She gave me a light punch on the shoulder and put her arms around me. We kissed, a firm long kiss, right there in front of all the guests, not caring who saw us. In that moment, all was right in the world.

❁ ❁ ❁

On the drive home, my phone rang and I answered it through the car's audio system. "Dutch, it's Bill Delahunty. Got some news for you."

"You're on speaker with Ginnie."

"Hello, Ginnie. How're you doing?"

"Getting better every day."

"So what's the news?"

"It's about Handford. She hung herself tonight. Used the sheets from her bed. You two won't have to testify, after all."

At first, I was angry that Handford wouldn't suffer in jail. She had caused so much suffering to both Ginnie and me that I thought it only right that she get life without parole. But then I realized she had suffered already: she had lost her husband and struggled to make sense of her life without him. Only by blaming me and taking Ginnie could she endure. She had wanted retribution. I would stay above such negative feelings and live without a dark cloud over me. I would find it in my heart to forgive her.

"Thanks, Bill. I appreciate your letting us know right away."

Ginnie reached over and held my hand. Her touch seemed to make everything okay. "I don't ever want to think of her again. Thank God she's out of our lives forever."

"I feel the same way."

A few minutes passed before Ginnie spoke again. "When things settle down, you know what I want to do?"

"What's that?"

"I want to have a baby. I had a lot of time to think about us and that's what I want more than anything."

"More than your career?"

"I can have both. Before, I couldn't see that but now I can. I'll take maternity leave; the station will give me plenty of time off."

"So does that mean you want to stay in Manchester?"

"I want to stay wherever you are."

My spirits soared as I pulled into the condo parking space. We were home, really home.

ACKNOWLEDGMENTS

I could not have written *Abiding Conviction* without the support of several people who read early drafts of the book.

My thanks go to Tom Beatty, Jeff Westmont, Norbert Chu, Mark Melton, and Doris Cheng for their insightful and helpful comments.

A special thanks to my editor Zoe Quinton, whose sharp observations and critical reading made this a much better book.

After reading one of the final drafts, *New York Times* bestselling author Sheldon Siegel offered numerous helpful suggestions. For his friendship and support over the years, I am eternally grateful.

I would be remiss if I didn't thank Michael A. Black for his guidance after reading an early draft of the first chapter as well as a synopsis. I was introduced to Michael through the Mystery Writers of America manuscript critique program.

Finally, thanks to Pat and Bob Gussin of Oceanview Publishing, whose enthusiasm for *Abiding Conviction* made all those years writing the book very much worth the effort.